When & Where

Far From Home: A Scottish Time-Travel Romance, Volume 6

Rebecca Ruger

Published by Rebecca Ruger, 2023.

This is a work of fiction. Names, character, places, and incidents are either a product of the author's imagination are used fictitiously, and any resemblance to actual persons, living or dead, events, or locales is entirely coincidental. Some creative license may have been taken with exact dates and locations to better serve the plot and pacing of the novel.

ASIN: B0CL37QR8M
ISBN: 9798864415252
When & Where
All Rights Reserved.
Copyright © 2023 Rebecca Ruger
Written by Rebecca Ruger
All rights reserved. No part of this publication may be reproduced, distributed or transmitted in any form or by any means, or stored in a database or retrieval system, without the prior written permission of the publisher.
Disclaimer: The material in this book is for mature audiences only and may contain graphic content.
It is intended only for those aged 18 and older.

Chapter One

Present Day
Chicago

"Are you out of your mind?"

"Of course I am not, but just think of—" Autumn Winters began, only to be cut off by her boss's blustery arguments.

"You want to be next? Five American women missing isn't enough for you? You'll be next, and then who will write the story? I asked you to write a piece on Megan West, our own hometown girl gone missing. I don't need you flexing your investigative reporter chops in the middle of an active criminal inquiry on the other side of the world." He paused, his thick caterpillar brows furrowing even more now after his small explosion. "I'll send Kennedy," he said after a moment.

Autumn rolled her eyes, planting her hands on her hips. "Billy Kennedy is about as subtle as a blizzard. He won't get any answers over there. The only reason he manages to be a semi-competent investigative reporter here is because his name is known—as are his strong-arm tactics. He still thinks he's in Boston, covering the mob in the eighties. C'mon, Eliot, you know I'm right. This will take finesse, a bit of charm, and more brain than useless brawn—and who better to do that than a Rivera-Walton Investigative Journalism Award winner?"

And now Eliot Treadwell rolled his eyes, throwing up his hands in frustration.

But damn right she played that card.

Her award-winning probe, which uncovered that a retired Chicago detective had fabricated and planted evidence to frame innocent people of heinous crimes over a span of decades had opened an enormous can of worms, leading to larger State and Federal investigations and the freeing of—so far—three innocent men from prison, one who had served more than twenty years. The final report, which was given a four-minute segment for three consecutive nights had been her proverbial big break overnight, though she'd quietly investigated for more than two years.

And what was the point of unveiling corruption—largely overlooked by supervisors to quickly close cases—and winning that award if she couldn't use it to her advantage? To take on more of the same, finding answers when so many things pointed in one direction, but the authorities were bent on looking in another?

She didn't blame Scotland for wanting to steer everyone asking away from the very obvious serial killer theory. But it really pissed her off that American authorities were not doing more to insinuate themselves into the ongoing but seemingly clueless probe into the missing women. The bewildering case struck home now with Megan West having gone missing, since she'd grown up and lived and worked most recently within a stone's throw of Chicago and WGRN news.

"Eliot, at least let me try," she pleaded. "This story is huge. Telling about her doesn't begin to scratch the surface of what the hell happened to her—or those other women by the way. Give me a week over there, with Adam and Peter—"

"Christ, no! We're not sending an entire news crew to Scotland," he hollered at her. "What are you going to find out that hundreds of law enforcement over there have not already?"

How could he be so outraged by her idea and not so much by the women missing in Scotland? Why was there not more outrage anywhere in the States? These girls were more than merely news stories—even Autumn, driven to make a name for herself, understood that. Why was no one on this side of the ocean more concerned about these missing girls and what was being done to find them? True, she'd love to break a story, but seriously, where was the outrage?

"I have her journal," she reminded Eliot. "I could—"

"Her journal? Her journal! It's a goddamn one-page, half-assed note that makes her look like she was smoking something pretty potent, that her friend should have never taken from the crime scene!"

His face was beet red. That happened sometimes—often—when he started yelling and forgot to draw breath.

Eliot Treadwell was a stereotype, but of the more commonly parodied large city newspaper editor rather than WGRN's news director, which he was, tall and lean with a towering personality, quick to anger, who shouted more than he spoke, who neglected his phone and intercom in favor of bellowing impatient directives from behind his desk. The news of the day was often measured by the state of his wardrobe. He began each morning in a suitcoat and tie. Then a bothersome traffic report might come in or the news station's website would go down and off went the jacket. The president might make a public gaffe that made America look foolish and the tie was wrenched from around his neck and tossed aside. A hurricane making landfall might unbutton the top of his dress shirt. A controversial bill passing or failing in Congress would roll up his sleeves. His favorite King Club sandwich from the deli near O'Hare Airport, eaten during meetings and invariably dribbled on his shirt, would see him swap out that shirt for one of the always-available extras he kept in his office, and the un-layering process would start again.

Damn. She'd known Eliot Treadwell would need some convincing, but she hadn't expected so violent a reaction.

His statement was false, though. Well, part of it was true. Megan West had only written on the first page of the notebook and the content could be misconstrued in so many different ways, and her friend *had* hidden it from the authorities. But the room at the inn where she'd been staying was not a crime scene, hadn't ever been declared as such since there was no crime known. Megan West had simply disappeared, and the inn was the last place she was known to have been. But it revealed little, no signs of a struggle or anything amiss, not a speck of blood, and aside from Megan's DNA, there had been too many other unknown samples to have been of any use.

"Eliot," Autumn tried again, keeping her voice firm, professional, "please reconsider. I just need a week to chase down what little the journal did say—"

"It said nothing!" He shouted.

Once annoyed or having expressed opposition to an idea, it was rare that sentences might be finished in his presence.

"Gibberish, all of it," he decided gruffly. "Some romantic notions of a clearly foolish girl. She's probably hiding out with the beefcake she met over there, now too embarrassed to show her face after all this fuss has been made about her disappearance."

He was showing his age—well past retirement, Autumn was sure—with the use of *beefcake* to describe the 'hot Scot'—as dubbed by Megan's friend, Jasmine Lane—whom Megan West had apparently met and spent time with in Scotland.

"Eliot, you can't believe that—"

"We know nothing, Autumn," he reminded her tersely. "And it's wasting time and resources to send you off on a wild goose chase. We've got enough going on here. You have other assignments, other Nancy Drew shit you could be sticking your nose into."

This! This is why she sometimes hated him, for how he belittled the investigative side of journalism. Despite the enormity of her crooked detective story, which she alone broke, Eliot Treadwell still treated her like a novice, and sometimes proved what a chauvinistic dinosaur he was. Leave the big stories to the big men, she was frequently made to understand.

"Very well," she said, understanding she wouldn't be able to sway him. She thought she might try again in two weeks' time. "Have a good day, Eliot. Don't forget I'm not here next week," Autumn said, maintaining her rigid posture, a constant in his company, which she believed effectively prevented her from jumping or jerking at every barked response or command.

"Not here? I just said you may not go to—" he began shouting again.

"I have scheduled time off," she informed him firmly. "It's been on the calendar for months. Jordan and I have a vacation planned." At his blank stare, she clarified for him, "You asked for a story on Megan West. I've done that, interviewed the friend who abandoned her, her co-workers, and three previous foster families, even the guy at the coffee shop at the corner of her street. Jason is finishing the editing now. My work here is done until I return," she said resolutely, not about to be bullied into forgoing her trip because of Eliot's maniacal whims.

Chances are she wouldn't be able to uncover what law enforcement had not over three years and five missing women, but she was since meeting with Megan West's friend, Jasmine Lane, regularly overwhelmed by a burning desire to at least try.

Eliot Treadwell snarled something under his breath. One more lip curl and then he waved his long arm toward the door. "Go on, then. Get out of here. But remember, Autumn Winters," he called out after her as she made her escape, "one award does not make a career! You've got a lot to learn yet!"

Yeah, yeah, yeah.

Despite his reputation—Eliot Treadwell rubbed elbows with presidents and celebrities, and in his youth with men like Woodward and Bernstein and columnist Jack Anderson—Autumn wasn't a fan. If her very close-knit family didn't all live and work in or very near to Chicago, if her own ambition were greater than her love of her parents and three older brothers and their families, she'd have sought out a job in another city or state. The Rivera-Walton award could have been her ticket to something bigger or better, but she couldn't imagine being anywhere but here. She loved Chicago, loved her family and Sunday dinners at her parents' house, and never wanted to be too far away from her nieces and nephews.

And then there was Jordan.

Jordan Charles Becker III, or more precisely, Autumn's boyfriend of almost three years who was, she was fairly certain, about to propose to her—possibly while they wined and dined their way along the Mediterranean on their cruise beginning tomorrow. And she was primed to say yes.

Having grown up in a wild house filled with too much testosterone, bad ideas, and noise, Autumn had almost immediately fallen in love with Jordan's quiet, reserved nature. She'd known him a year before he'd raised his voice—to shout out Happy New Year from a third story window to a friend on the street below. He was staid and solid and predictable. Autumn loved her brothers dearly, but she knew she could never be married to a man of similar character. They were truly guy's guys, exuding natural confidence and strength, a certain casual style, comfortable in their own skin, lacking only—and only sometimes—emotional intelligence. Though all three of her brothers were in their thirties, they still employed and were entertained by potty humor; though their rowdiness was harmless, they loved to prank each other; though they were dependable, they were sometimes unpredictable; though family came first, it sometimes had to be scheduled around the big game, the Bears or the Cubs.

Jordan was a tax attorney with one of the oldest law firms in Chicago. Her brothers teased her—and sometimes Jordan to his face, which wasn't always received well—that he'd managed to combine two of the most unpopular, satirized professions—taxes and the law—and join them together. Her brothers, Adam, Michael, and Sean actually gave her quite a bit of grief over Jordan. Though they were always polite to him, from the get-go they'd questioned if the match was good—good for Autumn, their baby sister. But Autumn knew that Jordan was earnest, honest, and ambitious, all the things she strived to be, qualities that she appreciated in others. He was a fine companion who respected her drive to succeed and her want to establish her career before she began a family, and who wasn't threatened by her small successes so far while his career took a more gradual, less flashy route to junior partner.

She finished out her day, determined that when she got back to work, she would try again to convince Eliot of the merit of her idea. Autumn was determined that fresh eyes and fresh thoughts—what had prompted and provoked her award winning piece—were exactly what was needed if any of those missing girls were ever going to be found. She left work, picking up her dry cleaning and stopping for gas so that she wouldn't have to do so when she returned from vacation next Sunday night. She texted Jordan but received no response, which wasn't unusual since he was often in meetings or with clients.

An hour later, sitting on the balcony outside her loft with a glass of wine, she received a text from Jordan, cancelling their dinner plans.

Sorry. Taking a late meeting with a senior partner and new client.

Autumn sighed, wondering if he still planned to spend the night. It would simply make it easier in the morning, getting to the airport. She dropped the phone in her lap, her bare feet propped up on the railing of the balcony, supposing that she shouldn't expect he would want to stay over simply to end his day by sleeping with her. They'd been together for almost three years; those days of not being able to get enough of each other had never been frantic and were since long gone. The sex was good, if routine, but was only a small part of their relationship, neither of them having personalities that were driven by physical desires. She liked that about Jordan, that he didn't think and wasn't governed by the organ in his pants. She wanted more in a relationship than simply that.

And yet sometimes she rather wished they were zealous lovers, that he couldn't get enough of her.

Or she of him.

Autumn frowned, wondering about that, and then shook herself free of that, not wanting to insert drama and questions when there should be none. Jordan was perfect for her.

But then a conversation they had just last week replayed itself in her mind. When she'd first mentioned about approaching Eliot about going to Scotland—she'd thought she might simply tack on another week in Europe after their cruise if Eliot had consented— Jordan had expressed doubts about her plan. Jordan always stayed in his own lane, didn't quite understand or appreciate the initiative of people who didn't.

He'd squawked enough—it wasn't her job to do the work of the Scottish authorities; how was she so certain she could help? having never been to Scotland, what did she expect to find?—that she'd teased him in response.

"Unless, of course, you want me here and near because you have some big date planned." She'd winked broadly at him, holding up her left hand and her bare ring finger.

Of course, they'd talked about getting married. Previously, Jordan had said they would get engaged when she finished her graduate school program, or when she was more established at WGRN, or when he made junior partner. And all those things came and went without a proposal. She didn't consider herself an enabler but sometimes entertained a bit of doubt, maybe even a certain sense of alarm that he did continually put it off—and that she let him. If he weren't so perfect for her, if she wasn't sure he'd make such a good father and good partner, she might have bailed some time ago.

"Autumn, we've discussed this," he'd replied last week, sounding a bit...off. "There's a lot going on right now and to add the stress of a wedding to the mix seems irresponsible."

She hadn't been stunned, but she'd certainly been a little surprised by the gravity of his tone. The tenor of his response would have been more understandable if she made a regular, annoying habit of bugging him about getting engaged. But she did not.

"I think you meant to say the excitement of wedding planning, the joy of the idea of a wedding—not the stress," she'd scolded lightly, meaning to get her point across but not wanting to start an argument.

At that moment he'd received a call from work that he'd likely been very pleased to take.

The conversation had not been revisited that night or since then.

Which forced Autumn now to examine why in the hell she was so sure he was going to propose to her on the cruise. Some of her expectation, admittedly, had been buoyed by her girlfriend, Amy, who'd suggested that Jordan's defensive response was likely an attempt to throw her off the fact that he did have something planned.

"If you don't walk off the boat with a ring on your finger," her oldest brother, Adam, had said at last week's Sunday dinner at their parents' house, which Jordan hadn't been able to make, "I'm going to call it. DOA. No more life-saving measures should be attempted. Can't find a pulse."

Autumn had tossed one of her mother's cheddar garlic biscuits at Adam in response.

She made some headway packing her suitcases and texted her mother, knowing that she couldn't call. Friday nights were still, after thirty-five years, date night for her parents. No doubt they were two drinks in, huddled together over dinner at one of their many favorite restaurants.

She was just finishing her shower when she heard the door to the loft open.

"Jordan?" She called from the bathroom.

"Yeah," came his answer.

He sounded tired. Autumn checked her phone. Almost nine o'clock. She hoped he had all his packing done.

Distractedly, she made a mental note that her and Jordan's passports were on the breakfast bar in the kitchen. Obviously, she didn't want to forget those.

When she left the bathroom, coming into the bedroom where one of her suitcases was still open on the queen bed, Jordan was there, lounged against the bedroom doorway, his shoulder propped against the doorjamb. His hands were in his pockets.

Autumn raised a brow at him. She'd known him for three years. She'd never seen him do that before.

He was still in his suit and tie. For a moment, she saw only the top of his head and it's short, wavy brown hair as he stared at the beige carpet on the bedroom floor.

"Did you pack already?" She asked, immobilized across the room near the closet by his odd behavior.

Jordan lifted his face to her, his brown eyes and narrow mouth tightened with tension.

Autumn's phone vibrated and she glanced down to see her mother had returned her text. She let it go, lifting her gaze back to Jordan, her eyes locking on his with a mix of concern and apprehension.

"Autumn," he began with the greatest of hesitation.

"Ah, shit." Her shoulders slumped, not caring that Jordan didn't like when she swore. "You've got to be kidding me. You're not going, are you?"

"I can't," he said, his words weighed down with an odd, utterly misplaced detachment. "Autumn, I'm sorry."

Very calmly, even as she felt as rigid as steel with her anger, she asked, "You can't, or you won't?"

Jordan straightened away from the doorway and made a face at her that suggested he viewed the question was childish. "It's just too demanding right now, with this new client. And you know that federal case is taking up a lot of my energy."

"And you realized this just now? The night before we're supposed to leave?"

"It's about priorities right now."

Nodding, smirking with her growing resentment, Autumn approached the bed, smacking the suitcase closed. "Priorities. Yes, of course." She spun the folded suitcase around, looking for the zipper. She waited for Jordan to comment on her remark, to catch onto his own error—Jesus, she hoped it was said in error, since he'd just suggested she absolutely was not one of his priorities.

Jordan strode inside the bedroom, grabbing onto the footboard post. "It's just the timing, Autumn. It's a really bad time to take a break."

Having failed to find the stupid zipper, Autumn gave up. She closed her eyes and lifted her chin. Taking a deep breath, she opened her eyes and stared at Jordan. She considered him intently, with fresh eyes, ones that red flags should have wakened long ago. She traced over the contours of his long face, looking for something—anything—that suggested that he was as upset as her about this.

And she waited. It wasn't on her to make this better. It wasn't on her to convince herself to understand. It was on him.

Silence hung heavy in the room as he appeared to struggle to find the right words—any words—his tense indifference finally giving away to a flicker of guilt.

Autumn smiled grimly.

Her brothers had been right all along.

"Actually, I think this is a perfect time to take a break," she told him.

It was time to set herself free.

Chapter Two

Autumn Winters sat near the window and balcony of Room 203 in the Lodge of the Loch, her elbows resting on the arm of the chair, her perfectly manicured fingers tapping a steady beat on the edge. She'd been here, in this spot, for more than twenty minutes, having only just checked in this morning.

The hotel room was non-descript, a worn commercial Berber carpet covered all the floor but the entry and bathroom. A pair of uninspired solid blue quilts covered the two queen beds. The furniture, this table and chair included, was dated but not attractive enough to have been considered vintage. The artwork on the walls was rather pedestrian, some wannabe photographer's prints of local scenery, hung poorly—crookedly in one instance—in cheap frames with no mats, small pictures lost on large walls.

According to Janet McLaren, the middle-aged, thin-lipped woman in the hotel's office, the police had combed over every inch of this 300 square foot space for more than three weeks, leaving Autumn with little to investigate. The room had only been released by the authorities ten days ago.

Megan West, the young American woman from Des Plaines who was the latest to go missing, might have sat in this very chair, she thought.

And now I am.

A prickling sensation raised the hair on the back of her neck.

Autumn ignored this. She was a reporter for the WGRN news station in Chicago, the rising star of the investigative team. She dealt with facts and evidence, not prickling sensations.

However, maybe she should have paid greater attention to her intuition and more than one nagging perception about Jordan. She *should* be sitting on the sun deck of a fancy cruise ship, sipping mimosas right now, but was here in this drab hotel room instead, chasing what she sincerely hoped didn't turn out to be nothing, a fruitless endeavor.

She was still angry and hurt about what she might now assume was her break-up with Jordan. And frankly, she wasn't quite over her shock. Despite several indications realized in hindsight, she truly hadn't seen it coming. Jordan not being able to get off work was one thing, not a deal-breaker at all, but Jordan's inability to convince her that he was bothered by it, had kind of filled in a lot of blanks.

Might assume was a break-up? She questioned herself.

She was torn. Part of her was dedicated to the idea that she was done. It was over. She deserved better. Another part of her bemoaned the loss of the dream: an entire life imagined with Jordan at her side. Yet a third part of her wondered still if there was any hope.

Jordan had left in a huff Friday night, and she hadn't heard from him until she'd gotten off the plane in Rome. His text was cool, defensive still. He hadn't extended another apology, heartfelt or otherwise. He hadn't closed with any mention or desire to see her and straighten out this issue when she got home, which had caused the most pain—and admittedly, a bit of desperation, that saw her texting him a lengthy communication that basically said, shit happens; she might have overreacted; his job was important, of course. All excuses, made by her for him. She was thankful now that she'd deleted the whole thing, had left Jordan's half-hearted olive branch hanging in the breeze. On her flight from JFK to Rome, Autumn had decided that she might just read into the entire thing what was meant to be known: his heart wasn't in it. And she'd be damned before she begged anyone to *want* to be with her, to *want* to love her.

She'd done nothing with their cruise tickets. That had been booked more than eight months ago, had been put on Jordan's credit card; that was his problem. But she'd kept her flight from Chicago to JFK airport and the transatlantic one, which had put her in Rome yesterday—thanks, Jordan, for that hop across the ocean—and then had promptly booked a flight to Edinburgh. It had made for a very long day of travel, but she was here, where she was thrilled to be, where she truly believed she was meant to be. Everything happens for a reason, she reminded herself.

Eliot Treadwell and Jordan Becker could kiss her ass.

Autumn glanced down at the journal in her lap.

Megan West's journal, which the missing woman's friend, Jasmine Lane, had hidden from the police.

Having been assigned the background piece on Megan as soon as it had become known that another woman was missing, Autumn had scheduled an interview with Jasmine Lane. For days prior to her return to the States, Jasmine had been enjoying her fifteen minutes of fame. *Had been*, until it was discovered that she was not merely the friend-in-mourning of the most recent missing American woman in Scotland, but instead was the shitty friend who'd made plans with Megan to vacation in Scotland, only to invite her boyfriend along once they'd landed. By all accounts—interviews with the glaring Janet McLaren, the driver Jasmine and her boyfriend had hired, and then the (now ex-)boyfriend himself, currently known around the world as Mc-Steamy 2.0 since he was a fairly attractive doctor—Jasmine had dumped Megan, had gone down to Edinburgh with McSteamy 2.0 and had left Megan alone here. Alone, that is, save for the 'weird hot guy' that the entire English speaking world was looking for. Almost hourly for the first few weeks, an e-fit of Megan's mystery man could be seen on any channel in any country including the US, he being the very first solid tip authorities had as a lead to follow after several years of women going missing. But Graeme—'MacSomething', according to Jasmine—was a phantom.

Autumn had interviewed Jasmine for the local news shortly after her return to Chicago. That had been *before* the truth had been made known, about how she'd ditched her friend. Jasmine's fleeting love for the camera had crumbled when the truth had come out. She was instantly vilified on the news, in the papers, and all over social media. She'd barely spoken to a soul since, hadn't worked, hadn't gone out, had even changed her phone number. Having met her, having built a fairly basic rapport with her, Autumn had written her a letter, asking her if she'd like to tell her story once more. She invited her to take the opportunity to explain what had really happened with her separating from Megan in Scotland, and not let the public at large fill in the blanks so uncharitably on social media, where Jasmine Lane was daily fodder for even those who weren't fanatics about the cases. Honestly, Autumn had been surprised when Jasmine had called her. In tears, she asked for Autumn to help her.

A week ago, Autumn had made her second visit to Jasmine's tiny apartment.

Though she wasn't supposed to feel for a subject, Autumn couldn't help but know some sympathy for Jasmine Lane. Even then, only a few weeks removed from Scotland, Jasmine was a shell of her former self. The vibrant, self-possessed camera-diva with the unnaturally bright red hair and sleeves of tattoos was now in dire need of a color-refresh, her light brown roots painting a strip over the center of her head. She wore no make-up, the once kohl-rimmed eyes now puffy and red-rimmed instead. She'd greeted Autumn in an overlarge t-shirt and baggy yoga pants. She'd looked like shit.

Before she'd even opened the door, Jasmine had announced she wouldn't talk with Autumn on camera, which had returned Peter and his camera to the station's SUV parked at a meter outside.

"Just you," Jasmine had said, her voice coming through the door. "And everything will be off the record."

Off-the-record put a damper on Autumn's mission, but she'd consented. As a general practice, she usually honored off-the-record agreements, wanting to be trusted by sources to share worthwhile news and background. In no way did she want her fledgling reputation stained by rumors that she was dishonest.

They'd met for forty-five minutes inside Jasmine's dark loft, where all the shades and curtains had been drawn and closed. Jasmine had cried through more than half of that. Guilt was eating her alive.

Autumn had asked her a series of questions, all the basics, most of which had been covered in their first interview.

How many days did you actually spend with Megan?

When was the last time you literally saw her? What was her disposition when you parted?

What can you tell me about the Scotsman she met? Was he there when you parted ways?

Autumn had been very careful to avoid using phrases like, *when you left her.*

Did it seem as if Megan were afraid at all of this man, Graeme? Did he strike you *as threatening? Dangerous?*

"Why didn't you give it to the Scottish police?" Autumn had asked when Jasmine had told her she'd taken Megan's journal from the hotel room in Scotland. It had required a herculean effort to show no shock or thrill at learning that Megan had kept a journal, and that Jasmine had it in her possession.

To her credit and despite the fact that she had essentially abandoned her friend, Jasmine Lane had been concerned when Megan had not arrived at the airport on the date and at the hour of their scheduled flight. Belatedly bit by the guilty conscience bug, Jasmine had missed her own flight to return to the inn to locate Megan, she being the first—and until she'd shared it with Autumn, the only person— to see Megan's small notebook.

"I didn't want them labeling her crazy," she said, piquing Autumn's interest. Jasmine held the journal, no more than four by six inches, against her chest. "I won't show it to you unless you promise this will never be published or discussed, or included in any article. This is off the record, or you won't see it."

Her anticipation nearly overwhelming at that moment, Autumn had given her oath that she would not publicly acknowledge the existence of the journal in any way.

"I didn't want them to think she was crazy," Jasmine had repeated when she'd finally put the small greeting card size notebook into Autumn's hand.

Skimming over the first page, the only one that had been written on, Autumn didn't blame her.

"I didn't want them not to look for her," Jasmine had cried—earnestly and unattractively cried; probably the reason she'd only agreed to meet with Autumn off camera.

It had been the right call to make, not alerting the authorities about the journal. It asked questions but didn't offer any help, in Autumn's estimation.

"What she wrote makes no sense," Jasmine had said, which was indeed true. "But that is Megan's handwriting," she confirmed.

Autumn still didn't know any more than Jasmine did about what to make of the words written in blue ink.

Reasons To Go back in Time with Graeme and *Just do it. Be brave. Take a chance. Go to the ruins of the broch with him and go back to the fourteenth century!* did not inspire confidence that the missing person wasn't simply in need of meds, that she wasn't strung out somewhere, needing not only to be found but in greater need of medical attention.

"But what is this about traveling back in time?"

"What? Oh, that." Jasmine had dismissed with a shrug. "Makes no sense. She read quite a bit. Maybe she was planning a book."

"But she met this guy, Graeme," Autumn had reasoned, "and she's written his name down here."

"Yeah, but obviously he was lying about his name. The Scottish cops looked everywhere, found three Graeme MacQuillans. I'm pretty sure—well, mostly sure—that was his name. Or what he claimed it was. I was dragged down to the police station here to look at photos the Scottish police sent over and none of them were him." Her bottom lip quivered. "He lied. She fell for it." She'd fought against a rising tide of emotion, and lost, crying,

"It's all my fault. I shouldn't have left her. If I'd been with her, if I hadn't dumped her for Kyle—that asshole—she wouldn't be missing. Wouldn't be dead."

Autumn didn't do well with crying scenes. She tried, she really did, but she was too unemotional, too focused on the job at hand, always the story. She winced a little, giving Jasmine a moment to compose herself. But she couldn't imagine any words to ease her guilt. Autumn was creative, but not in that regard.

She'd asked a bit about Jasmine's ex-boyfriend, Kyle, but had been satisfied that he was simply a jerk. He'd been happy to take advantage of a trip to Scotland to see his girlfriend, and possibly had relished his own fifteen minutes of fame as McSteamy 2.0, but that all came crashing down when his *other* girlfriends—plural—had been discovered. Apparently, he'd been sleeping his way around almost every floor of the Des Plaines hospital—shacking up with nurses, doctors, PAs, anything with a vagina.

"But you would know that guy—Graeme McQuillan—if you saw him again?" Autumn had asked.

"He'd be kind of hard to miss. He was super hot, and he carried a sword and dressed like a weirdo."

Autumn had blinked. "I'm sorry. Did you say he carried a sword?"

"Yeah," Jasmine had replied indifferently, as if a sword-wielding man was a normal thing. "He was kind of weird about it. Like Megan had to beg him not to bring it down to dinner. But honest to God, despite the sword and several other things, I thought he was harmless. He seemed like he was into Megan. I thought, *good for her*. She never dates, hasn't had a steady boyfriend in years, while I've gone through several."

"Did you tell the Scottish authorities that the man carried a sword?" Autumn had asked.

With a nod, Jasmine had revealed, "They were just as surprised as you, but I promise, I'm not making that up."

Autumn had chewed on that. She'd love to know what the police had made of that very alarming piece of information. And she wondered as well why that hadn't been made public.

"Is she...is there any reason for you to think that maybe she just ran off with him?" Was the last question she'd put to Jasmine last week.

"None at all, I promise you," Jasmine had answered, an earnestness in her voice. "She wasn't reckless like that. I'm telling you she's that guy's sex slave or she's already dead." She'd started crying again and Autumn had, shortly thereafter, taken her leave, once more promising that she wouldn't make public anything about the journal.

Presently, having learned little from the sterilized hotel room, Autumn stood and collected her shiny gold rolling suitcase. It was tiresome, always lugging it around, but she needed it. Inside was her small digital camcorder, her regular digital camera, her laptop, several steno books and an entire pouch of her favorite ergonomic roller-ball pens. She smoothed down her camel-colored pencil skirt and yanked on the hem of the matching jacket—not navy, she wasn't a politician; not gray, she wasn't an attorney—and paused at the bathroom mirror to freshen her Yves Saint Laurent lipstick—Conflicting Crimson, which was best suited to her coloring and showed well on camera. She examined the rest of her face and hair, giving a quick spray to her blonde hair, hoping it wasn't too windy outside.

The three-inch heels of her designer shoes tapped along the tiled floor and then were muffled on the short-pile carpet of the hallway as she made her way downstairs, taking the tiny and dubious elevator.

Janet McLaren was no more pleased to see her now than she had been an hour ago—"the inn is nae a tourist attraction, Ms. Winters," had been her reply when Autumn had asked if she might be shown around, to places Megan West had visited.

Presently, pretending she had no agenda at all, Autumn asked if there were any ruins of brochs nearby that she might visit. Twenty minutes later, having wasted much of that time explaining to Janet McLaren all the reasons she was not prepared to "find yer way on a bicycle", Autumn had a semi-detailed hand-drawn map from the grumbling woman, illustrating how she could get there by car.

She tossed her rolling luggage into the back seat and set out in her rental car, having quickly grown accustomed to driving on the left side of the road, as the drive from the airport to this inn had taken several hours. After thirty minutes, a few wrong turns, and nearly getting stuck while backing out of a muddy trail that was not a road, Autumn finally found the ruins.

She pulled off to the side of the road, hoping the car didn't get swiped or smashed by someone speeding around that last bend on this very narrow road and stared out her window, up the hill at the ruins. Brochs, she'd since learned after a bit of internet searching, were found only in Scotland and were thought to be from the Iron Age, roundhouse totems to Scotland's prehistory. Having no idea how much daylight she might have, she exited the car, retrieved her luggage, and wheeled that up the hill, having to walk on her toes to prevent her heels from sinking into the marshy ground.

As far as tourist-y things went, she considered this one unimpressive. Of course the age of it was remarkable for having stood for so long, minus the collapsing front half, but it was rather bleak, gray and overgrown, no care taken with the vegetation surrounding it. Across the street sat a barn, very close to the road, another contradiction with its new, gray metal roof and its ancient stone walls, which were covered in lichen and almost blended in with the pasture surrounding it.

And yet as she neared it, she...felt it. Or felt something. She was not a history buff, didn't get excited over ancient things, was more apt to be wowed by the performance of a fine orchestra or the display at an art gallery, or perhaps be impressed by a more modern castle or mansion, so she wasn't sure what she felt was any reaction to the site, to its mysterious history.

Still, there was a current, some altering of the air or the way she perceived it. Suddenly and just here within only a few feet of the broch, the air had a distinct richness and depth. Or maybe she had simply failed to notice the air in Scotland until now, she could not be sure, but then could not discount that this present awareness left her a little rattled.

She turned away from the ruins, meaning to grab her camera and take a few pictures before she scoured the area, looking for anything that might clarify Megan's cryptic words in her journal.

As Autumn turned her back to the ruins, she felt a greater, inexplicable, creeping consciousness, this one larger and more urgent, lifting not only the hair at her nape but also the ones on her arms.

"Hello...?" She called out weakly, her hand clutched on the handle of her luggage.

But she was alone. There was no one around here. It was almost eerily quiet.

And yet she clearly heard—felt, actually—someone say, *Dinna go, lass. He's coming for ye.*

Autumn twirled around, unnerved by the whispers that couldn't possibly be real.

Were they her own consciousness? Had she heard or sensed something and now attached a narrating voice to it?

Had Jordan come to surprise her? –was her next thought. Had he been undone by guilt and now wanted to make amends? She dismissed the idea almost as soon as it was born. Jordan did not make a habit of surprises. So not his style.

But...

She felt again another cryptic message, given in a craggy voice.

Ye will nae escape him, lass. Ye will nae want to.

A whimper of fright escaped her, and she spun around again, terrified that either she was losing her mind, or someone was playing a really nasty trick on her. Still, there was no one about, not a soul in sight.

And yet she was seized by some frantic notion that she should run, that she was being chased. Her lips trembled and she began to run down the grassy hillside, back toward the rental car.

Oh, she most certainly did want to escape!

She stopped, came to a sudden halt, when she was still twenty yards from the little sedan. Was stopped, actually, by a piercing pain in her shoulder. Autumn closed her eyes in agony, tipping her head back while she clamped her mouth tightly to keep from screaming at the inexplicable pain.

After a moment, when she opened her eyes again, nothing was as it was.

Chapter Three

September 1304
Near Inverness, Scotland

Clumps of peat were furiously kicked up and just as swiftly flopped back down, the ground disturbed by the bruising pace set by Marcus McInnes. No sooner had bits settled than they were agitated just as violently by the thundering army that followed in his wake.

"There!" Called out Gibbon, riding closest to Marcus. "The glint in the trees!"

Aye, Marcus saw it, and supposed as Gibbon did that it might well be a reflection of the bright sunlight off the sword of any one of the callous marauders who'd just visited an unholiness upon the wretched souls of the Darrie village, the attack carried out at the break of dawn, the devil's hour.

Marcus's lip curled as he spurred on his destrier. He would show no mercy, would grant no quarter, just as these brigands had done inside Darrie. He'd leave their bodies to rot in the autumn sun, would mark them with black soot as traitors to humanity—making war on their own bloody people!—would incite the devil to collect their souls before any feeble-minded angel might take pity on their faithless carcasses.

The humble village of Darrie was nestled deep within the rugged heart of the disputed land of the McInnes and the MacPhail, a place where the very landscape seemed to echo with the ancient songs of the earth. Darrie stood as a lone bastion of autonomy, governed by history and lore more so than it ever would be by any man or clan. Small, thatched cottages, built to withstand the fierce Highland wind and mean winters and huddled together like old friends, now smoldered as ruins from the unprovoked and unprecedented MacPhail attack. Long before the McInnes and MacPhails had laid claims to the surrounding lands, Darrie had stood free and proud, a haven for those who sought refuge from the never-ending land wars in the north. Today, it had been reduced by half, in people and edifices, but Marcus could make no sense of it. Decimating Darrie did nothing to further MacPhail's claim to the disputed land, naught but incense those who survived—possibly to finally take a side—and enrage Marcus to strike back, hard and deep.

But mayhap that was what they wanted. Mayhap all-out war was what MacPhail was after.

Gibbon cursed something unintelligible and then exhorted the army behind them, "By my oath and my order, lads! No mercy! Naught but death!"

The victors would now become the vanquished.

Compelled to larger urgency by these words, several of the McInnes archers let loose as they rode, wild volleys meant not as warning—the enemy would not be allowed to escape—but as a hint of the might and power of the McInnes army. The fleeing enemy didn't need to know that Marcus had but two units with him presently. They would bring hell to those MacPhail raiders, who would find no place to disappear, no escape inside the forest of pines into which they'd apparently gone. Another arced stream of missiles flew overhead while they were still a hundred yards out.

Marcus narrowed his eyes, a wee surprised that even through the dense boughs of greenery he detected no scattered movement, saw not one more glint of sun off steel, could discern no figures scrambling for cover or incited to flight. The tree-covered beinn before them was motionless.

Damn, but he and his men might be further behind them than they'd guessed.

Straightening in the saddle, slowing his mount to be able to navigate the trees without mishap or misstep, Marcus was the first to enter the forest, the first to begin the upward climb on the braeside, and had progressed not more than twenty more yards when he was brought to a crashing halt by the sight before him.

So vigorously did Marcus jerk on the reins that the destrier's front hooves were lifted off the ground. The steed shook his head with displeasure, but Marcus paid him no mind, unable to lend consideration to anything but the apparition that stood directly in front of him.

A woman....

Or a ghostly specter of one. Oddly garbed and seemingly unruffled by the coming of his army though already she was apparently a victim of its furious reprisal for the harm done at Darrie.

While his army came to a crashing halt all around him on the gentle slope, Marcus met and held the bright but stricken gray eyes of the woman. Her peculiar fawn-colored garb, indecently bared legs, and the unusual gold box attached to her white-knuckled hand by way of a black metal rod were of little significance presently.

Nae, the swan-feathered McInnes arrow protruding from her left shoulder and the circle of vivid red blood growing larger around it, darkening her fawn surcote, was what held so much of his attention.

"Blessed Màthair of God," Gibbon breathed at his side.

Marcus grunted. "Whatever she is or nae, she is nae that, mate."

"I think I..." the woman said, her voice so small as to almost be unheard. She blinked and looked directly at Marcus, a frown of confusion wrinkling two precisely shaped eyebrows. "I've been shot."

Bluidy hell.

At Marcus's side, Gibbon drew in a hiss of breath.

"Are ye a MacPhail?" Marcus asked, hoping that she was and that this incident—the wounding of the strange woman—would be accounted as necessary, justified even, whether she played an active role in the massacre or not.

"I've been shot," she repeated dumbly, lifting her left hand and extending only her forefinger until the underside barely touched the feathers. "Oh, my." Her gray eyes lifted again, skimming over Gibbon before returning to Marcus. "I might...I'm going to be sick. Or pass out."

Marcus's gaze was briefly fixed on her fingernails, all ten of which were coated with a bright red paint. He blinked at her words, though, and focused again on her face.

She did appear a wee bit wobbly.

"Are you a MacPhail?" He asked again, the words growled, wanting to know if he should entertain satisfaction or remorse. And if he and the McInnes men would help her or not.

"A MacPhail? No," she said, shaking her head. "I'm...Autumn Winters....WGRN News."

Her voice was soft—weakened by fright, Marcus guessed. Her accent was unusual but gave credence to her claim that she wasn't related to the infidels. While she didn't sound at all Scottish, her speech was refined, not common at all.

Marcus met and held her wide, glassy stare, able only to discern her quiet shock and little else from those unusually pale gray eyes.

Her frown increased, tainted with a bit of angry disbelief. "Are you going to stand there, staring at me? Or will you...?" she paused, cautiously adjusting her feet, widening her stance upon a pair of shoes tilted with remarkable height, the back end of each lifted by a thin stick painted red. Possibly she was becoming weaker and sought stability. She blinked again and appeared to put forth great effort to focus. "Did *you* shoot me? Why would you—oh, shit. I think I'm...I feel very lightheaded."

Marcus dismounted smoothly and approached the woman. She tipped her head back as he closed in on her and filled her line of vision.

She was a very contrary specter, pristine in appearance—tidy and well-manicured, dressed in sumptuous fabrics—but then so peculiar for how tasteless was her garb and for the whore's paint she wore all over her face.

The circle of red surrounding the entry point at her shoulder was larger now.

Her breaths came short and quick through pursed, bright red lips.

"Might better sit, mistress," he said, lifting his hand toward her, "ere ye fall."

Her calm was shattered as she stared at his large hand coming near, her fright becoming more obvious. Tears gathered in her eyes. "But tell me what's going on first. Why…why are you dressed like that? Why am I shot? And with an *arrow*? What is happening?"

She was so wretched with bewilderment that a rare occurrence of sympathy scratched to be known inside him.

"Chasing MacPhails, we were, mistress," said Gibbon, who'd come to stand beside Marcus. "Looks like ye got caught up in the pursuit. But we'll see ye made—"

Gibbon cut himself off with a curse just as the woman's gorgeously bare legs gave out beneath her.

Marcus reacted first and quickest, closing the small distance between him and her before she crumbled completely. He reached for her arms, connecting with the smooth fabric of her surcote and solid flesh beneath, able to prevent her from dropping hard. For lack of any other idea about what to do with her, he lowered her to the ground. The shaft and feathers of the arrow were inadvertently bumped and moved by his arms and chest.

The woman groaned, her anguish plain, and went limp in his arms as her eyes rolled back in her head.

"Christ almighty," Marcus seethed, going down on one knee with the woman in his arms.

Carefully, he laid her on her back. He straightened away from her but remained there at her side, on his knee, his gaze raking over the fainted woman. Fairly quickly, a crowd surrounded her.

"That's yer shot, Lewin," said one of the men, Wilfrid. "Finally hit something, dinna ye?"

"Weel, we ken it dinna come from ye," said Aelred. "Couldnae hit the backside of a plump whore, nae within ten feet of her."

Wilfrid shifted his square and short body toward Aelred, frowning as he pointed loosely toward Aelred's left arm, at the end of it, where a hand should be but had not been for many years. "And we ken it was nae ye, ye one-armed bastard."

"One-handed," Aelred corrected mildly, scarcely disturbed by the slight. "How many times will I explain all the parts of the body to ye?"

"Whole arm is useless, with nae hand attached to the end of it," Wilfrid maintained.

"Haud yer wheesht, will ye?" Gibbon commanded.

Silence followed. Indeed, many went completely still. Though he looked amiable and laughed easily, Gibbon was not known for suffering insubordination.

Marcus ignored all the fuss and furor around him, his searing gaze making loose with the woman's face and body.

Her mouth caught and held his attention, being smeared in a shimmery red paint that highlighted the shape of her lips, the top and bottom being wide and plump, and parted to reveal glimpses of impossibly white teeth. Little could be discerned from her closed eyes, save that they were liberally caked with cosmetics, her long lashes coated in black while her lids were covered in strokes of brown and a glistening gold powder. Marcus narrowed his eyes, wondering who this woman was and why she felt the need to employ paint. A curtain of hair, lighter and brighter than straw, lay about the earth around her head in golden waves. While one slender hand was yet clenched around the handled kist, the other had flopped next to her face and was utterly still, the red fingernails almost an exact match to the shade of her lips.

Her pale complexion was so immaculate that he might presume more cosmetics concealed any blemishes that plagued her. He moved his gaze downward, over the ivory skin of her neck and to the triangle of flesh available to the eye where her white tunic was unbuttoned above her breasts. Her surcote had fallen open when he'd laid her down. Her breasts pressed against the silk of her thin tunic, firm and round globes encased in a lace fabric, easily visible beyond the virtually sheer fabric of her tunic. Her waist was trim and her hips lean, her figure boyish if one discounted the nearly indecent but generous display of bosom. As he skimmed his eyes lower, Marcus amended his opinion. Beneath her crudely short skirt, bare legs of sun-kissed skin were lithe and toned. Not boyish at all, but appearing as velvet might, begging to be stroked.

Marcus's frown of confusion over her appearance swiftly evolved to one of displeasure.

She was tiny but not very young, beyond the age that might have suggested he address her as *lass* and not *mistress* as he had. But who the hell was she? And what was she doing in the middle of nowhere, in the vast, disputed woodland between the McInnes stronghold and the MacPhails fortress?

After a silence that stretched for possibly as long as half a minute while all the McInnes men stared at the fallen woman with equal bewilderment, Eadric, standing somewhere behind Marcus, spoke up. "What's she wearin'?"

"Kirtle, is it?" Suggested someone.

"Mibbe aye," guessed another. "Mibbe naw. Dinna cover 'er shanks."

"But how's she painted?"

"Dinna look like she needs—"

"Will we only gawk at her, trying to figure her out?" Young Lewin interjected with unchecked edginess. "Or shuid we attend the injury we've caused her?"

"And will we allow the MacPhails to get beyond our reach?" Osgar, standing beside Gibbon, wanted to know.

Marcus's straight dark brows furrowed lowered, fathoming a baffling sense of recognition. Or more aptly, a familiarity. He stared hard at the fainted woman, knowing he'd never seen her or the like before. But then why did he feel so intensely that he was not meeting her now for the first time but that they were reuniting? Of course it made no sense, not any more than the voice that offered a suggestion inside his head.

Your soul knows her.

Shaking himself free of his absorption with the unusual woman and these most fantastic thoughts, Marcus stood and announced his intentions, which would then become those of his men. He addressed these to Eadric. "It's on ye, mate. Do what ye can." Since Robert McInnes had perished last year, Eadric was the closest thing they had to a surgeon. "I'll leave Lewin and a few others with ye while we pursue them. Abide here, await our return." He glanced down at the lifeless woman again, putting off just now what seemed to be his responsibility. "We'll decide then what's to be done with her."

As Marcus made his way to his steed, Gibbon issued further instructions, separating a few more men to stay behind with Lewin and Eadric.

Returned to the saddle, Marcus spared not one more glance at the fallen woman but led the party away from the scene, and once more in pursuit of those wicked MacPhails.

The woman and her injury were of little concern to him, he swiftly concluded. The folks at Darrie—those that lived yet—and punishing the perpetrators of that horrendous crime were where he would concentrate today's ambitions.

His jaw remained clenched though for another ten minutes.

He considered again words that had been known internally, that had come unbidden.

Your soul knows her.

Bluidy gray eyes and bright red lips, Marcus seethed.

***

She dreamed someone was removing her clothes, and she fought wildly to stop them. Or she thought she did. She couldn't be sure. Pains stabbed at her, but she didn't know what hurt or why. She thought someone was speaking to her in a thick Scots' accent but was unable to comprehend the words or intent of the person.

She had a sense that some time had passed but ideas such as that—time and place and what and who—remained elusive so that she existed for some time in the space of a happy fog. This was decidedly uncharacteristic, she being a journalist, answers being her bread and butter, her life's goal.

When she woke finally to a place and condition that insisted she question her circumstance, she was groggy and unsettled. Still, Autumn had an initial, wispy notion that something terrible had happened but at first was unable to recall what that might be. But her stomach was knotted with an unknown or unremembered dread, she recognized that almost immediately, even before she'd fully taken in her surroundings.

Wakefulness came slowly, her hazy awareness followed swiftly by more bewilderment as a jumbled profusion of thoughts accosted her.

Autumn didn't move immediately, but remained perfectly still, trying to grab at some memory that felt as if it should have come easier to her—something unexpected but awful had happened, she was sure, but couldn't remember immediately.

Nearly the entirety of her vision encompassed a coarse, creamy canvas, that which was stretched above her. She blinked several times until she was able to focus. And how strange that she should understand fairly quickly that she was inside a small and short tent—the canvas suspended above her with a smooth rod—since she'd only ever been tent-camping once in her life and that had been when she was very young, seven or eight years old maybe.

Though she'd woken with that foreboding dread, she hadn't been aware of her heart hammering, but it did now, confusion and fright being to blame for that. She lifted her right hand to her throat, her eyes widening as she encountered only flesh and not any fabric. She moved her hand around, horrified to discover that she was half-naked; her hand found only scraps of material, and none of it was the silk blouse or the light polyester jacket she was certain she'd been wearing. Instinctively, she made to rise to a sitting position, but this elicited a sharp whimper for the acute pain felt in her shoulder at this undertaking.

Autumn fell back down, her head landing on what she supposed was a pillow, though it was very stiff. She moved her fingers again over her front, finding a rough fabric—linen?—had been wrapped around her arm and over her shoulder before it crossed her chest and was threaded under her right arm, presumably joined at the back.

While her chin quivered with dismay, she moved her hand further, only slightly relieved to encounter the strap of her bra and then the lacy cup and then the other. She was not naked, but still wore her bra at least. A further examination, moving her hand lower along her body, offered more relief, finding she still wore her skirt as well.

Everything came back to her in a rush, mercilessly flooding into her, images and sounds and the strangeness of it all. That illusory voice she'd heard—*Dinna go, lass*; running toward the rental car, down that hill that should have only been grass but then was crowded with trees; an arrow—*an arrow, for crying out loud!*—suddenly protruding from her shoulder; that horde of men in their simple but strange clothes, all of them riding horses, looking as if they'd stepped off the pages of a book set in the middle ages; the dazzling but formidable presence of that one man, who looked all at once ruthless and too handsome to be real but then so frightening for how intimidating was his size and glowering stare.

She shivered even now, recalling the piercing regard of his brown eyes. He was a savage, or looked the part, wearing a medieval leather jerkin, an item of clothing she had never known existed before two years ago when she'd ordered one online for Jordan as part of his medieval warrior Halloween costume. This one, on this man today had been of much better quality, possibly made of actual leather and not some synthetic. A strap had crisscrossed the man's chest and affixed to that had been what appeared to be a sheath holding an embossed silver-handled blade. The guy was impressively cut, with wide shoulders and a broad chest. His arms were bare and chiseled with muscles, an impressive sight that did not escape even Autumn's dazed attention earlier. But he was rather scruffy, which possibly added to her opinion of him as ruthless and intimidating. His hair was long and dark but hung in strings and strands around his sharply angled face. His cheeks were covered not only in many days' stubble but in dust and grime and what she was pretty sure had been spots of blood. Sweat dripped from his temple and glistened on his throat.

It was no wonder then that she recalled him in particular and so specifically, when she could remember little of any of the other forty—fifty? more?—men that had crowded the hillside forest around him.

Autumn's body wracked with a shiver at the recollection of his cold brown eyes, at the way they'd made her feel so...so undressed and lacking and insignificant. Good Lord, but she prayed that man had no regular meetings or interactions with children. Talk about the devil of your nightmares.

But then all that was only wasted energy and time, deliberating about that savage man. Her last notice of him had been when she'd felt herself slipping into a faint. She'd known she was falling, losing consciousness, but couldn't have done anything about it. The last thing she remembered now was seeing the frown he wore actually swell dramatically when she'd started to wither downward. As he'd lunged toward her, he'd looked downright pissed that she hadn't been strong enough to stand on her own two feet.

Purposefully, she dismissed him from her mind now, needing instead to get her bearings.

It was night, she realized, possibly with a good moon, since she'd been able to identify the canvas of the tent so clearly. She'd been shot, but first aid had been administered. She didn't remember that she'd noticed any women among the army of men that had surrounded her earlier—today?—but she was fairly confident that though her general impression of that group had been as one of alarming savages and though it seemed her blouse and jacket had been removed, she'd not been violated in any way.

But where was she? Why had she not been taken to a hospital?

She was a logical thinker. That was her job, making sense out of snippets of information, forming complete pictures from all the puzzle pieces she collected. But this—whatever this was, whatever was happening to her—made no sense. Or she could not make sense of it.

An army on horseback, cavalry she supposed they would be.

Using bows and arrows as if they were from some earlier period in time.

Dressed as they were, those men she'd met, in clothes that might have been mistaken for authentic medieval costumes.

The one seemingly in charge, appearing as more a fantasy-inspired warrior than an actual living, breathing man.

What sense could she make of that?

Was she alone? The tent was large enough for only one or two people and presently, thankfully, she was the only person occupying it.

Autumn breathed intentionally, trying to relax her heart rate. She wasn't normally known for leaping straight toward panic and she didn't plan to start now even though this situation was possibly the most unsettling she'd ever faced.

With greater intention and a returned awareness of her injury, she tried to sit up. It proved more painful than difficult but she managed it, her hair brushing against the inside of the tent wall near the ridge pole. Once upright, she noticed in the gloom of nighttime gray that she was covered from the waist down in a blanket, a tartan patterned thing, which she'd expected to see more of in Scotland but had not. A pile of crumbled things in the corner of the tent near her feet drew her attention. She reached forward with her right arm and hand, pleased to find her blouse and jacket wadded up there.

Putting on her blouse proved as uncomfortable as sitting up had, but she managed that as well and felt immeasurably better already simply to be fully clothed. She buttoned up the blouse and threw the jacket over her left arm since she'd already realized it felt better to keep her arm bent near her waist and because she didn't plan on moving the arm or using it for anything else. She thought she might fashion her jacket into a sling but didn't take the time now to do that. A rather thorough search around the tiny tent did not give up her shoes, for which she was doubly upset. Not only did she not relish going barefoot around where ever she might be, but the price tag of her Christian Louboutin leather, pointed, red-soled pumps had her cringing at their loss.

Since she could not stand up inside the tent, Autumn tossed off the warm wool blanket and butt-scooched forward until she could peer beyond the loose flaps at the opening.

She wasn't sure what she expected to find or if any idea about her location had even began to develop in her brain, but discovering that she was yet in a forest, a dark and eerie woodland of shadows and spooky silence, hadn't occurred to her. But there it was, just outside the tent, a fog-shrouded landscape, spotted with tall lines of pitch black and lesser, translucent lines of gray, the trees and their shadows. Silence was felt and not heard; no birdsong pierced the night, no rustling of leaves or animals could be heard, the air was fresh but uncommonly still.

It took a moment for her eyes to adjust from the expanse of creamy canvas to the darkness of the night but soon after she recognized the remnants of a small fire by the slow moving plume of gray smoke that rose from its embers. Around the fire, she presently distinguished more tartan blankets and comprehended they covered bodies, likely those of the army she'd met, one of whom might have been responsible for shooting her but also, one of whom might have tended her wound.

The nagging, nearly frightening questions of who they were, why they'd shot her, if she were safe with them were just enough to recommend that escape, away from these people, was in her best interest.

A sudden cough startled Autumn, and then a low and steady rumbling of someone snoring obliterated the complete and creepy silence. Carefully, Autumn scooched forward some more and then gingerly got to her feet. This was not easily accomplished but was not as impossible as she had imagined it would be. She used one hand to push herself up from the ground and then stood perfectly still just in front of the tent, waiting to see if what bare noise she'd made might have disturbed anyone. When no one challenged her leaving the tent, Autumn glanced around the immediate area for her shoes but when she could not find them, she began to tiptoe away from this most absurd situation.

As the opening of the tent faced the remains of the camp fire and the men who'd made their beds around it, Autumn walked noiselessly, one step at a time, around the side of the tent and headed steadily away from the band of brothers or whoever they were. Vaguely she wondered if she would ever have a clear picture of what had happened and why on this crisp day in September in Scotland.

When she was much younger, walking barefoot would not have troubled her in the least. Now, after years spent honing a carefully polished image of fledgling news reporter, a woman who had it all together, who sometimes—she charitably allowed—and with the help of filters, looked like an Instagram picture walking, Autumn never went barefoot. Certainly not in a sinister forest in the dead of night while trying to slip away unnoticed from a gang of men for whom she could not even conceive a collective name.

Good grief. All this harrowing business and she'd not yet even seriously begun to investigate the disappearance of Megan West.

Beyond the tent, the trees seemed to thicken. Of course she had no sense of direction or of which way she should want to head, and so she only snuck away, hoping soon she would meld into the fog and shadows and trees unseen.

"Ye dinna want to do that."

Autumn froze at the sound of the deep voice, instantly recognizable, hardly able to be forgotten for the way it washed over her like a warm wave on a Key West beach. She stopped moving completely, barely dared to breathe. Maybe he would go away. Or allow her to.

"Ye dinna want to strike out on yer own, into the forest," he said instead.

A slightest rustling, a small crunch of gravel or stone, came with his voice as he moved unhurriedly toward her.

She willed herself to turn and face the man, though every fiber of her being screamed with fright.

Swallowing down her worst fears, she lifted her chin and met the glistening midnight gaze of the awe-inspiring man.

Chapter Four

Good God, but how could a guy be so incredibly hot and at the same time instill a person with so much foreboding? It wasn't like he'd brandished a weapon at her or had made any threat against her. And it wasn't really as if he were *that* handsome—he was, frankly, too unkempt, too savage to be truly and classically attractive. Possibly, it was simply that he *looked* so big and mean; hence the menace assumed. Maybe she should resist fear until he gave her reason to know it. But then, perhaps it was her intuition, a gut reaction to him, that wisely warned her to be wary.

Something was not quite right about him. Or about anything since she'd stopped to check out the broch that Megan West had mentioned in her sparse journal.

She took a hesitant step backward, her mind racing as she tried to make sense of his mood, his intention right now while he tried to prevent her from leaving.

"I—" she began but then was forced to clear her throat to make her voice work properly, without croaking. "I need to get back."

"Back to where?" He asked, his tone unreadable.

"The Lodge of the Loch," she answered mechanically, her own voice dull.

"And now ye will go? In the deep of night?"

He stepped forward, along a sliver of bare earth that might have been a trail, moving until he stood within three feet of Autumn.

She gulped down a swallow of horror, realizing what had escaped both her earlier notice and her persistent memory, the fact that he wore a sword on the belt at his waist. Had others in his company had a sword as well? A sword, she mused internally. What the hell? That *was* a sword, wasn't it? That long, narrow leather-clad thing which was nearly as tall as his long legs. His hand sat atop it now, on the hilt, looking as if it rested there often, as if he regularly was outfitted with a sword.

"I need to get back," she said after a moment, when it dawned on her that while she struggled to grasp the very idea of the presence of a sword, he was waiting on a reply from her.

"Aye, so ye've said," he allowed, narrowing his eyes at her. "But now ye need to go? With nae an escort?"

Autumn nodded. "Yes, I do. Can you just point in the direction of—" she let that thought go, laying her hand on her chest as another forgotten thing came to her. "Where is my suitcase?" She couldn't abandon her luggage. The equipment was hers, not *borrowed* from the studio as she sometimes did, but it represented a personal investment of thousands of dollars, which she would rather not lose if she could help it.

The thick, straight brows of the strange medieval-looking warrior angled downward at the top of his straight and bony nose. He shook his head as if he didn't understand her.

"My luggage," she clarified. "The gold case with the wheels." She tried to make motions with her hands to indicate its size but winced and stiffened when her thoughtless movement wrenched a muscle near her shoulder or the wound itself and she was once again knifed by an intense pain.

Autumn closed her mouth, clamping her lips together. Funny how sharp pain could also produce instant nausea.

The man bent his arm at the elbow, pointing his thumb over his shoulder. "'Tis there yet, nae gone."

Autumn waited, for both the nausea to pass and for the man to offer to bring the hardside spinner suitcase to her. Somehow she was not surprised when he did not.

"I canna allow ye to travel by night."

Autumn's brows lifted. "But...you really can't stop me." *Could he? Jesus, would he?*

"I would hope that guid sense might give ye pause. Unless...mayhap ye've nae been gifted with a plentiful supply?"

Autumn's eyes widened. The question, if on paper, might have read as a joke. But here and now, delivered in his decadently rich, arrogant voice, it sounded more like a smug reproach.

"Nice," she said pertly. "Nice try, anyway, that manipulation. I suppose that might work on—who? Seriously, who would fall for that?" Christ, she couldn't even slap her hands on her hips to punctuate her annoyance. The barest movement of her left arm caused excruciating pain.

"Will ye nae wait until morn, just a few hours away, and we'll walk ye down the hill and out of the forest?"

"But...the road is just at the bottom of the hill," she argued mildly, wondering frankly why he cared. "My car is there. It'll be warm and can take me someplace even warmer."

"Ye dinna make so much sense, mistress," he told her. "Has me speculating ye're nae quite yerself. Fever might get ye if it has nae already."

"Oh, my God. *I* don't make sense?" She was prompted by shock to protest. "*Me?* Okay, and fever? Yeah, all the more reason to be on my way. I should probably find a hospital—who did this anyway?" She asked, pointing to her shoulder and the bandage. "Was it even cleaned? Won't I need an antibiotic?" She drew in a sharp breath and then bit her bottom lip, an idea coming to her. "Oh, shit. You're worried that I'm going to the police. That I'm going to press charges." She most certainly would. That might even be her first stop before she found a hospital or an urgent care place to check out her shoulder. These reckless men needed to be reported. "I promise you I'm not. I just want this day and whatever...whatever happened and...all of it—I want to put it behind me. I'm super confused and even the reporter in me isn't looking for answers so much as she and I just want to get away..." *from you*, she finished internally. At his darkening scowl, Autumn added in a small voice, "Nothing personal."

He nodded slowly, piercing her with the force of his gaze briefly before he turned and walked away, blending in with the shadows of the nighttime forest.

Blowing out a release of breath, Autumn waited an entire minute before she followed tentatively, meaning to collect her suitcase herself. She hoped its contents were still within, hoped none of these men had stolen anything. She didn't make it all the way back to the tent in which she'd found herself when she'd first woken, but was met by the man returning to her, suitcase in hand. He held it completely off the ground by its short handle, ignoring the telescoping handle that was still fully extended.

Autumn supposed if someone had snooped around inside they might first have lowered the walking handle.

When the man stood again within a few feet of her, he brought forth his other hand, in which he held her pumps.

"Ye dinna forget these, did ye?"

While his expression was indecipherable, his tone suggested he knew that she'd abandoned her shoes in favor of making a hasty exit.

She lifted her chin. "I didn't want to wake everyone asking what had become of my shoes."

When she made no moved to claim them, he lifted his hand and his brow, presenting the shoes to her along with an unasked question about whether or not she was afraid of him.

She was.

But she stepped forward anyway and retrieved the shoes. He set the suitcase down, gave it a strange look, as if he'd never seen anything like it, and then glanced up at Autumn again.

"Well, thank you," she said. For what, she wasn't precisely sure.

His hand returned to its position atop the hilt of his sword—a friggin' sword!—and he only nodded in response.

"Good night," she said. "Good bye, I mean," she clarified quickly, a bit flustered, willing to blame him for that, for the way he devoured and terrorized a person with his penetrating, gleaming gaze.

He made a sound that was hard to interpret—not even imprecisely enough to say that it was positive or negative.

"Okay then." She curled her fingers around the suitcase's drawn-out handle, knowing there was no way she could carry the thing through the forest, at night, and with only one good arm.

And while she contemplated fleetingly an indistinct worry that he might now spring, might try to prevent her from leaving after all, she was also softly seized by some other emotion at the idea of simply walking away from this man, and leaving behind with him all that had happened and all that had perplexed her on this day.

Naturally, it made no sense that she should feel—what did she feel? She didn't feel bad for leaving, for wanting to get away from the hot weirdo. But she felt something. Maybe she only supposed she'd been kind of bitchy when in truth the arrow was in all probability an accident and he and those men with him hadn't harmed her but had helped her. So yeah, she did feel kind of guilty for expressing her confusion and fear to this man as a bitchy persona.

"I'm sorry if I seem rude." She sighed and meant to change that. "I didn't get your name."

"I dinna give it."

Autumn rolled her eyes. The bitch hadn't departed after all. "Do you want to?" Weirdo. "So that I know who to thank for...for your, um, your care." She released the suitcase handle and struck out her right hand. "I'm Autumn Winters." She waited for the inevitable, some mention about her two-season name, or what her parents had been smoking when they'd given it to her, or the predictable question, if she had just made that up. Only her name and face on the news in her hometown kept the locals in and around Chicago from questioning it. Almost at the start, when she'd first gotten the job at WGRN, she'd made a Facebook post about her name, getting the elephant in the room out of the way. Little was made of it these days, not much more than the occasional joke, most often from the evening anchor, who sometimes pretended to slip up and called her Summer Winters, at which she always pretended to laugh, but secretly she wanted to punch him in the face. Until that one occasion almost a year ago now, when she'd ended her piece with, "Back to you, Slim Whittaker," because his name was Jim, and he was nowhere near slim. He'd not ever referred to her as Summer Winters again.

The man in front of her now stared at her hand as if he didn't understand why she'd extended it. It was hard to tell in the darkness, but she thought he narrowed his eyes even more at her. At length, he did reach for and clasp her hand. The initial touch was shocking for how warm his hand was. She'd not realized how cold she was. And then, some curious feeling assailed her, but she could not say if it was fear or just the opposite, what she felt at having her hand clasped so warmly, so tightly, in his firm and strong grip.

"Marcus of the McInnes," he introduced himself.

Marcus? Marcus.

Yes, she supposed that was fitting. Certainly Norman or Walter or Clark would have been incompatible with the image he presented, with what he was, whatever he might be aside from the obvious: huge, strong, brooding.

Marcus was suitably masculine to represent this man.

He cautioned her once more. "The forest is hostile enough during daylight hours and only more treacherous at night. My guess? Ye get lost or find yerself surrounded by folks nae as kind as the McInnes—"

"You are the *kind McInnes*?" She interrupted, saucy now since he'd returned to that, to telling her what was best for her, what she should do. "You and all those men? The ones who shot me with an arrow? Yeah, thanks. I think I'll take my chances."

"Mayhap meet up with night prowlers or ravenous beasts," he went on, as if she'd not interrupted him. "And I'll wager my last farthing ye tear open Eadric's bonny stitches ere the cock crows at sunrise."

Ere the cock crows crinkled her brow once more. Who the hell was this guy? Who talked like that?

"My guess," she responded pointedly and without missing a beat, "is that you'd like that, that any or all of those things happened to me. You look like one of those guys who can never be wrong, who knows everything, and whose orders must be followed. Well, Marcus of the McInnes, I'm from the States and we American girls don't so much like people telling us what we can and can not do. Good bye," she said as she pivoted on her bare foot and began marching away from him. "And good riddance," she murmured when she was sure he couldn't hear her.

***

Marcus was teased by a rare grin of amusement. Though he didn't allow it to emerge fully, he did entertain the idea of it for a moment. At least he contemplated the reason behind it.

Autumn Winters—strange name aside—was certainly diverting. There was something to be said for a lass of her station —he reckoned her as wealthy, spoiled, useless, too beautiful to be anything else—fighting the intrinsic urge to blanch in front of him. Fighting *and* persevering against that innate fear that had warned her to be wary of him, arrow through the shoulder notwithstanding. But damn, if she hadn't just spoken most impertinently to him as few would dare, as if she knew no fear at all. He'd been certain she'd rolled her eyes at him. Rolled her bluidy eyes at him! Had she no fear? Did she not know better?

Marcus sighed as her figure and lesser shadow disappeared into the growing fog, moving deeper into the forest. He toyed briefly with the idea that he should have detained her, should have insisted with more authority that she not take leave just now. It dawned on him that aside from her name and despite all the time devoted to her inside his head over the last eight hours, she walked away as much a mystery as she had been when first he'd encountered her.

Though plenty of speculation had taken place all day throughout the ranks of his men and within himself, no answers had been discovered about the woman or her circumstance.

The hunt for the MacPhails had proved fruitless, their trail ending at the fast and frothy river Lochy. Marcus had returned to the temporary camp made atop the lower beinn to find a small crowd gathered round Eadric as he'd tended the woman's injury. It was deemed beneficial that she'd remained passed out as Eadric had been obliged to remove both her strange short surcote and the gauzy tunic beneath it. Marcus had not been the only one rendered stiff and mute at the sight of her then, the top half of her at the time covered in naught but a stunning and wispy confection of lace and silk triangles, whose sole purpose was, it seemed, to contain the lavish bounty of her breasts. He'd been compelled by an irrational annoyance at the leering of Niall, at the lad's nearly grotesque smirk as he'd ogled her. Marcus had sent him off with harsh commands, bidding him to fetch and erect his laird's tent rather than reprehensibly eyeballing the woman.

Marcus had remained, had even flinched as he'd watched Eadric capably pierce her tender flesh with the long bone needle while sewing her wound. He could not say what had prompted him to offer his own tent as shelter but had done just that. And then, knowing Eadric and his pronounced limp and Aelred and only one hand and even Lewin with his reedy frame—not wide enough to bless himself, it had been said—could not have transported her, Marcus himself had lifted her into his arms and conveyed her to his tent.

She'd been lightweight in his arms, and he hadn't known her name then, hadn't met her but an hour before, but still experienced a mystifying sense of responsibility for her. Her head had lolled against his shoulder, her blonde hair disheveled and matted with dirt and debris, the end of one lock caked with blood. Beneath the powder of cosmetics her delicate features had been pale, and yet her eyes, closed in unconsciousness, had been squeezed tightly as if her faint had not relieved her of fright. Her body was slender, almost fragile, and he could feel even now the warmth of her skin, where his bare arms and chest had met with the soft warmth of her flesh.

Even half-clothed, she'd been but an incomprehensible person in the daytime, an unknown entity, mysterious for how peculiar she appeared and for how unusual was her speech, and more so for the stunning effect she'd had on him.

But nighttime....

Autumn Winters was a different creature entirely in the night, soft and hazy, imbued with courage to stand up to him, with nary a cry for her plight, whatever that might be beyond the very obvious arrow wound, brave enough to strike out on her own—or simply and mistakenly terrified enough of him and his men that she deemed it safer to depart the safety of their numbers. She'd stood before him with her blonde hair cascading around her shoulders and shimmering with a life of its own under the charitable moonlight. Her gray eyes, like mysterious pools, had held a depth that seemed to hint at countless untold stories, at some fantastic life lived.

Of course it was beyond ridiculous to ponder even vaguely that sense inside him that he knew her. Or that he *should* know her. However, he could neither ignore nor escape the needling energy that seemed to work as some invisible force, guiding him toward her, toward wanting or needing to know her.

All rubbish, he decided and turned away from where she'd walked away into the night.

Marcus dismissed all this fanciful conjuring as idiocy, as time wasted, and blamed it on his heightened anger at losing track of the MacPhails. He was riled to enhanced awareness of everything around him when his wrath was aroused.

He returned to his tent and was greeted by the soft floral notes of the heady fragrance that was hers but slept little that night. The despicable injustice done to the people of Darrie warred for time and space inside his head with the image and perception of Autumn Winters. Resolutely, he pushed thoughts of the woman from his mind.

But then he didn't worry so much about the MacPhails escaping justice today. He knew where to find them.

He would return to Balla Àrd and regroup and make preparations for the full scale battle that MacPhail apparently craved. This morning, the sparse smoke plumes spotted from the walls of Balla Àrd had suggested little more than an out of control fire at Darrie, which sat miles away from the McInnes fortress. Marcus had assembled only two units, forty men, to accompany him to lend aid to their plight. Never would he have guessed that MacPhail would have ordered an attack on Darrie. Possibly, the old bastard had led the strike himself; Marcus wouldn't have been surprised. When he'd reached Darrie and it had been made known to him what had transpired, Marcus had chased the infidels intuitively, driven by rage, even as he'd known he hadn't a force large enough to properly confront them. But he would remedy that, would go home and assemble his entire army, and he would make sure neither MacPhail nor any of his wretched kin ever again made war on innocent people.

Well before the sun rose, Marcus abandoned his tent and the unlikely possibility of sleep. He prowled the camp and the woods restlessly, and then nudged his foot against his captain's toe, wanting to get moving.

Gibbon woke as he always did, his thick white-gray hair tousled but not laughably so, his eyes and mind immediately sharp. He stood, bringing his plaid with him, rolling the breacan neatly while he listened to Marcus's instructions.

"I canna wait on the sun," Marcus said. "Let us move now. We can be home and outfitted and on the move again before the noon hour."

"Aye," replied Gibbon. "And straight at the snake in his lair."

"Aye. He'll expect it," Marcus presumed. "He must. But we've no choice. The assault can nae go unanswered."

Gibbon nodded. "Might want to send word to the Nicholson, should it nae go our way."

"I will." The Nicholsons were not the next closest clan or neighbor, but he was a valued friend of Marcus, who would be expected to both avenge the McInnes and protect their interests in land and people if this fight went in favor of MacPhail, as Marcus would do for Reid if the need arose.

They left the beinn and its forest straight away, traveling quietly over gently rolling hills and shallow glens of dew-dampened green grass, but could not escape the prevalent scent of moss and pine. Birdsong tracked their movement, creating a rhythmic cadence that seemed to harmonize with the soft hoofbeats of the McInnes steeds.

An hour later as the sun began to break through the cool fog that crept about, the sound of rushing water grew louder as they neared the banks of the River Lochy, which represented one section of the imprecise and long-disputed border between the McInnes demesne and the MacPhails land. Often Marcus thought the river flowed like a moat protecting the McInnes lands. Other times, he had to consider that it might well be serving the MacPhails as much as the McInnes for how it so ably kept the two clans away from each other.

Osgar and Wilfrid served as the leads, turning north at the river's banks, steering the party toward Yopin's ford, that generally shallow place with good footing where crossing was easy. As soon as they crossed, they would again be upon McInnes land. Rarely had Marcus made this crossing without feeling an immediate sense of peace, a connection to the land, as if the very earth beneath him was alive with the spirit of every McInnes who'd come and gone before him.

And though today's encounter was no different, the peacefulness was short-lived.

"Why does he insist on going bare-headed?" Gibbon, at Marcus's side, asked.

No doubt he referred to Osgar, who for as long as Marcus had known him could scarcely claim to have more than a few strands of hair on his head, and who had taken to shaving his pate completely. And though his head was agreeably round, not oblong or otherwise misshapen, his ears were overlarge and considerably pointy so that the overall image of him was sometimes likened to an elf or several other fey creatures.

"Och, Goblin," called out Gibbon good-naturedly, addressing Osgar as he routinely did, "throw a blanket over it, will ye? Ere the reflection cast us all into blindness!"

Without turning around, Osgar held up his hand, making a crude motion overhead, which elicited several guffaws from those between and around the two men, and then a less than serious derisive snarl from Gibbon.

He chuckled at Marcus. "Tell me true, is nae the day wasted if I canna give the goblin some grief?"

Marcus smirked indifferently at his captain. Even as he was vaguely pleased for Gibbon, for all of them, who seldom suffered foul tempers when returning home, no matter how long or short their absence had been, he was just then needled by an awareness that something in the air had changed.

In the next instant, just as Marcus realized that the birdsong had quieted, Osgar fisted and stiffened the hand raised above his head and drew his majestic black destrier to a halt. He went rigid enough in the saddle that at least an inch was added to his seated height.

Marcus did not pause to wonder what concerned him, did not listen for answers, but rode ahead to the river's edge. Before he'd fully gained Osgar's side, Marcus simultaneously took note of two alarming facts, either of which might have been the basis for Osgar's pause.

Across the river and to the right, upon McInnes land, stood the wooded vale that stretched for hundreds of acres and followed the curved path of the river as it traveled east and then rose north. Emerging from that wilderness in the east came a massive army wearing the familiar and despised red and black of the MacPhail tartan. They charged hard, a thunderous rumbling growing as they materialized from the woodland, the trees no more absorbing the sound.

Tragic enough, the sight, the idea of what would come. Nearly slack-jawed, Marcus estimated a force more than a hundred strong.

"Son of a..." Gibbon breathed, having followed Marcus to the water's edge.

The bastards had circled around, separating Marcus and his men from home, just far enough away that no one there at Balla Àrd, even guards atop the curtained wall, would be aware of what happened here and now at the River Lochy.

Tragedy indeed, about to occur. He and his men would likely die today, each of them, upon the wretched blades of depraved MacPhails.

And yet the second thing of which he'd taken note at almost the exact same time, somehow even more alarming, might have been what actually caused his heart to skip a beat. Standing in the midst of the sun-dappled grass of the meadow across the river, in the direct path of the charging MacPhails, a solitary figure stood frozen with her back to the McInnes. 'Twas a woman, unmistakably, said the slender frame and the wealth of long blonde hair draped down her back. At her side, a golden, wheeled trunk sat unmoving. From this distance Marcus could only imagine, by way of recollection, her delicate hand white-knuckled on its handle. He might also suppose her gray eyes were alive and wide with horror.

His battle mien came unbidden, simply as an innate reaction. He wasted not a moment more in shock over the sight of either of these things—another chance meeting with Autumn Winters or the MacPhails on McInnes land, about to slaughter him and his forty men—but twisted his features into rage and squeezed his knees into his destrier's side at the same time. He issued a guttural "Yah!" to the steed and plunged them into the river and beyond, intent on reaching Autumn Winters before the MacPhails did.

Chapter Five

Though the trek was tedious, surely having more to do with her injury, her bare feet, lugging the suitcase over rough terrain, and having had little sleep but that which she'd gained from her faint, Autumn had not thought the hike particularly challenging. Still, she'd been frustrated, imagining she might actually have wandered in circles overnight with no sun to guide her direction. Come morning, she'd sadly spent less time marveling over the woods themselves—a tapestry of vibrant greens and browns with tall trees forming a protective canopy overhead, where the sunlight broke gorgeously through the thick foliage and cast evershifting patterns of light and shadow on the forest floor—than she had trying to escape them.

She'd walked for miles by now she was sure, had climbed a friggin' mountain to get her bearings, and...and nothing. She saw nothing that looked even vaguely familiar. No roads, no buildings, not the broch, not that long barn with the gray metal roof that stood across the road from the broch. Where had those McInnes men taken her? How had they traveled so far without her being aware of it? And Christ, why hadn't Marcus McInnes told her *oh, hey, you're not anywhere near where we first met you*?

When finally she'd emerged from the forest, it hadn't been long before she'd found the river, where she'd drank greedily and had sat for quite a while, trying to make sense of her location—no luck there—and then lamenting the state of her person and her belongings. The rising sun had shown the complete annihilation of her suit jacket. Nearly one half of the subtle herringbone of light and dark camel was awash in blood. A ragged hole an inch wide pierced the left shoulder. Same with her blouse, the hole and the blood, but little choice had she but to wear them, the temperature overnight dropping dramatically that her want and need to keep moving had been precipitated not only by wanting to find civilization again but to retain what little body heat she'd still possessed.

During her rest at the river, she'd worked up the gumption to peek under the linen bandage, gagging down her reaction at the sight of the jagged line of beige, mostly bloody thread that crisscrossed the skin just below her shoulder. Good God, those men were Neanderthals. Didn't they carry with them a basic first-aid kit with *actual* bandages? And what the hell had they used as antibiotic? The stitched hole in her body had been slathered with a bilious concoction that looked like green slime and smelled like rancid milk.

Were they some kind of survivalist group, eschewing all things modern and practical? Did Scotland have characters, fringe societies, like that?

She'd been forced to pee in the woods overnight and prayed to God she found a road, a car, or maybe a helpful person who might steer her toward the Lodge on the Loch before she needed a bathroom for anything else.

Her feet were scraped and caked in mud, the baby toe of her right foot red and swollen from when she'd caught it on an exposed root. Likewise, her face and hair and arms had suffered many meetings with bristly branches and underbrush, until she felt there wasn't a square inch of her not chafed, lacerated, or otherwise manhandled by the unforgiving forest. Her suitcase was dinged and dented and had lost a wheel, and she'd lost one of her shoes after her pit stop, when she'd thought she'd grabbed both of them from where she'd dropped them on the ground but apparently had only retrieved one. She'd tossed aside the other when she'd notice its mate was missing.

But oh, how happy she'd been when the trees had thinned, when the mist had dissipated, when she finally stood and then sat directly in the morning sun, hungrily sucking up its limited heat. She'd allowed herself only a short break at the river, maintaining as she had all night a genuine desire to put as much distance between her and Marcus and all those McInnes men.

She'd walked along the river banks until she'd found a crossable spot, had gingerly made her way to the other side, and then....this.

Beyond confused, Autumn's shoulders slumped as she sighed wearily and stared at the approaching—what was it? A swarm? A marauding army? A horde of zombies?

At this point, she wasn't sure any one of those could or would surprise her.

Her ambivalence toward the approaching throng was swiftly replaced by a new surge of panic as they drew closer, as they came into focus.

At first it seemed only a dark splotch against the backdrop of yet another forest. But then the splotch began to shift and sway, and she realized it was a mass of mounted men. Men riding horseback, wearing dull metal helmets and what appeared to be suits of armor, or parts thereof. But this was not the McInnes men, was it? No, there was a lot of red and black before her, not any of that vibrant blue and green of the McInnes tartans.

Suddenly, the air was filled with a raucous sound, men shouting battle cries, their voices rising like a cacophonous chorus of rage-filled sports fans. A gleam of weapons, broadswords and foot-long knives, caught the sunlight and flashed like jagged lightning in the dark storm of this nightmarish delusion.

Autumn's brain tried to make sense of what she was seeing. Otherwise, she was stunned, immobilized by her confusion. And quite frankly, she was more attuned to the concept of her own bewilderment than she was to the cause of it, the cause being the fantastic sight of what looked to be a medieval army bearing down on her.

What the actual—?

"Autumn!"

Her name being roared, and with a volume and rage as she'd never heard in all her life, pulled her from her frozen reverie. The loud bellow did not echo, but the sound of her name seemed to fill the air with considerable substance so that it was easily heard over the deafening noise of the approaching army. Mechanically, she turned, facing the river she'd crossed not more than five minutes ago, and immediately recognized this much smaller group of mounted men as the McInnes, noting the colors of their plaids.

Not surprising at all, Marcus McInnes led the charge, being several horse lengths in front of the next closest man.

Autumn's mouth fell open at the sight. He hadn't looked even remotely friendly yesterday, not once, hadn't even looked sheepish or guilt-ridden when she'd first met him, not even as she realized that the arrow sticking out of her body was very similar to ones carried in quivers on the backs of the men in his company. But now—Jesus, *now*!—he looked ready to murder, was ten times more terrifying for the homicidal rage painted across his face. His features were contorted with an unholy fury, the angular lines sharpened with contempt. His lips were pulled back, his teeth bared like a snarling dog ready to defend its human.

He's coming for ye whispered inside her, bringing with it some hazy realization that she wasn't actually surprised to see him just now, as if subconsciously, she'd known they would meet again.

It was his face that finally startled her out of the immobility of her incomprehension and into a full blown panic. This was no game. No joke. No cinematic endeavor.

Autumn finally moved, putting one foot in front of the other, running directly toward Marcus McInnes. Still, she was befuddled enough of mind yet that she bothered to drag her suitcase along behind her, which seriously slowed her down so that she was sure that those armored sword-wielding men might actually reach her first. While her heart pounded in her chest and her pulse reverberated in her ears, she kept her gaze locked on Marcus.

Even as he bent low in the saddle and compelled his huge horse to go faster, Marcus McInnes's scorching brown-eyed gaze was unwavering.

Autumn finally realized that her hand was still attached to the suitcase and let go, leaving it in her wake as she continued to run. She was too shocked yet to cry and too stunned to wonder why she was running toward *this* man. Likewise, she hadn't thought far enough ahead to wonder what might happen when she reached him, or he reached her. Would he take her up on the horse with him? Christ, and at this speed?

She winced a bit in expectation of being run over as the McInnes bore down on her. At the last minute, Marcus yanked on the reins, coming to an abrupt halt. The horse's hooves lifted and pawed at the air only a few feet away from Autumn's face.

Other McInnes men continued on, the sound strident as forty men passed on either side of her.

Marcus did not extend his hand to bring her onto the horse with her, which she realized at that moment was exactly what she wanted. Something awful, something terribly perilous was about to happen. She wanted to be with him, on his horse, with escape an option, not on the ground, able to be run down and mowed over.

Autumn raised her hand to him, hope in her terrified gaze.

"Nae," Marcus said curtly, leaning down toward her. He pointed behind him. "To the river, lass! Run and dinna stop. Head west." He moved his hand to the right. "Half a mile and—"

"No. Can't I stay with you?" Without thought, guided only by fear, she put her hand beseechingly on his thigh. "Please."

"'Tis nae safe and I canna fight true with ye in the saddle," he clipped shortly. He pointed again. "Head west half a mile, then turn north. You'll find Balla Àrd soon enough. Run and dinna look back."

"But I—"

"Go!" He commanded, his frown severe. "Run!"

And then he was gone, chasing his men to meet that other group. As confused as she was, as improbable as the obvious seemed, Marcus's brusque harshness confirmed this was real, whatever was about to happen.

Self-preservation moved her now, same as it had moments ago. She sprinted toward the river and hop-skipped across it. Ahead of her, just at the fringe of the forest, two McInnes men stood with several feet between them, letting arrows fly one after another. Neither paid her any attention. Autumn watched as the closest one blindly retrieved an arrow by its feathered end from the grouping he'd struck into the ground at his side. Closing one eye and squinting the other, he drew back and held that stance momentarily, moving only the bow and nocked arrow, presumably along with a sighted target, releasing when he was ready. He didn't pause to see what became of that missile or its target but reached for the next arrow and lined up his next victim.

Autumn turned right and continued moving. She wouldn't have stopped, would have kept right on running, might have run all the way back to the airport if someone had pointed its direction, but that the noise from behind her gave her pause. She yelped when the first resounding clang of metal against metal reached her ears. Autumn crashed against an old oak tree and hugged its trunk while she stared back across the river. And despite the harrowing last few minutes, she was wholly unprepared for the sight that greeted her.

In the green grass of the brilliant sunlit meadow, the fortyish men with Marcus McInnes met an army of what was clearly more than a hundred. Arrows whistled swiftly through the air, straight and level, no arc in their trajectory. Screams sometimes identified their victims. Swords clashed against shields or other blades; some warriors fell, their cries of agony piercing the riotous din; blood stained the ground, mingling with the vibrant green grass. Marcus was easy to pick out among the colliding warriors, being larger than most, his sword a massive weapon of brightly polished steel. He was a towering figure with wild black hair and a deep war cry that rose above every other sound.

As Autumn watched, her mouth hung open, Marcus fought with savage intensity, every movement precise and effective, a sure testament to his skill and strength. He parried with a man now, countering with powerful thrusts and jabs until the enemy was sliced to ribbons and fell from his horse. Before the dying man had hit the ground, Marcus had moved on, cleaving his sword through an enemy's armor as if it were only paper. He was a force of nature, a whirlwind of death and destruction, laying waste to everything in his path, battling with such immaculate passion.

Autumn removed her gaze from Marcus and took in the entire scene, her lingering shock giving way to the truth, that this was real, this was happening right before her eyes. This was a battle, an all-out war between these two armies. The blood was real, the dismembered parts and pieces were real. The lifeless bodies, bloodied and broken, were real. The scent of blood and sweat and fear wafting across the river was not imagined.

But Marcus and the McInnes men were losing, had never stood a chance actually. Not against an army two or three times their size. But why had Marcus and his army raced toward the fight and not away?

At this moment, hiding behind the old oak and watching this horrific scene, Autumn was revisited by the words of Megan West's journal. In her mind's eye, she saw the words clearly on that first page, the only one Megan had used, written in blue ink, the handwriting small but neat.

Go back in time with Graeme.
Go back to the fourteenth century!

No, Autumn resisted. That was not possible. Of course it wasn't.

No. Just no.

Rejecting the very idea, Autumn returned her complete attention to the battle. The desperate urge to run away no longer gripped her. She put her hand to her throat, watching as one McInnes after another fell.

Get up. Fight! Her mind screamed.

Her gaze again searched for Marcus. She found him just as he was knocked off his horse, being overpowered by three men. In sudden agony, she watched as he was kicked from behind when he tried to get to his feet and then she became distraught when an enemy combatant approached on horseback, lifting his sword to land a killing blow. The loud scream that came at that exact moment, she realized, erupted from her and she clamped her hand over her mouth just as the man with the raised sword was struck in the chest with an arrow and toppled to the ground.

Autumn barked out a cry of relief and turned to see those McInnes archers still at work. Possibly they had saved as many lives of their own men as they had taken of the enemy.

Marcus stood with his back to the river and Autumn, taking slow steps backwards, still holding his sword and that other blade at the ready. He moved at an angle and Autumn wondered if this was done to give his archers a clear shot of the many men who slowly, tauntingly pursued him, some still in the saddle, some on foot. Horrified, Autumn realized Marcus and only a handful of others were the last McInnes men standing. If the other McInnes were not all dead, they were certainly incapacitated. She saw the bald-headed man that she recalled from yesterday and that one who was portly, downed but still moving. Another that she remembered, with an incredible head of gray hair, was trying to stand while blood seeped from his gut. Only a few other smaller hand-to-hand fights took place in the background, but otherwise, Marcus was the last man standing.

Twenty men and then more stalked Marcus as he continued to slowly back away. At least ten yards separated him from them, but the distance was dwindling. The ridiculously loud din of battle faded to grunts and groans and the random whinny of a horse. Arrows continued to fly from the archers on the same side of the river as her. Occasionally they found their marks but still there were simply too many for Marcus to take on by himself.

He stopped moving backwards, which curiously paused the slow pursuit of his enemy. Shoulders that had slumped a bit with fatigue or hopelessness now squared noticeably. Autumn was able to see only a sliver of Marcus's profile, and that from a distance, including a trail of blood oozing from a gash at his temple. He wore a savage lip curl and his chest heaved as he tucked the long knife into his belt and then planted his feet wide. His spine stiffened as he lifted his sword with both hands, assuming a battle pose. Blood was noted on almost every part of his body, arms, legs, face, back.

He was an impressive figure, but Autumn saw only a lone man standing before an army of many. Her fingers dug into the bark of the tree. Tears spilled from Autumn's eyes at the image of Marcus. The view was terrifying, him standing alone, a solitary man about to be confronted by dozens of heavily armed men.

Oh my God! Why didn't he just fall down and pretend he was dead? Why not run?

Frantic, she turned to the archers twenty yards away. Why weren't they still shooting? She found one of those men on the ground, an arrow sticking out of his chest. She hadn't even realized the enemy had been firing at them. The other man—barely more than a kid by Autumn's estimation—wasn't even facing the battle, but turned around, staring into the forest with his jaw gaping. Autumn opened her mouth to scream at him, but before she might have, she recognized more noise. She looked down at the ground, believing it vibrated beneath her. But...why? The surreal fight hadn't shaken the ground so what did now? Her head swiveled quickly back and forth. Marcus hadn't turned around, but still faced the enemy. Those red and black tartan-ed men were looking beyond Marcus toward the forest. The McInnes archer kid scrambled suddenly to grab the unused arrows from the earth and took cover in front of a tall pine tree at the forest's edge.

And then she saw it, shadows dancing among the dense trees, flashes of swiftly moving things.

Oh, you've got to be kidding me.

Another army came, she realized with a terrific awe etched on her face, as dozens and dozens of riders exploded at top speed from the forest with their weapons brandished over their heads or in front of them, swords, axes, hammers, and spears held at the ready. They didn't stop, didn't even slow to cross the river but galloped at it and through it as if no water moved there at all. A primal war cry was called out by one and then answered by hundreds as they raced into the dwindling fray.

Marcus never turned to see who came but sprang forward while the enemy stood rooted to the ground, jubilation at their assumed victory drowned now by shock. A mad scrambling took place as those closest to Marcus tried to escape his mighty wrath while others sought out their lost horses, presumably meaning to evade this newest combatant.

Autumn was as confused as ever. Not that she understood the first fight and its players, but who was this new group now?

Marcus raised his sword and brought it down on a man attempting to flee and then swung it sideways with rigid control, nearly taking off a man's head. It then became more and more difficult to track his movements with the addition of so many horses and men. She fidgeted against the tree, going up on her toes and then leaning far to the right. She caught sight of him again, with his sword struck into the ground and he leaning upon it, his face twisted in pain or exhaustion. His leather jerkin was mottled with blood. He wobbled for a second as the re-ignited battle swarmed around him before he dropped suddenly to one knee as if he simply could stand no more. He put both hands on the hilt of his sword and tried to pull himself to his feet again. He made it halfway and then collapsed completely.

Stay down, Autumn begged desperately as tears streamed down her cheeks. *But please don't die.*

Much later, Autumn would guess that both parts of this battle from start to finish had not lasted more than fifteen minutes in total. Presently though, it was an agonizing wait before the clang of swords and the guttural shouts of those struck came fewer and farther between. Eventually though, the noise diminished again, the once pristine meadow littered with a greater multitude of bodies. There had been no question about who the victor would be. Whoever that late coming army was—only a few wore any tartan fabrics and they were not the same color as the McInnes—they clearly sided with Marcus and his army. Autumn couldn't say if even one of them had been killed or had suffered any injury.

When in her periphery, she saw the bow and arrow kid begin to move and then run across the river, she assumed it was safe and moved hesitantly away from the tree.

She couldn't say what drew her across the water or why as she walked among so many dead and dying she was not more sickened or outraged by the gory scene, except that she was governed by an intense need to find Marcus McInnes. Without a word, she picked her way carefully around the tangle of bodies, knowing exactly where Marcus was, where he'd fallen.

Neither affection nor desperation moved her forward, but simple human compassion. Marcus had shown some degree of kindness to her, had not visited upon her the same rage he'd just unleashed upon that other army. He'd appeared genuinely concerned for her when he raced toward her before the first clang of swords. He'd fought bravely, tirelessly, despite the overwhelming odds, had not given up. He should not die alone, staring at a cloudless sky and with no one to hold his hand.

Men turned their heads as she passed them, but no one questioned her or tried to stop her.

Some loud voice calmly called out orders to all the standing, uninjured men, about moving bodies and finding survivors. He ended his list of commands with an order to, "slay any still-breathing MacPhail."

A sickening chill ran down Autumn's spine.

Halfway through the sea of the fallen, spurred by a dread that Marcus might not have much time, she began to run. She stumbled twice, her legs being weak and rubbery, but picked herself up and finally saw him, motionless near his still standing sword. Autumn ran to him, crying his name as if she hadn't just met him, as if he would recognize her voice. She crashed to her knees next to him.

"Oh…Christ," she breathed, surveying the damage done to him. "Are you…?" How did one ask a person if their injuries were life-threatening?

His raven-black hair, streaked with crimson, clung to his sweaty brow and his piercing brown eyes now held a distant, haunted look. Blood oozed from multiple wounds across his body. His leather jerkin was torn and beneath it, his chest gave evidence of his desperate struggle today. A deep gash marred his left shoulder and a jagged wound snaked down his right thigh. The grass around him was muddied with blood. One large, calloused hand, which had wielded his sword with such relentless power, now trembled as it lay on his stomach. His chest rose and fell rapidly, and his mouth was open as he appeared to try to steady his breathing.

Marcus met her gaze, possibly too weak or dispirited to exhibit any surprise.

Autumn covered her mouth with her hands until she remembered that her intent was that he shouldn't die alone. She picked up his hand from his chest with both of hers and squeezed her fingers. She tried to smile at him but feared the attempt was pathetic and possibly raised his concern and not his spirits.

She wanted so badly to ask him what the hell had just happened and why. She was desperate to ask him what year it was, crazy as that sounded, but found herself instead giving a better effort toward her smile, telling him, "It's done now. You'll be fine." She continued to weep, though hadn't any idea why, unless the mere idea of so vital and vibrant a person as Marcus McInnes dying was what destroyed her now. "The army doctors will come now, right?"

"I'm nae dead and I'm nae dying," he told her.

If she knew him better, she might have been a better judge of his tone, but just now she wasn't certain whether she detected a sardonic slant to his tenor or not, and if so, whether it was directed at her for thinking he might have been killed or toward the enemy for their failure to effect his demise.

"Few cuts, nae deep, mayhap a broken rib or two. Winded, that's all," he said, this wheezed, indeed sounding more breathless than weak. "I told ye to run,"

"I...I couldn't," she said weakly, which of course made no sense. Self-preservation was generally ingrained pretty deeply in her.

"Stay by the Nicholson now," he said, ignoring her question, briefly closing his eyes. When he opened them he stared straight above and not at her.

"The Nicholson? What is that?"

"Who, nae what," was answered.

He closed his eyes again.

And didn't move at all. Autumn stared hard at his chest.

"Marcus," she cried. "Marcus?" She relaxed only minimally when he squeezed her hand lightly.

A shadow fell over his lifeless body. Autumn turned her face toward her shoulder and found the imposing figure of a man standing over her, his countenance gruesomely severe as he stared at Marcus.

"They've gone to the keep for a litter," the man said, the words meaningless to Autumn.

When he moved his gaze to her, his frown did not lessen. He was quite rude in his thorough examination of her, from her bare feet and legs—dirty, scraped, and scratched—over her skirt and jacket and their miserable condition, and onto her face.

"Who are ye?" He asked, his tone becoming ruthless.

"Au-Autumn. Autumn Winters. I was just trying to—"

"Bluidy hell," he cut her off, dropping quickly to his haunches. He snarled gruffly but quietly at her, "Are you one of those bluidy time-travelers?"

Chapter Six

Stricken by both the harsh manner of the man—more brutal than an uninjured Marcus McInnes—and his absurd question, Autumn could only stare at him.

When she didn't answer quickly enough for him, he rose to his full, considerable height and uttered a smattering of unintelligible words before turning, waving his hand and shouting at someone. "Dinna only stand there, gawking, Simon! *Jesu*, help Gibbon over there. Put some pressure on that hole in his gullet. Nae one wants to see what he ate this morning." He stormed off, murmuring, "Bluidy hell," before he turned sharply and pointed at Autumn. "Dinna leave his side." And then he moved further away, issuing more commands in his rich voice. "Eamon, get on back. Fetch my wife and the wagons."

Autumn returned her attention to Marcus, finding his eyes open and steady upon her.

"What did he say?" He asked.

"He...he wanted someone to help someone named Gibbon with his—"

"Before that."

"I don't know," she lied. "I couldn't hear very well—his accent—who was that?"

"The Nicholson."

"Oh. And he's...well, obviously you trust him and vice versa, I suppose, since he came to your rescue. But Marcus, where are the doctors? Why is no one coming to..." *save you*, she initially thought but instead used, "help you."

"Litter coming from the keep," he said, squeezing her hand with a greater firmness now, lodging his elbow into the ground as if he would sit up.

Autumn reacted automatically, pushing at his shoulder, one of the few areas of his body that wasn't splattered or dripping with blood. "Are you kidding me? Do not sit up. Just wait." When he settled again, surprising her by not arguing against good sense. She asked, "What does that mean, a litter from the keep?"

Briefly, Marcus wrenched his mouth as if in pain. He closed his eyes again, and another few seconds passed before he answered. "A travois. To convey the wounded. How does Gibbon look?"

Reluctantly, Autumn removed her gaze from Marcus, fairly certain that he was much paler than she'd known him to be, but not completely sure since she didn't suppose her recollections should be trusted; when first they'd met, she'd just been shot, and when next they'd met, it had been dark. She surveyed the carnage all around once more, deliberately focusing on living and moving men, including the wounded ones, trying to find him an answer.

"Is he the gray-haired man?" When Marcus murmured a low affirmative, Autumn informed him, "He was standing a minute ago but is now sitting. But he's awake, looks alert. Someone's there with him." She continued to scan the remains of the bloody scene, her brain still unable to comprehend the carnage all around. "Who's the bald guy? He's got blood on him but he's up and working, helping some young guy to wrap his arm—aw, God, his arm looks like someone tried to saw it off."

"Osgar," he said, identifying the bald man. "He canna be killed. Ye've nae ever witnessed a skirmish?"

"I'm sorry, did you call this a skirmish?"

"'Twas nae premeditated," he reasoned. "Nae large scale."

"It is—or it was—a blood bath," she argued.

Unbelievably, she thought she saw Marcus McInnes's strong and square jaw quiver with emotion. She knew him hardly at all, but for a handful of words exchanged and by some inexplicable sense that their paths had crossed for a reason, but she'd bet her lost Christian Louboutins that this man didn't ever cry. And yet he looked like he wanted to now.

Absently, she rubbed the forearm above the hand she held.

"I'm so sorry," she finally thought to say. "All your...friends...."

"*Jesu*, how many gone?"

"One thing at a time, Marcus," she said, having no true idea how to address this properly. "Let's first tend the wounded and make sure as many are saved as can be." Good Lord, how had those words fallen so easily from her lips? "The... ah, the Nicholson gave orders to kill any breathing MacPhail. Is that—was that—the first army we came upon today?"

"Aye."

"And...they are your enemy? Or *were* your enemy?"

"Are. The laird was nae here today, did not lead the attack."

"How...but why—?" She paused, not even sure what she wanted to ask, what she *should* ask, the reporter in her still trying to wrap her head around what seemed so unbelievably obvious and yet so ridiculously impossible that she was, frankly, afraid to sound like an idiot by assuming anything. She switched gears, focusing instead on him and his condition. "Marcus, are they going to be very long, whoever is bringing the litters? I'm worried...there's so much blood here. Should I be bandaging something. I'm sorry, I know nothing about field dressing."

His response was a long time coming. He regarded her thoughtfully for a long moment with his magnificent brown eyes. "Why do ye fash about someone ye dinna ken?"

Context helped her translate his question. Strangely enough, she wasn't entirely embarrassed or didn't feel it made her vulnerable, her genuine concern for him. She thought of him roaring her name earlier when she'd been in the proverbial line of fire, and the way he'd ridden hellbent to her rescue. The scene had only needed that universally adored hero's anthem, *I Need a Hero,* blaring overhead to have made his arrival this morning perfect—perfect, except for all the unimaginable tragedy that had followed.

"Why did you?" She asked him.

Once again, he was slow to answer. "Ye come to Balla Àrd now, when we go," he said, closing his eyes once again, his voice getting weaker, "and we'll see about that."

Autumn sat with him, believing he really did sleep now. Carefully, she laid her palm flat on his chest, pleased to feel a strong and steady heartbeat. For a while she stared at him, contemplating his enigmatic statement.

Come to Balla Àrd and we'll see about that.

Had he just acknowledged experiencing something similar to what Autumn had mysteriously felt about him, which she'd yet to understand, but that felt as if either she already knew him or that she was meant to know him?

While Marcus slept she scanned the disturbing aftermath of the fight once more. Soldiers who had come with the Nicholson, essentially the only ones standing and uninjured, were busy around the site, many of them kneeling over a wounded McInnes man, doing whatever could be done, she guessed. All the dead and dying MacPhail soldiers were left unattended.

Her gaze encountered the man named Gibbon again, still sitting up, listening to whatever the Nicholson said as that man and another crouched at his side. Gibbon possessed a head of absurdly gorgeous gray hair, thick and with a perfect curl to it, swept perfectly off his forehead and away from his face. He sported a beard and moustache to match, both trimmed short and close to his face. Autumn couldn't decide if he were over fifty and just extremely fit with a youthful complexion or if he was much younger and only prematurely graying.

Gibbon was nodding at whatever the Nicholson was saying and then turned his face and looked directly at Autumn, narrowing his eyes, his nod slowing.

Autumn met his gaze steadily, not sure what to make of his speculative stare.

And then all eyes turned toward the trees again, from where the McInnes party and the Nicholsons had come, from where now was heard the telltale sound of horses on the move. While Autumn braced herself, fear springing to life yet again, the Nicholson chief patted Gibbon on the shoulder and rose to his feet. Without any urgency, he made his way toward the river, watching as yet another party emerged from the woods.

This meadow, Autumn thought with a hint of exasperation, was like Grand Central Station.

This party consisted of more than a dozen riders but came with no great hurry, it seemed. She didn't know anything about horses but judged their speed not a gallop but a cantor. In the very center of the group rode a woman, hazy from this distance but clearly distinguished for the way her long skirts floated about her legs and for the wealth of loose, auburn hair that bounced around her shoulders. Just then, Autumn recalled that the Nicholson had asked someone to fetch his wife. It did not escape Autumn's notice how tight was the formation of the circle of soldiers around the woman, nor the fact that her husband had left so large a contingent with his wife, away from the battle to which he'd so freely and valuably ridden.

Intrigued by the presence of the woman and her husband's care of her, Autumn squinted as she watched the woman and her party cross the river. Though the woman scanned her eyes over the horrendous sight just beyond her husband, her gaze quickly settled on the formidable man, her brow crinkled with concern until she discerned that he was unharmed and a brilliant smile of relief lighted her features. She released the reins rather too soon, Autumn thought, falling sideways toward her husband as she came upon him. Thankfully, the man caught her, pulling her off the slowing horse, bringing her into his arms.

Autumn arched a brow, absorbed by the sight. Nicholson held her so that they were face to face, but that kept the woman's feet easily a foot off the ground. She took her husband's face in her hands, and they exchanged muted, somber conversation for just a moment before the Nicholson kissed her lips and then her brow. The woman then laid her head against his shoulder, closing her eyes in what Autumn suspected was supreme relief.

Autumn supposed the Nicholson must have said something else to her, against her ear, when the woman gasped and lifted her face, gaping at her husband. Autumn was no lip reader but clearly saw the woman ask, "What?" of her husband. The Nicholson inclined his head toward the right and the woman was not subtle as she followed his direction, casting her gaze across a sea of bodies until it landed with unerring astonishment upon Autumn.

Seemingly transfixed, she all but ignored her husband's presence as she disengaged herself completely from him. Or tried to. The Nicholson only let her go after saying something to her that was issued with a serious frown and in a curt manner. The woman nodded dutifully, her eyes locked with Autumn's, and then allowed her husband to lead her by the hand to where Autumn sat with Marcus.

Whoever she was, aside from obviously being the Nicholson's wife, she was almost bizarrely beautiful, like way too pretty to be here, now, in the gory, untidy chaos of this place. She was petite and slender, with long red-brown hair that shone with a healthy radiance, with a sleek, disciplined wave, the ends of it laying in perfect curls over her shoulder. The concerned eyes set upon Autumn were a light green and sat over a nose that was slim but not pointy. Her mouth was made of heart-shaped lips, the upper one having a prominent cupid's bow while her lower lip was full and well defined. Beneath, the center of her chin was dented with a shallow dimple.

She was dressed oddly, wearing a long gown of cornflower blue wool, which seemed so much less conducive to horseback riding and bloody battles than would be, say, jeans and a T-shirt. Autumn thought this even as she knew—had known—that she was the one who truly stood out as dressed inappropriately in the settings of both yesterday and today.

The woman was simply stunning, or maybe she appeared so beautiful for the expression of genuine compassion that arrested her features as she closed in on Autumn.

Autumn supposed it would have been impossible for any person to have mistaken the look in her returned gaze for anything other than what it was: chilling apprehension.

Fleetingly, the woman scanned her pretty green eyes over the entirety of Autumn, same as her husband had a while ago, minus the scathing judgment, and then promptly clasped her hands over her mouth. Her eyes were bright as her brows wrinkled. She lowered her hands when she stopped half a dozen feet away.

"Did you...did you just arrive?" The woman asked haltingly.

"I..." Autumn began, until she realized she wasn't sure what the woman was asking.

But the woman didn't require a response, it turned out.

"Of course you just got here," she said. "I can tell by the way you're dressed, and your doe-in-the-headlights look. Oh, you poor thing."

God, how she wished whatever was going on would just be clearly spelled out to her. Autumn's puzzlement was not being minimized at all, only increased. She glanced at the Nicholson but found no help there, nothing more than his still-hostile glare.

The woman took a step closer. "I'm Charlotte," she said, holding out her hands unthreateningly, as if she approached and addressed a frightened child. "Charlotte O'Rourke—well, Charlotte Nicholson here in this time. I'm so sorry that this is what greeted you in the fourteenth century. It's awful enough to be moved so unbelievably—so helplessly—through the centuries, but to come to this—" she stopped, lifting both arms to indicate the remnants of the violent carnage.

Autumn's brow furrowed sharply. "I...you...you're kind of freaking me out."

"I'm sorry. You're probably so confused. I remember my first few days—crap, my first few hours. It was really awful." She glanced around. "Well, not this awful, but close. Anyway. Go ahead. Ask me whatever you want. I'm here for you. You're not alone. We'll get you through this."

Autumn's shoulders shrank inward, her entire body deflating and resisting the impossible concept suggested by this woman and her cryptic words. "I don't know what you're talking about."

Charlotte was unruffled. "Okay, we'll slow it down. It's scary. I get it." She cleared her throat and asked, "What is your name?"

"Autumn."

"Nice to meet you, Autumn," said Charlotte. "And now you...you do understand you are no longer in the twenty-first century, right?"

Jaw tight, Autumn shook her head. "That is not—I don't find that at all humorous," she said, quite willing to dislike the woman despite how pretty she was, despite how kind she pretended to be.

Nicholson snapped something in a language Autumn neither recognized nor understood.

Charlotte turned on him. "C'mon, Reid. Can't you see she's traumatized? Go. Go away," she said, pushing at his thick arm with her hand. "You're not helping, standing here looking so...so intimidating, like you're going to take her head off at any moment."

The Nicholson—whom Charlotte had just called Reid—scowled down at his wife, scoffing at her attempt to remove him. "I am nae leaving ye with her, nae until we ken what she's about—"

"Clearly, she doesn't know what she's about, Reid," Charlotte O'Rourke Nicholson said to her husband, amazingly indifferent to his brutal bearing. "She's terrified but not dangerous. Go...go bandage something. Or someone. Or sharpen your sword. Shout commands. Arrange transport. Just go."

He didn't budge, not until Charlotte Nicholson turned and laid her small hand upon his chest. "I'm fine. I can guarantee you I am not in any danger whatsoever. Give me just a few minutes. Seriously, Reid, she doesn't know you. You come across as very...well, you're very scary. You know that; I've told you that. Let's not needlessly torment the poor woman."

Reid Nicholson's lip curled as he glowered at Charlotte, who looked up at him with great and effective appeal, her fabulous green eyes probably very useful at getting her way. He nodded, almost imperceptibly, and took himself away, throwing several glances over his shoulder, which Autumn could see but Charlotte could not since she was facing Autumn again.

"Ignore him," Charlotte advised. "He gets cranky when people are killed so indiscriminately."

Autumn's eyes widened. Finally, something that made sense. Yeah, she was cranky, too, for what seemed a senseless and unprovoked slaughter.

Returned to the matter of utmost implausibility, Autumn declared tonelessly but firmly, hoping her insistence would make it true, "It is not the fourteenth century."

"It is," Charlotte said, wincing, as if she were sorry to have to impart this fantastic news.

"That's impossible."

"It should be," Charlotte concurred. "It seems preposterous but I'm sorry to be the one to tell you that it is very real—time-travel—and that you are standing—kneeling, as it were—here in the fourteenth century. Just barely, anyway. It's 1304."

"But how did this happen?" How *was* it possible? "Are you—" She clamped her lips, refusing to actually put forth so outrageous a question. *Are you from the future, too?*

Two men skirted close to Charlotte, walking just beyond her, carrying the lifeless body of a third man.

Charlotte pulled a face, as agonized as Autumn it seemed at the sight of the dead man's eyes, which were open yet and staring inertly. Charlotte moved herself out of their way and maybe with some mind that their ludicrous conversation not be overheard. She went to her knees on the other side of Marcus, who remained sleeping between them.

"I came here two years ago," Charlotte confided. "Like you, I didn't believe until it became impossible not to. And the strangest thing, well one of the strangest things is that the more time that passes from when I arrived, the less I remember. Not of my previous life, that I still recall vividly. But of what exactly happened the day I was moved through time."

"But why didn't you just go back?"

"I don't know how. I don't know how I traveled through time in the first place. I didn't set out to do so. I don't remember the actual...journey, if you will. Oh, hey. What year is it now? I mean, from when you come?"

Stricken, Autumn stared at her. How could she ask such questions with so casual a tone, as if they were not extremely weird?

"You'll get used to it," Charlotte said, as if she'd read Autumn's mind. "It just becomes another event in your life, like a wedding or birth or death. Big deal at the time, but the enormity of it dissipates after a while."

Autumn blinked. "It's, um, 2023."

"No shit," Charlotte said. "That's weird. I know I've been here two years. It was two years last month. But I left the future in 2019. Hmm." She shook herself from that curiosity and asked, "What do you remember of your journey?"

Autumn shrugged, nonplussed. "Nothing—or nothing remarkable enough to have..." she let that trial off, still unable to say the words. She glanced down at Marcus, whose eyes were still closed. She still held his hand with one of hers, and the hand she'd rubbed consolingly up and down his forearm now was laid over his wrist, where she felt a warm and steady pulse. "I was at these ruins and...I don't know, I just felt a change in the air, like it got real heavy. And then I felt, rather than heard, a voice speaking. It freaked me out and I started running. I don't remember the area around me changing but suddenly I was running through trees where before there had been none. And then...then I was shot with an arrow. That was yesterday."

"Shit, that's awful," Charlotte replied, her green eyes wide. "That's what this is, then?" She asked, pointing to Autumn's shoulder. "I figured, since the blood is dried, looks less fresh than everything all around us."

"He shot me," Autumn informed her in a quiet voice. She didn't release Marcus's hand but lifted one finger away and pointed down at him. "Or rather, one of his men did." She'd yet to see Marcus McInnes wield a bow and arrow.

Charlotte winced again. "Yikes. Not exactly a memorable meet-cute."

Autumn frowned again, nearly insulted by Charlotte's misplaced and untimely idea of romance. What the hell!

"I'm sorry. I'm not making light of it. But obviously, since you're holding his hand and Reid said you were *fair wretched with worry*, I assumed something was going on between you and Marcus."

The day and this conversation only became more surreal. "You know him, then?" She asked of Charlotte, removing her hands unhurriedly from Marcus, laying his hand back on his stomach.

"Yes, he and Reid are like brothers. He's meaner and more volatile than Reid, but honestly, he's a really good guy. Salt of the earth, my grandmother would have said about him."

Autumn's incredulous frown returned. *Meaner and more volatile than Reid?* Whose own wife had asked him not to look at Autumn as if he were going to take her head off?

"I still…I don't understand how this happened or honestly, what's going on, or if I even believe any of this."

"But it's kind of hard not to, isn't it? When you're sitting in a blood-soaked meadow in the aftermath of a foul battle between two rival clans?"

"How are you…how are you able to behave so…normally?"

"As I've said, I've been here for a few years. And honestly, what choice do I have?"

"But…what do I do now?"

"For right now, we're going to get on to Balla Àrd," Charlotte said, rising to her feet again. "Talk about perfect timing. We were only coming to visit Marcus—what dumb luck. We thought we'd drop in on Marcus. Reid wanted to catch up with him before we all settled down for winter."

"You brought an army with you," Autumn felt compelled to remind her.

"We don't go anywhere without them. Dangerous clan business such as this aside, there is another war going on, Autumn. The one with the English? It's a dangerous time to live in Scotland."

"But I don't want to be here. I don't want to go to Balla Àrd, whatever that is."

Charlotte dropped her shoulders with a bit of sympathy. "I would argue that you *do* want to move to Balla Àrd with us. That's Marcus's castle. You can't stay here with all these dead MacPhails. Obviously, Marcus needs the healer. Don't you want to stick around to make sure he recovers all right?"

Autumn gritted her teeth, detesting the blatant manipulation.

"I suppose I have to stick around because I wouldn't know where else to go. If you're telling the truth—"

"Autumn, I promise you I'm not lying."

"—then I don't know how to get on in the fourteenth century. If you're lying, I still don't know where I am and will need to get back to the place I was staying and then the airport." She was overwhelmed by a sudden and distinct want of home. She didn't want to be in Scotland anymore, not in any century. She wanted to be home with her mother and father, with her brothers and their families. She wanted to curl up on her parents' sofa with a cozy blanket and have her mother give her a hot mug of cocoa and tell her everything was going to be fine.

With the unexpected attack of homesickness came more tears, which Autumn swiped at angrily. She got to her feet, deciding she didn't want to engage with Charlotte anymore. She wasn't sure she trusted the woman even as her crazy explanation made more sense than any reason Autumn could think of to explain the way people dressed and talked, the lack of roads or any other kind of civilization, so many horses and swords, and most specifically the very real and wholly terrifying battle she'd just witnessed.

Very gently, Charlotte said, "Autumn, I don't have half the answers you'll be looking for. No one did when I came here. The best guidance I can give is to keep an open mind and just take it one day at a time. It will get better, I promise you. You'll figure it out and I'll be here for the next few days with you. I hope that helps."

Autumn nodded curtly but said nothing, not particularly worried if she hurt the woman's feelings.

With her hands on her slim hips, Charlotte sighed and glanced down at Marcus. "Here come the litters from Balla Àrd, Marcus. You can quit pretending you were sleeping or unconscious for the last ten minutes and didn't hear every single word Autumn and I just said."

Chapter Seven

Marcus did not open his eyes and thereby confirm Charlotte Nicholson's suspicion that he was awake and had indeed overheard almost every shocking statement and question exchanged between the two women.

Instead, he struggled to keep all the disbelief and incredulity from his expression, exerting great effort to keep his entire face and specifically his brows and eyes from moving at all, more difficult than the battle had been, he was beginning to imagine. More than once over the past ten minutes he'd wanted to open his eyes and throw an incredulous scowl at either woman, demanding clarification or compelling them to admit they spoke nonsense.

At first he'd thought he must be dying after all, despite telling Autumn that her fear for him was unnecessary. Aye, he must be dying, must have become delirious with weakness from loss of blood. For a moment and because his breathing had been labored and painful, he'd assumed one of his broken ribs might have punctured his lung, and that his life breath was slowly seeping away from him causing disorientation, which had allowed him to imagine the entire extraordinary conversation. Otherwise, in his mind there were only two other available explanations for what he'd just heard. One, Charlotte, knowing he was somewhat alert, had invented the entire odd narrative to taunt him, thus chastising him for eavesdropping. Or, two, what they'd spoken of was truth as each of them understood it. Strangely enough, though the second option was the more preposterous choice, Marcus had to assume it was the case, since he didn't know Charlotte to engage in devious schemes and couldn't imagine her using this moment on this day, believing now a good time to teach him a lesson about eavesdropping.

As support of his decision to even consider that anything spoken between the two women might actually have some footing in reality and while he continued to pretend to be asleep, Marcus did consider that Charlotte *had* always seemed a little...odd.

Mayhap not odd, he decided, as she was a perfectly agreeable person and a worthy mate to Reid, but unusual for her forthwith manner and the dialect of her English, never before known to Marcus but so unlike anything he'd encountered in all his years—until he'd met Autumn.

Would that explain that feeling he'd known since meeting Autumn, vague and yet so strong, that she was not what she seemed? That there was something mysterious and incomprehensible about her? Truth be known, he'd thought her foreign, obviously not born to Scotland, but possibly not even of English origins despite the fact that she spoke a form of that language. Choosing to believe that she hailed from another time altogether would explain her manner of dress, that unearthly wheeled trunk she'd carted around for almost twenty-four hours, and her seeming confusion about every blessed thing.

Marcus recalled just now what Autumn had denied hearing, what he was quite sure he'd not mistaken: Reid, his tone both incredulous and displeased, asking Autumn, *Are you one of those bluidy time-travelers?*

Frankly, this only raised more questions. Why had Reid never shared with him this most incredible news? Charlotte herself was from another time? He didn't take Charlotte as one to blather senseless twaddle, or to spew falsehoods, to invent so fantastic a tale. Likewise, Marcus didn't suppose Reid would have wed a woman who was either simply daft or shockingly cracked in the head. But this...this was beyond comprehension.

Jesu, could this actually be true?

Or by unfortunate chance, were his wounds far graver than he himself believed? He couldn't be sure but decided that merely entertaining the idea of such a ludicrous claim only exhausted him further.

He sighed and gave up his pretense of sleep, opening his eyes to find Charlotte and Autumn still standing fairly close but now with their backs to him. From his vantage point on the ground, the closest thing to him were Autumn's bare legs. He studied them intently, as much as he was able in his condition, wondering what he should glean from her exposed limbs. Wearily, his gaze moved upward over the scanty yet rich fabric of her skirt and surcote, unable to avoid wondering if this was truly how people in the future dressed.

Charlotte pointed to the north just as a group of riders came into view over the petite hill at the far side of the pasture. His vision was blurry now, the faces of the riders unrecognizable, but as no fuss was raised by any nearby, Marcus assumed the men from Balla Àrd had come.

The creaking and groaning of wagons caught Marcus's waning attention. The carts came from Balla Àrd and by way of the McInnes army, all who remained, those garrisoned at the castle who'd not traveled with Marcus to Darrie yesterday, answering that call they'd initially thought might only be a nuisance fire. Balla Àrd's captain of the house guard, Gilchrist, led the coming troops, his booming voice heard above any other noise until it stopped abruptly. Marcus thought he might have been quieted by shock when he came upon the scene, likely unprepared for the McInnes wreckage strewn about.

He would have let his mind return to the slaughter, and what necessary and vicious reprisals he would plan and exact against the MacPhail chieftain, but that Autumn turned and faced him.

Her mouth formed a small *o* before she closed the distance between them in a few steps.

"You are awake," she said, her tone suggesting she might not have believed Charlotte's conjecture. She knelt again at his side but did not touch him. "The ah, the wagons are here."

"Is it true, what Charlotte alleged?" Was foremost on his mind, numb to all the pain that wracked his body.

Though Charlotte had clearly stated that she believed Marcus *had* overheard them, Autumn still managed to appear taken aback. After a split second of her lips moving without any sound, she asked, "Is it really 1304?"

Magnus nodded, his scowl deepening. He locked his gaze onto her gray eyes, which appeared to mist immediately at his confirmation.

Grimly, she responded, "Then yes, it appears to be true."

"'Tis nae possible," he said, searching the depths of her expressive gaze for some hint or evidence that she lied but finding nothing to support this frail theory. Instead, he decided her tears were enough to melt a heart of stone.

Autumn laughed, the sound tinkling and scathing at the same time. "I agree. Trust me, I don't *want* it to be true. And...well, if you did hear everything, then you know that I have no idea how it happened."

"Or how to correct it," he guessed, aware that just beyond Autumn, Charlotte was walking away, possibly to greet and organize the litters and the wagons. "Ye might better keep that between ye and Charlotte," he proposed to Autumn. "And the Nicholson and me. A tale such as that will only invite unwanted and undesirable attention."

Autumn nodded swiftly.

He was troubled enough by her distress that he thought to distract her with something other than the preposterous notion of her supposedly having moved through time.

"How is your shoulder?"

The question seemed to startle her. In all likelihood, the events of the last hour had removed all recollection of her own wound from her mind.

"Oh, um, it's fine," she told him, glancing from the hole in her surcote and all the old, brown blood around it back to Marcus. "I mean it hurts...but I'm in better shape than you are presently."

If Reid Nicholson hadn't come, even if they'd somehow miraculously received rescue by Gilchrist and the McInnes army, Marcus would have been compelled to be on his feet to make things happen that needed to happen. Reid's formidable presence, his innate ability to command, prioritize, and effect results for what needed to be done in the wake of the skirmish had allowed Marcus to remain as he was. Marcus supposed for this he should be doubly thankful for Reid's timely arrival—*dumb luck*, Charlotte had called it—that allowed Marcus to rest here and not aggravate any or all of the wounds he'd not been able to avoid.

Possibly, he would realize more appreciation that he hadn't stood yet, hadn't been able to take in the full scope of the massacre, could not properly see all the McInnes bodies scattered about the pasture. A familiar sadness came over him again, a great and tragic sense of loss and fury that he'd known too many times in his adult life.

He startled, brought back to the present, when Autumn once more laid her hand over his.

Marcus met her gray eyes again, compassion clearly perceived in her tender regard, as if she understood where his mind had gone. She said nothing though, just touched him, rubbing her thumb back and forth on the back of his hand. No words were needed for him to comprehend her empathy.

"Stay with Charlotte now," he advised levelly. "Nae doubt the Nicholson and she will abide at Balla Àrd for a wee spell. Charlotte will show ye how to get about." Though her plight was inconceivable and the timing of it most unfortunate, he imagined to some degree he did feel—and was—responsible for her, reasoning that she should be housed at Balla Àrd for the foreseeable future.

"All right." She turned, finding that Charlotte had left the area. Facing Marcus again, she asked, "Should I be helping with anything now?"

Marcus moved his head from side to side on the ground. "Nae. Ye wait until the wagons are filled and then ride with Charlotte. Dinna approach anyone just yet and raise questions now...with yer garb and yer speech."

A dazed expression overtook the compassion of her gaze. She was pale and forlorn, and suddenly appeared especially young and vulnerable. "Okay," she said in a voice very small.

"All will be well, Autumn," Marcus said to her, truly meant as a vow more than a dismissive statement.

Even as he was battered and bruised and would surely leave a fair amount of blood here in the meadow, even as exacting revenge against the MacPhails would be his first priority, he felt a desire to make this true for her.

"Thank you," she said, giving him a wobbly but bonny smile.

***

At length, Marcus was carefully lifted onto what looked to be a very primitive stretcher by men who only stood out presently because they were whole and well and not covered in blood. Neither of the two men who'd come to collect Marcus spared more than a puzzled glance at Autumn, their concern obviously for the wounded man and not her. They spoke a language Autumn did not understand but which she expected must be Scots' Gaelic, and Marcus answered in the same foreign tongue and then briefly reminded Autumn to stay near Charlotte before he was carried away.

She didn't need to be reminded. As the wounded were methodically evacuated from the field of battle, she found herself standing amid a sea of dead men, enemies to the McInnes, and with a sickness in her stomach picked her way carefully through the flattened grass, wet with blood, on bare feet toward Charlotte. She looked down at the earth and not at any of the dead faces watching her move among them. She'd forgotten all about her suitcase and the gear within until she happened to stumble upon it in her path. Though she had no idea what use the camera, laptop, and her notebooks and pens would be in the year 1304, she bent and wrapped her fingers round the handle and pulled it along behind her once more.

Two wagons had already begun to move away from the battlefield, laden with half a dozen wounded McInnes men each. Dozens of men on horses followed them, heading north—the direction not known by Autumn instinctively but recalled from Marcus's earlier instructions—but still another twenty or thirty Nicholson and McInnes men remained, though few were idle. Another wagon had been brought nearly to the epicenter of the fight and was now being loaded with the bodies of McInnes men who had not survived the battle.

Charlotte was just laying some injured man's sword next to him on a stretcher and sending the man and those conveying him off with a seemingly unruffled, "They'll take good care of you up at Balla Àrd," when Autumn caught up to her.

Charlotte wiped her hands on her skirt and nodded at Autumn. "This way," she said. "My horse is just over there with the others. Oh, but your case," she said and then chewed her lip as she glanced around. "Here, give me that," she said, reaching for the handle. "I think it will fit in that closest wagon." She walked away, rolling the case behind her, asserting herself with quiet authority once she reached the wagon so that one of her husband's men nodded amiably and without question—he gave the suitcase and not Charlotte a good frown, though—lifted the suitcase up into the front of the wagon.

"I don't know how to ride on a horse," Autumn alerted Charlotte when she returned.

"It took me six months just to be comfortable riding without Reid," said Charlotte as she untied a wool blanket from where it was rolled up against the back end of the saddle. "And then another six months before I felt truly in control, as master of the horse." She handed the blanket to Autumn. "You'll want to wrap this around you like a sarong so that when you throw your leg over, you're not showing the fourteenth century more of your thighs and ass than you want them to see."

This was delivered with twisted grin that Autumn rather translated as, *In this time we have to think of things like that.*

Charlotte then climbed up into the saddle, making it look pretty easy, while Autumn unrolled the blanket and secured it around her waist. She left it folded in half, and it still managed to cover her legs down to her calves. She tucked the front end inside the section that was pressed against her belly, same as she would when securing a towel to herself after a shower.

Charlotte reached down her hand to Autumn at the same time she disengaged her foot from the stirrup. "Put your foot in there and hop up. And swing around behind me."

Autumn scoffed good-naturedly because Charlotte had given that instruction as if such a maneuver were just that easy. But it wasn't terribly difficult after all, and she was able to seat herself on the horse just behind Charlotte. The blanket had become loose and began to fall just as she sat down, but she was able to keep it in place and was very grateful then for Charlotte's foresight since her skirt had ridden up to her hips as predicted and would have left little to the imagination.

When Charlotte clicked her tongue and the horse began to move, Autumn automatically put her hands on Charlotte's waist. They moved toward Reid Nicholson, where he was conferring with another man.

While the man with the Nicholson stared unabashedly at Autumn, his narrowed gaze resting for quite a bit on the blood and hole just below Autumn's shoulder, Reid Nicholson spared her only a glance before moving his gaze with some thoroughness over Charlotte. Autumn was seized by an impression of a husband always vigilant about his wife's well-being and safety.

"We're heading up," Charlotte said. "We can help in the hall with the wounded. It'll be chaos there right now."

"Aye, and I'll nae be long," said Reid. He turned a quarter step, whistled curtly, and then called out, "Eamon! Call up your men. Escort your lady to Balla Àrd."

Men jogged from several different points around the battle field to the area where the bulk of the horses stood waiting, those men obviously not of a mind to idle and possibly incur Reid Nicholson's wrath. In no time, Charlotte and Autumn were surrounded by an army of twenty men.

"Aye, lass, and ye keep to the center, ye ken," said a middle-aged man with a thick head of wavy brown hair and dark blue eyes.

Receiving Charlotte's nod of affirmation, the man rode on ahead, leading the party forward. At least half the men went on ahead of Charlotte and Autumn while the rest followed in their wake. Though Autumn received a few more sidelong glances, and some much less subtle, for the most part the soldiers escorting them kept a polite distance, for which Autumn was thankful.

They rode straight as an arrow through the trees, fairly quickly catching up with and then passing one of the wagons that carried the dead. Autumn averted her gaze.

When they were well past that hearse, and because Autumn was thinking about Marcus's suggestion—and what might have prompted it—that it was probably a good idea that she not run off at the mouth about any of this unreal and horrifying time-travel business, Autumn asked Charlotte, "Why did you say all that in front of Marcus if you knew he was awake?"

"What? About the time-travel?" Charlotte asked over her shoulder and then shrugged. "I figured the sooner he understood, the easier it would be for you. You will need someone of his stature—a chief, a laird—to take your part if needed. Honestly, I'd felt bad every time we've met him, not disclosing so fantastic but integral a piece of news to him. Like I said, he and Reid are super close. I know it tore Reid up, to essentially lie to his best friend, so...well, this puts us back on even footing with Marcus."

Autumn had another concern. "He's going to think I'm crazy." *If he doesn't already.*

"Actually, he's going to think *I* am crazy," Charlotte proposed instead. "I did most of the talking. Or he's going to think Reid is crazy, for marrying me. But he won't think you're crazy. Just play dumb, act scared. He won't be able to resist. His natural inclination to protect, his keen sense to shelter a damsel in distress—it's a real thing in this century—will kick in."

"Oh, my God. Is that how you got by? Or how you got the Nicholson to marry you?"

Charlotte laughed. "I wish it had been that easy. At least the first part. Getting by was very difficult when I wasn't so lucky as to meet someone who'd already done this, come from the future, someone who could explain all this to me. How I got Reid to marry me?" She shook her head. "Not quite, but that's another story for another day."

One she apparently wasn't willing or interested in divulging now. Instead, Charlotte asked, "Obviously, you're American. Were you simply vacationing in the Highlands when you were moved?"

"I'm from Chicago."

"I'm from Florida. Were you with a group, family or friends, that will have immediately noticed your disappearance or might have witnessed it?"

"No, I was working, essentially," replied Autumn, startled that she just now recalled the reason for her visit to Scotland. A handful of different ideas ran chaotically through her head when she recalled her purpose. "Are there others like us? Time-travelers? Christ, that sounds so...bizarre. I was actually, unofficially investigating the disappearance of an American woman, Megan West," she explained. "Do you know her?"

Charlotte shook her head. "Is she from the future?"

"Christ, stop saying that," Autumn pleaded. "It sounds so...unreal." And then she heard herself ask, "Do you know any others from the future? Five women—all Americans—have gone missing in the last two years."

"Including me?"

Confused, Autumn shook her head before she realized Charlotte couldn't see that response. "No, you would make six." She frowned, considering. "And I guess I would be seven. Wow."

In front of her, Charlotte sighed. "I had wondered if my disappearance had even registered."

"What do you mean?"

"I don't really have any family and I went to Scotland on a whim, traveled solo."

Because Charlotte didn't sound too upset about it, because she offered no more than that, Autumn asked, "Jesus, are they all alive, those missing women, but were just...stolen? Taken back in time?"

"Possibly. It's a big country. Neighbors are not just a short drive away, not just around the corner. There might be a hundred miles between you and your neighbor here. Sadly, the McInnes and MacPhails didn't have the luxury of so much distance between them."

They were quiet then for a while, the only sound that of the rustling of leaves, the soft footfalls of the twenty or so horses, and the wind which seemed to be growing more forceful the further along they went.

"I'm really freaked out, Charlotte," Autumn confessed. "Actually, I'm terrified."

Charlotte was quick to assure her, "It's not awful. I mean, it won't be. You have Marcus and—"

"Have Marcus?" Autumn gasped. "I don't have Marcus. I don't have—or want—anyone. I want to go home."

"It's weird, I know," Charlotte said, which sounded utterly insufficient to Autumnn's ear.

It wasn't simply *weird*.

Charlotte continued, "Isn't it fascinating though as well? I mean, think of all the things we call science fiction that might also be real. Big foot, aliens, the Loch Ness Monster—I did ask about Nessie since we are here in Scotland, but no one seemed to know what I was talking about. But honestly, if I see a unicorn I'd be like, yeah, sure, that's possible."

Autumn decided not to comment on any of that, supposing since Charlotte had two years to grow accustomed to living in a century seven hundred years in the past, she might have lost most of her inability to believe and much of her fear.

"But don't you miss things? Like running water and coffee from your favorite cafe?"

"Every day," Charlotte answered promptly but then qualified, "but they're only things. Yes, I bemoan the lack of them. But to go back, to not have Reid..." She shrugged and then her voice sounded incredibly young and then almost apologetic, "that's not a life worth living, I've decided. I don't ever want to be away from him."

"But...but this is so violent here. What if he were killed?"

"He won't be and don't ever say that to me again. He won't be killed." Her shoulders slumped. "I could not live without him."

"In this time, you mean?"

"Ever. In any time. He is everything to me."

Autumn thought fleetingly of Jordan, unable to prevent herself from wondering if she'd ever felt that strongly about him, even when she had been nuts about him. Maybe she simply wasn't made that way, to put so much stock into another person, to have her happiness controlled by the existence of another.

"Maybe Marcus and you will—"

"Why do you keep trying to make us a couple?"

"I'm sorry. You just seemed so...very concerned about him."

"I literally just...arrived yesterday, just met him yesterday."

"I fell in love with Reid the very minute I saw him."

"That's just, I don't know, that's both improbable and suspect."

Rather than being offended, Charlotte laughed. "Okay, truthfully, I was terrified of him, but only because I was terrified in general, not understanding at the time what had happened. But honestly, it didn't take me long to trust him, to depend on him, to see beneath that super crusty exterior of his. He's actually a big softie, you've probably noticed, same as Marcus. Oh, don't get me wrong, they can kill with their bare hands and probably have—many times in this war, I'm sure—but they're good men and never resort to violence without provocation."

Autumn tried to reconcile *big softie* with that image of Marcus flying over the river on his massive horse, with that look of utter viciousness on his face. Like, how had anything in his path not simply withered and died of fright at his feet?

Autumn swatted at a flying insect that got too close. No sooner had she thought she'd be thrilled if she never saw the inside of a forest again, than the pines and oak and birch trees began to thin and then were diluted completely as they emerged from the woods. She sighed wearily, very uncomfortable upon the horse, wondering how much further she would be required to be on it.

And then Charlotte lifted her arm and pointed straight ahead.

"There's Balla Àrd."

Autumn peered around Charlotte's slim shoulder, her jaw dropping.

If any doubts had lingered about the veracity of Charlotte's claim that they were now in the fourteenth century, they were all shattered as she gazed ahead at the magnificent sight.

Chapter Eight

Balla Àrd was perched atop a rugged, windswept hill, the castle and wall surrounding it seeming to emerge from the very stone of the earth, the imposing fortress silhouetted against a moody Scottish sky, which was blown in by the swelling wind. The towering walls were cast of rough-hewn stone, the gray warmed to a golden hue whenever the sun's grace fell upon it. Upon its craggy, flat-topped hill, the fortress commanded a breathtaking view of a vast lake that curved around the hill and castle in a serpentine manner. Turrets and battlements rose defiantly above all else while a massive drawbridge spanned one arc of the lake. The castle's entrance was guarded by a looming portcullis, giving the impression of an impregnable barrier.

As they continued on, moving closer to the castle, Charlotte remarked, "What a shame. To be attacked so close to home, so close and yet so far from the safety offered just here."

Though she never took her gaze from the impressive fortress, Autumn frowned and challenged, "Close to home? We just rode for almost an hour from the scene to get here."

"It wasn't more than a few miles," Charlotte reasoned. "As I said, that's considered close in the Highlands."

The horse beneath them increased his speed, either at Charlotte's insistence or because the men in their party had.

The castle loomed larger and larger as they neared. Atop the tallest and foremost tower, a massive flag bearing the image of a fisted hand holding a cluster of arrows, rippled defiantly in the breeze. A winding path led to the castle's imposing gates, which were flanked by two towers three stories tall, between which two massive wooden doors were bordered by iron torch sconces. They crossed over the drawbridge, the hooves of the horses making a clippety-clop noise, and Autumn glanced down into the murky waters of the moat beneath them, part of that winding lake.

The doors themselves were battered, seeming to bear the scars of countless sieges, the wood showing depressions, chop marks, and other cuts, few of those higher than any man might reach by hand.

A cobbled courtyard lay just ahead inside the gate and the sound of the walking horses changed from a dull thump over wood to a click-clack noise that echoed off the cold stone walls. The courtyard was a picturesque blend of medieval grandeur and an impossible-to-believe realism. The scent of woodsmoke filled the air while people bustled about, all dressed in period clothes, their faces creased equally with grime and concern, as a group of them worked to unload a wagon of wounded that had reached the castle before Autumn and Charlotte and their party had.

Yet overcome by awe, Autumn glanced around, noting a series of arched doorways and entrances, leading to various parts of the castle. The largest of these, possibly the main door, stood ajar, the wooden door fitted with huge iron hinges. Beyond it, Autumn saw nothing but a barely lit interior. Lifting her gaze showed men armed with bows and arrows standing guard above the courtyard, elevated on the battlements, indistinct figures with their backs to the interior of the wall.

It was hard then to disavow any claim that this was the 14th century. Everything looked so...authentic.

The men of their party dismounted swiftly, handing off reins to young boys who came running from a slope-roofed structure attached to the castle that might be the stables. Some of those men dashed up a set of stone stairs that climbed the wall just inside the main gate, to the right of the open door.

"Of course, we need to make ourselves useful," Charlotte said as she, too, dismounted.

Autumn followed suit, performing what amounted to more a graceless scrambling off the rump of the horse than a competent dismount. She brought the wool blanket with her but unwrapped it straightaway, as soon as she'd yanked down her skirt to a decent length.

"They'll set up the hall as the infirmary," Charlotte said, waiting as a boy came running toward her to take the reins in her hand. ""We can help with the wounded as they come—thank you, lad—and shroud those who've passed when we have time."

Shroud those who've passed?

Charlotte faced Autumn, an air of purpose about her now that strangely had not been noticed before, even as they'd met under pretty harrowing circumstances.

"What did Marcus tell you about Balla Àrd?"

"He didn't tell me anything." Autumn informed her. "I just met him. I spent about thirty wakeful minutes total with him. I know nothing but his name." And that his eyes were a gorgeous chocolatey brown and that his hand was twice the size of hers, had felt warm and comforting when she'd held it even as her intention had been to bolster him.

"He is what I call a bachelor orphan," Charlotte said quickly, using her hands as she spoke. "You see it a lot. People die young here, so his parents are gone. He lost two brothers to the war against England. I think there was an old aunt who lived with him. I remember Reid telling me that, and Marcus was very close with her, but she died shortly before I met him. Of course, he should have married, he's like 30, I guess. They marry pretty young here, in this century. He was betrothed, actually several times, but they never worked out." She waved her hand dismissively then, as if that was all she would say about that. "He does have a sister living, but she married and moved to London, but that was a decade ago, if I have it right. I don't think he's seen her since. Anyway, I say all that to let you know that he maintains the household of a bachelor, with only a skeleton staff, so to speak, and I can only think of one or two who might be helpful with all these wounded."

Autumn's eyes went wide. "And you think *I* might be helpful? I'm a reporter, a journalist, not a nurse."

Charlotte paused, her purposeful expression lightening briefly. "I was a kindergarten teacher. Anyway, we're modern women," Charlotte reminded her, taking her hand and leading her into the castle. "They've likely summoned or sent for the healer—their version of a doctor, though not really. Anyway, she will be well-versed in battle wounds and indispensable for her knowledge in that regard. But we—you and I—know that dirt and grime are the major contributors to death. Infection causes more deaths than the actual wounds do, I've come to realize. So I always make it a point to sterilize everything, tools and such, as best I can, and to clean the wounds before slopping on any of the noxious but mostly helpful ointments they employ."

"I'm not sure I have the stomach for this," Autumn groaned as they stepped inside the castle.

"You do," Charlotte said with confidence. "You just witnessed what I'm sure was a pretty horrendous battle and you're not catatonic with shock. You can do this."

Autumn tried, she really did, but could not restrain herself and had to ask, "Why didn't his engagements work out? Marcus's? What happens in the middle ages that betrothals fall through?" Weren't people simply ordered to marry someone and they did so without complaint? That had always been her impression. Although to be fair, her exposure to the middle ages, of literature, art, or academia had been limited by her lack of interest in the subject.

Charlotte did not answer her but paused when they emerged from a short narrow corridor and stepped into a vast open room with extremely high ceilings. Charlotte's shoulders slumped, possibly at the chaos inside.

Autumn forgot her own question when she realized that this was likely the dining hall of the immense castle but that presently the tables and benches were being used as gurneys and hospital beds. Possibly there were fifty or more people inside this room but more probably less than half of them were uninjured. There seemed to be no order and no one specifically attending any wounded though several able-bodied men did stand near to or with certain injured men.

"Oh, shit," Autumn murmured unconsciously.

"Exactly. I'll get to the kitchens and make sure they've got kettles of water boiling. Just do what you can, Autumn. The servants and villagers will want to be helpful," Charlotte said in a hushed and hurried voice, lifting her finger to punctuate her thought. "But don't let them start sawing off any limbs. They are sometimes a little too hasty with their swords—all with good intent," Charlotte was quick to clarify when Autumn shot her a horrified look, "intending to save their kin, but...well, they seriously are sometimes a little too quick to chop things off."

"Oh, my God."

"I'll be right back," Charlotte said, ignoring Autumn's growing alarm. "Maybe start a triage, if you can, prioritizing those whose needs are most urgent."

And then Charlotte left her.

Autumn watched her hurry away, wanting so badly to follow her, wanting more than anything not to be left alone here, awkward and unsure.

But then men were injured, some were dying, and none of the non-injured seemed to be doing anything useful. Except maybe for that young boy who was busy making the fire in the hearth bigger and brighter. And there was a crying young woman—girl maybe, surely not more than sixteen or seventeen—crying over an unconscious, perhaps dead body on one of the long wooden tabletops. At least she was using her apron to stem the flow of blood from the young man's chest.

Autumn inhaled and exhaled slowly, trying to calm herself. She had three older brothers; she had nearly perfected the art of diffusing hot-blooded tempers and untidy scenes, had become very adept at lessening unruliness to calm.

She had one time witnessed a terrible car accident, had been the first person on the scene in fact, hovering over the man who had been ejected from his car from the rear window and then had lain in the middle of the four lane highway. Without thinking, she'd begun to organize the gawkers who'd spilled out of a nearby restaurant into traffic cops, charging two shocked men with diverting the traffic—which had disgracefully driven around the body and the mangled cars. She'd hollered at another to call 911 when no one seemed to have done so. She'd yelled at a woman not to touch the man on the ground, not knowing if his neck or back had been injured, and then had assured the seven-month pregnant woman inside one of those cars involved that she was fine, that everything was going to be okay. For a full minute in the immediate aftermath, the only voice heard had been Autumn's, clipping off one instruction after another.

She glanced around now at the chaos in the hall and drew in another breath, this one to fortify herself.

I can do this. Men shouldn't die because I'm baffled and terrified.

With great purpose, stiffening her spine, she approached the closest wounded McInnes man, who was seated on a long wooden bench, swiftly determining that the slice in his arm was not life threatening. The man next to him had a cut in his thigh that was bleeding but not profusely. She paused there, saying to him, "I'm just going to wrap this around it so the bleeding stops," as she removed her jacket. She knelt beside him, ignoring his perplexed frown, which sat heavily upon her, and wrapped her expensive but ruined jacket around his thigh, tying it tightly on the underside of his leg.

Next, a young man with a blaze of red hair, who'd cautiously watched Autumn's approach, and whose forehead sported a big goose egg with a bloody gash in the center of it, waved his hand to dismiss Autumn's inspection, mumbling something that she supposed might have been the medieval Gaelic equivalent of, "I'm fine."

She went from one to the next, developing her own triage system, which existed and evolved fully inside her head. She imagined four separate categories. The first were simply those already deceased or expected to become so without urgent and likely impossible treatment, impossible in this time without professional interference; next, those who needed immediate treatment and might be expected to survive if they received it. In a third group, she lumped those with injuries that were serious but not life-threatening and in the last group, which she privately labeled *the walking wounded*, she mentally registered all those with minor injuries.

And now she had to relocate each group according to her very basic classifications.

An unwounded man, possibly a Nicholson, happened to walk by Autumn. She grabbed at his sleeve.

"We need to re-arrange these wounded men in a way that—"

He stared at her as if she spoke...well, a language he didn't understand.

"You don't speak English, do you? Shit." Improvising, she pointed to a gravely wounded man and attempted to make motions to show that he should be lifted and moved closer to the fireplace. She wanted the most seriously wounded near the fireplace for light and warmth and because she assumed eventually boiled water would come there as well. But clearly this man didn't understand what she was trying to impart, or possibly he was suspicious of her; his puzzled gaze had traveled up and down Autumn and not with any benevolence.

Frustrated, Autumn waved him off and turned, facing the middle of the room, calling out, "Does anyone speak English?"

Most all the walking wounded glanced around, first at each other, then around the room, and ultimately back at Autumn. Finally, a young kid raised his hand. Autumn waved impatiently at him, annoyed by his slow and hesitant response. "Come. Hurry up." She thought she recalled him as one of the McInnes men, vaguely noticed in the fringes of her awareness when she'd been met by Marcus while an arrow protruded from her shoulder. He was about her height but possibly weighed a bit less than her, with stringy brown hair and a lean face, his features nearly feminine. As he limped toward her, Autumn noticed her jacket tied around his thigh, recalling him from a few minutes ago.

"Hi," she said. "What's your name?"

"Lewin, Mistress," he answered promptly.

"I am Autumn," she introduced herself. "I'm not a mistress. Okay, I need to rearrange all these wounded. Tell everyone if they can move, if their injuries are not life threatening, they need to move to the far side of this room, down to that end. I need to see and have access to all those who need immediate, life-saving care."

"But, mistress, the healer—"

"Is not here," Autumn told him. "If you want these men—your friends, I assume—to be saved, get them moving now."

"But the laird—"

"Marcus? He's not here either. But these men can't wait for everyone to get here and for everything to fall into place. Go ahead, repeat what I said. Use a loud voice." She reminded him of what action she needed. "If they can move, get to the far side."

For half a second longer he stared at her but then did turn and face the congregation and called out a string of foreign words. Another small space of time elapsed without any reaction. Autumn clapped her hands brusquely, calling out, "Chop, chop, people. Move." And then a quiet, unhurried scrambling took place, whereby at least half of the population inside rose and shifted to the back of the room.

"Great," said Autumn to Lewin. "Now, pick out four guys, strong and able to lift others who cannot walk, and follow me."

Expecting the kid to follow her orders—he looked a little afraid of her—Autumn pivoted and caught sight of the man they called Gibbon staring at her from where he lay on the table-slash-hospital bed. Moments ago, as she'd triaged him while his eyes had been closed, she'd put him in the second category: he would survive but only if something were done to save him. Though he didn't move at all but seemed to be beckoning Autumn with his bright blue eyes, Autumn went to his side.

"You're at the top of the list to be treated," she told him. Frankly, she didn't have time to spend with each individual, simply to assure them that something would be done for them. Once around the room had shown how dire was the need of almost a dozen men. She saw again the bloody rag that had been pressed to Gibbon's side, under which she'd peeked and winced at a few minutes ago. It was at about stomach height but off to the right, and might have hit a kidney or his ribs if it were as deep as it looked.

He didn't respond to her assurance but looked beside her, causing her to notice Lewin had followed her.

"Do as the lass bids ye, lad," said Gibbon. "Bring some order to this disarray."

"Aye, sir," Lewin acknowledged firmly, with much less hesitation, and then was off.

"Who are ye?" Gibbon then bluntly asked Autumn.

She gave him a grimace of a smile, noticing just now a scarf or cloth wrapped around his neck, which was tucked into the padded leather vest he wore that presumably had been buttoned at his front but had been unfastened and opened, possibly shortly after he'd been struck while still out in that meadow. "I am no one, sir," she said, pulling gently at the cloth to remove it from around his neck. "Just Autumn. But I have no injury and so I can be helpful, I hope."

Gingerly, she removed the soaked rag from his side and replaced it with the fresh, dry cloth. She picked up his hand and laid it over the cloth. "Hold that firmly," was one of the few essential instruction's she knew to give.

Gibbon lifted his other hand without hesitation as if he weren't so weak as his injury would suggest and pointed to Autumn's shoulder and the brown stain and the tear in her blouse. "A wee bit grazed."

Aiming for lightheartedness, Autumn scoffed with a grin. "'Tis but a scratch," she teased, quoting an old Monty Python movie and a scene that had been re-invigorated by memes in recent years.

"Of course, ye fib," he accused but not with any rancor. "I have nae breath to exert volume, lass. But call out for Osgar, will ye?"

"He's the bald guy, right?" When Gibbon nodded, she informed him, "He's not here. Or not here yet. He was fine, or fine-ish, all things considered, last I saw him, but he hasn't yet made it to Balla Àrd. Nor has Marcus—er, the laird, though he insisted to me that he was not in any jeopardy of dying."

"Nae worries then. But smile down at me, lass," Gibbon instructed. "and I'll gie ye my best simpering puss. Will serve one or two goals. Either it'll be the last bonny thing I ken, or it will function as a dubbing, me bestowing power upon ye. The lads'll do yer bidding once they see yer kindness to this auld man and perceive my returned favor."

She did smile but more so because she liked him. "Very clever, sir, and thank you for the endorsement. Don't forget to keep pressure on that cloth," she reminded him before she moved on, meaning to get the entire room and all its occupants settled before—if or when—the actual doctor arrived.

***

From the shadows of the east end of the hall, Marcus sat unmoving, watching Autumn. When he'd come to the hall a few moments ago, he'd recognized immediately the back of her, her hands filled with the two feet of poor young Hamish, not likely long for the world if the amount of blood dripped in his wake as he was moved closer to the hearth were any indication of the probability of longevity.

Gibbon had been found upon the trestle table closest to the door, his lids heavy over dull eyes. Marcus and he had clasped forearms, no words necessary to reveal their gladness to find each had survived.

"She is nae a miracle worker," the captain of the McInnes army remarked to Marcus, following the trajectory of his gaze, "but she might be if only she were surrounded by any other with such competence—the Nicholson's bride naewithstanding."

"Gormlaith has been summoned?" Marcus had inquired, sparing only a glance at Charlotte, who was at that moment in conversation with Autumn, nodding agreeably at whatever the latter was saying.

"Aye, made that the first concern nae sooner had I cleared the gate." Gibbon had said.

Marcus had tasked Gibbon only with resting well until the healer came before taking his leave of his captain. And he might have approached Autumn then but was advised by a red-faced and stammering Lewin that as he was wounded but yet able to walk, he was expected to abide at the east end of the hall with the others awaiting their turn, and thus Marcus had slipped quietly into the shadows. He might have gone straight away to his own chamber, might have requested an ewer and basin and thread and needle to address his wounds himself, but he had not. He needed now to be with his men. He needed to assess the fullness of the tragedy, wanting very desperately to stew just here. He and his men were safe from further destruction by the MacPhails and yet still overwhelmed by the weeping and groaning of the wounded, by the stench of blood and gore and death.

He sat now in the shadows on the long bench that sat against the east wall, with Osgar on his left and Aelred on his right. And he watched everything that went on in the hall, making notes of the condition of those gravely wounded, easily recognized by their placement around the hall, which had been Autumn's doing, as told by Osgar.

"In the shadows for us," Osgar added to that explanation. "Mistress wants those who can wait to do so out of her way. Is she a healer then?"

Marcus didn't know what she was and so made no response.

"Strange bird, she, eh?" Remarked Osgar.

"Undeniably," he said before he thought better of it.

"What do ye make of her?" Asked Aelred, his voice as hushed as Osgar's.

Marcus considered this but didn't for one minute think he would share with Osgar or Aelred the impossible truth as he was made to understand, that she had traveled backward in time from a distant, unimagined future.

"Too soon to tell," he said evasively. "But we will judge aplenty her deeds here today, will we nae?"

"Aye," agreed Osgar, sighing as he leaned his head back against the wall behind them.

"Amen to that, Laird," concurred Aelred.

They exchanged no more conversation for several minutes so that Marcus was free to observe Autumn carry on about the hall. He was no more or no less shocked as any other who watched her with such dedication—and he understood there were more than only a few in her audience. It would have been difficult to ignore her presence, even if she had been familiar to them, she being dressed so garishly and being barefooted, and with black circles around her eyes. Despite the grime and the rip, and the blood now a day old, her tunic was yet abnormally bright white and clashed sharply with the present surroundings. Her hands, small and gentle, moved deftly, as she arranged the wounded, her demeanor calm and collected even as all around her, men breathed their last or fought valiantly not to. The flickering flames of the fire and the additional torches that had been lit cast an ethereal glow to her complexion and turned her gray eyes golden.

Who was this woman?

Mayhap she was a general, or a chief in her own right, in her time. She behaved as such, issuing orders with ease, firm when she needed to be, so that after a while those witnessing her actions might have begun to differentiate between the assorted tones she used. A crisp and clear voice demanded an immediate response, in action or words; a quieter, thoughtful tone was her advising or suggesting; the soft, melodic tone, one a mam might employ with her bairn, was used exclusively with men whose eyes she would eventually close for the last time, who would then be covered with a shroud.

Though Charlotte worked just as tirelessly and with equal confidence and utility, Marcus only had eyes for Autumn.

His wounds throbbed, a reminder of the battle that had turned Balla Àrd's hall into a makeshift infirmary, and ultimately a graveyard of the McInnes. But even in his weakened state, he couldn't tear his gaze away from her. Autumn's vibrant blonde hair framed her face like a halo as she visited like an angel of mercy each wounded McInnes man. Her eyes, though mostly filled with an admirable determination, were sometimes dulled by a sadness that tugged at Marcus's greater awareness.

Nearly perfect, was she nae? Save for the foul matter of being from the future.

After another half hour, in which time Marcus only grew increasingly annoyed with himself for his inability to resist watching every move Autumn made, he slipped quietly from the hall.

Chapter Nine

She should have slept like the proverbial baby—although why was that a saying? did that mean that you woke every few hours needing to poop and wanting to eat?—but she did not. Instead, her brain regularly relived each horrific detail of the last thirty-six hours and then Charlotte's crazy, still hard-to-digest news that she'd somehow traveled to the fourteenth century, as Charlotte herself had done, though with much happier results.

Autumn rolled over on the mattress, thin and lumpy but then not as uncomfortable as she might have expected to find in the middle ages. Not that she had anything to compare it to, and certainly not as if she wished to bounce around like some medieval Goldilocks, evaluating mattresses in this time.

"What am I supposed to do with this impossible, implausible information?" She wondered aloud, staring at the vaulted timber ceiling of the bedroom she'd been given—a chamber, Charlotte had called it when she'd brought her here last night, well after midnight. Though it never quite left her mind yesterday, she'd hardly been afforded the opportunity to give it the full weight of her concentration. And when she had, all through the night, no answers came screaming at her. Not to why she'd been thrust so rudely through time or how she might return to where she belonged, or even if there was or should be some mission attached to her journey. True, all her beliefs about time travel were governed by the few fantasy novels she'd read or movies she'd watched, but wasn't there supposed to be some reason or justification for journeying through time?

Charlotte's suggestion from last night, the last thing Charlotte had said before she'd departed to find her husband and her own bed, had been, "Remember to take it day by day. You don't need and shouldn't expect to have all the answers at once. Possibly, you should prepare yourself that you might never have answers—like me—and need only to figure out what you're going to do with and in this new circumstance."

With those parting words, Autumn had not bothered to give voice to the rant that she'd wanted to go off on, about the unfairness of it all.

Charlotte had found love with her brave and valiant knight, or laird, whatever Reid Nicholson was. Of course she could afford to be indifferent about how intolerable Autumn found it all.

But maybe Charlotte had the right of it for the time being. Balla Àrd and its residents had suffered greatly, and Autumn had assumed what she considered to be a valuable and appreciated role, even as she felt at times there must be more she could do. The healer had eventually come, more than three hours after the first casualties had arrived at the castle.

Gormlaith was a woman with pitch black hair and saggy skin, though she was thin and reedy, who was about sixty years of age if Autumn had been asked to guess, and with a temperament that had Autumn wondering if crotchety-ness were simply a common behavior of people in this time.

Shortly after her arrival, shit got more real, as Autumn had irreverently thought yesterday. Autumn had done little more than arrange the wounded, holding their hands, and wrapping open injuries as best she could. Gormlaith, after her initial quizzical reception of Autumn and her description of her triage system and the location of each group, had gotten immediately to work. Gormlaith quickly proved that she was a learned and capable healer and had proven equally adept at bossing around Autumn and Charlotte and another girl named Lorain, a young girl surely not more than sixteen or seventeen, who had been culled from the kitchen at Charlotte's behest, and had, much like Autumn, looked as if she'd have rather been anywhere else in the world over the next few hours. Orders had been given frequently and tersely, fetch this and hold that, watch this and do just that, while Gormlaith stitched and sewed, and cauterized flesh and set or relocated bones, any and all of which turned Autumn's stomach until her belly felt as if it were constantly in motion and about three seconds and one more glimpse of broken body parts away from heaving all over everyone and everything.

Abruptly, Autumn sat up, throwing her legs off the side of the bed and planting her feet on the smooth wood floor. She needed to act, not think. Possibly that was all that would keep her sane. She couldn't keep reflecting on yesterday's tragedy—either one of them—but needed to *get action*. That had been Theodore Roosevelt's approach to life, one that Autumn's parents had taught and instilled in her brothers and her. *Get action*, the one-time president had either said or written. Autumn's parents might be sad to know that she'd forgotten the exact quote, but maybe would be pleased that she remembered the gist of it. Get busy to stay sane. Use time wisely. Act, move, make something of each circumstance in which you find yourself. Get action.

Deciding she would very quickly go nuts if she did nothing but sit around and wallow in this most untenable circumstance, Autumn stood, determined that she would indeed do something. *Do something, even if it's wrong*, her father was fond of saying.

It would have been easy then to give full rein to indulge the tears that once more wanted to overwhelm her. For right now though, she simply couldn't think about her mother or father, or her brothers and their families, none of them. She'd be rendered immobile and inconsolable if she allowed herself the luxury of that kind of wallowing.

Once standing, however, Autumn wasn't sure what her first step should be. Chewing her lip, she glanced around the large but sparsely decorated room—chamber—deciding home décor wasn't something people in this century gave too much thought or attention. Possibly, the whitewashed walls, which looked to be made of very rough plaster, was the only nod toward decorating. The floor was clean but bare, the wood not even varnished. It matched the ceiling almost perfectly, save for a few worn paths on the floor around the bed where the wood was darkened by regular footsteps, naturally not repeated on the ceiling. The bed itself was more correctly a cot, a raised wooden piece with a mattress that hung several inches over each side. It was larger than a twin bed in width but not so wide as a queen, Autumn guessed. Thankfully, the bed had been made with a cover over the mattress and the small pillow and had been topped with a wool blanket and a heavy fur throw. One sniff had advised that the fur was an authentic hide, not some nifty and washable find at the local Home Goods store. Aside from the bed, the only other furniture in the room was a trunk that sat against one wall and a small writing desk, complete with a myriad of ink stains but presently no ink pot or pen—er, quill?

Her indecision about how and where to begin to get action was thankfully short-lived, interrupted by someone's perfect timing, as a small and quiet knock came at the door.

Half expecting that she might find Marcus on the other side but not quite sure why she would imagine he would seek her out, Autumn was both a little surprised and then somewhat relieved to find Charlotte there in the hall, holding a medium sized, shallow bowl of porcelain that was filled with water while a bunch of fabrics were draped over one arm.

"Good morning." Charlotte's greeting seemed to be teeming with more hope than confidence, which was clarified when she added, "I would ask how you slept but even if I couldn't see the dark circles under your eyes, I would have guessed you tossed and turned all night."

"Bingo," Autumn allowed, with as much good nature as she could muster, pulling the door wide to admit Charlotte, "and good morning. I was just wondering how or where to start the day."

Charlotte stepped inside and deposited the basin onto the writing desk and then plopped the fabrics onto the messy bed. "I have the how," she said, turning from the bed, showing that she still held one more piece of cloth in her hand. "Here's water and a washcloth to wash away the grime—and FYI, when your face and whatever else are washed, then you use this linen to scrub your teeth." At Autumn's cringe, Charlotte laughed and thrust the linen cloth into Autumn's hand. "It's not as bad as it sounds, actually. I find that a good gargling also helps but you'll figure out what works best for you. Also, I brought an outfit of mine," she said, pointing toward the pile on the bed. Her mouth twisted with a bit of regret as she explained. "I'm sorry I'm not taller,

Autumn. This kirtle is going to be pretty short on you, but it's all we have right now."

Autumn considered Charlotte's very petite figure. "Forget the length. I'll be shocked if I fit in any part of it."

Charlotte shrugged. "You're taller but thinner than me, so it should work overall. Unless you want to wear breeches and a man's tunic, we'll have to make it work."

"Right."

Autumn was thrilled to be able to wash her face and got right to it, leaving the wrung cloth laying over her face for a moment before she scrubbed away grime, blood, and what remained of the make-up she'd applied two days ago. Her esthetician was likely going to cry when Autumn finally got back to her.

She washed her face and neck and soaked her hands, asking over her shoulder, "I will be able to get a shower—or a bath, I guess it would be now—sometime in the near future?"

"Absolutely," Charlotte said. "Just give it a day or two until things settle down. The castle has a garderobe—where baths are taken—but again, this is a bachelor pad, so to speak, and there are no doors there in that chamber, only a series of corners to turn so that it isn't completely open. Anyway, a bath takes some doing, lugging tubs and water up the stairs and all that."

"No problem. I understand it's the least of anyone's concern here. I just wanted to make sure I wouldn't have to wait like a week or more. That would—oh, God, I hope I'm not still here in a week."

Charlotte made no response to that, which gave Autumn pause. But because she wasn't yet ready to question if she could actually get back home to her time, afraid of what the answer might be, she clamped her lips and finished with her washing, wringing out the cloth and laying it over the edge of the basin when she was done.

When she turned around again, Charlotte asked, "Do you want me to leave you alone while you—"

"No, it's fine," said Autumn, stepping forward to consider the items Charlotte had brought. "Or rather, I don't mind if you don't mind. But um, what do I do about panties. I only have the ones I'm wearing now."

Charlotte grimaced again, as she did almost every time she was compelled to deliver what she no doubt considered bad news. "I don't suppose it will come as any surprise to you that they don't wear panties or underwear as we do. With all the layers, some people don't wear underclothes at all. I have since had something close to panties made for me at Kingswood. But I don't think you want to wear my underwear."

Though Charlotte was lovely and seemed to practice hygiene better than any other person Autumn had met in this century, the idea of borrowing underwear from a virtual stranger sat about as well with Autumn in 1304 as it would in her own time. "No worries. I've gone commando before." Oh, God, she didn't even want to ask what that would mean when she had her period. Hopefully, she'd be long gone by then since she didn't expect it for another two weeks, returned to all the modern-day conveniences, or necessities as she saw it.

As Charlotte politely pretended to have a keen interest in what might be found outside the window, Autumn removed her torn and dirtied clothes that she'd now worn for two whole days and took a moment to peek under the bandage just below her shoulder. Whatever salve had been applied had either evaporated or soaked in so that she saw clearly the sloppily stitched hole in her flesh. What little blood she saw was dried and brown and the flesh immediately around the wound was pink and maybe a little puffy but not angry red, which her mother had always said indicated infection.

She flattened the bandage again and then tried to make sense of the different layers, having to ask Charlotte what went where, and then put on the linen shift first, which was sleeveless and floated down over her hips closely but not too tightly. It landed just above her ankles. At Charlotte's instruction, a linen kirtle of an earthen russet hue followed, a scoop-necked gown with long, tight sleeves, with a fitted bodice and flowing skirt that likewise fell far short of nearly reaching the floor as Charlotte's did. The kirtle's neckline was trimmed in a band of silk ribbon, embroidered with a vine of leaves and roses. A matching band of silk circled each arm of the dress about midway between her shoulder and elbow.

While she dressed, she fought and eventually lost the battle against asking about Marcus. Despite all the commotion of yesterday, she must have looked at the door to the hall a hundred times, watching for him. When she could no more bear the inexplicable worry over a man she'd just met, she'd broken down and approached Reid when he'd shown himself in the hall in the early evening.

"Should have been back hours ago," had been Reid's scowling response to her inquiry. "I'll look into it."

Whether he did or not, Autumn did not know. But she saw Marcus a short time later, making his way from one patient to another. While it didn't appear he'd bathed fully, he had changed his clothes and washed up a bit. The gash at his temple, wiped clean of dripping blood, looked much better, possibly not even deep enough to require stitches. His hair had looked as if he'd only run his fingers through it to push the length of it off his face. He'd been wearing a tunic with sleeves so she couldn't attest to the state of the injury to his shoulder but had asked about it when she'd approached him as he stood at Gibbon's side.

Marcus had lifted his gaze to her, inclining his head as a greeting, but instead of answering had asked first about his captain, who'd been sleeping.

"Gormlaith felt fairly confident about his prognosis," Autumn had informed him. "She ah, she had to sew up things inside as well as his flesh externally. I suppose we'll just be watching for infection." And she didn't know if the meaning behind it would be appreciated by him, but she'd added, "Charlotte and I have been very careful all day to make sure everything was sterilized. Boiled clean, free of germs," she clarified when he'd only stared blankly at her.

She'd again expressed her concern about his injuries, including what had seemed a terrific gash in his thigh.

Marcus had waved off her worry. "'Tis wrapped tightly and will keep until the lads are mended."

"What about your rib?"

"I dinna fear it's cracked, after all," he'd said.

Though she'd wanted to insist he be looked at next while the healer was still making her rounds, Autumn hadn't pushed him then. There had been a hollow sound to his voice, and she was pretty sure that mournfulness and not weakness was what had dulled his complexion, and even the usual fierce intensity of his gaze. He was still reeling in shock over the brutal attack and the loss of life. She'd been desperately sad for him just then, her heart aching for the depths of sorrow that lurked behind his brown eyes.

She'd been peripherally aware of him over the next hour, her gaze constantly drawn to him as he made his way around the hall and spoke with each of his men. He even paused at each of the covered bodies, laying his strong hand over the linen. Autumn wondered if he said prayers for them. Or maybe, he only committed to avenging their deaths.

Presently, she asked Charlotte, "Have you seen Marcus this morning?"

"I haven't," Charlotte answered. "But then Reid was up with the sun and gone from our chamber. I'm sure he met first thing with Marcus and if I know Reid—and Marcus for that matter—they'll be out scouring all of Balla Àrd and the McInnes estate, looking for any sign of more trouble from those stupid MacPhails."

And yet another shock came Autumn's way, a sudden internal gasp of anxiety about Marcus. "He wouldn't have gone by himself though, would he? Or even with only Reid? They'd have taken the entire army, right?"

"Oh, God, yeah," Charlotte answered quickly. "Well, not the entire army. All the house guards are here, of course. Marcus would never leave Balla Àrd unprotected."

Knowing a bit of relief for this response, Autumn pulled over her head the last layer, which Charlotte called a surcote, but which was simply another sleeveless linen gown, this one a deeper claret color, also close-fitting and expected to reach the floor but only dropping so far as the other two dresses, not quite to her ankles. And now her shoulder, which had only been a nagging nuisance of discomfort all through the night, ached and throbbed in protest over the continued lifting of things over her head.

"All set," Autumn said, which turned Charlotte from the window.

Autumn hadn't yet glanced down, which would only tell her so much, but read fairly quickly in Charlotte's gaze that she looked ridiculous. She wasn't freakishly tall, was just over average at five foot seven, but standing next to Charlotte, who surely wasn't more than five-three, Autumn did feel like a giant freak in too-small clothes. Nervously, she smoothed down the skirts, grabbing more than one layer and attempting to make them longer.

This was about as far as she was ever going to be—she sincerely hoped!—from Dior, her Louboutins, her Prada handbags, and every over-priced but well worth the luxury article of clothing she owned.

"Oh, you look wonderful," Charlotte lied, almost convincingly. "I apologize that I haven't any shoes to loan you, but we'll figure something out. Somewhere here at Balla Àrd, or from someone, we should be able to find you some footwear."

Autumn shrugged now. "I was barefoot during all that awful business yesterday," she told Charlotte. "Another day won't bother me." Not half as much as the certainty that she looked so ridiculous right now.

"Nicely done, Autumn," Charlotte said. "You're doing great with all this—my God, if I'd been greeted by what you were when I first came, I'd have curled myself into a ball and died."

Autumn acknowledged this with a wry grin, mostly for how ridiculous were half the things that came out of their mouths. Otherwise, her endless optimism, and what had been ingrained in her since childhood, that there was a solution to any problem, lived strong and loud in her. She *would* figure this out.

"Let's go," Charlotte said. "The hall is still being used as the infirmary, but we can go down the back stairs to the kitchen and get breakfast before we begin our shift, pretending to be nurses."

Autumn nodded and followed Charlotte out the door, not quite enjoying the weight of the three layers of skirts swishing around her legs. In all likelihood, that would take some getting used to. She couldn't help but notice how graceful and, well, put together Charlotte was compared to her. Her outfit looked period perfect, while Autumn was convinced she looked like she was playing at something she was not, which she guessed was essentially true, since she most certainly wasn't five foot three and was not born in the middle ages.

As they wound their way down the spiral stairs, Autumn said, "Charlotte, while I thank you heartily for the clothes, I have to laugh as it reminds me—rather painfully, I might add—of my part in the Christmas play when I was in the third grade."

To her surprise, Charlotte stopped and turned on the stair, being two below Autumn so that she seemed even shorter and smaller. In the dim light of the stairwell, she threw up a quizzical glance at Autumn.

"Well, you've got me curious. How on earth could a third grade Christmas play compare with these clothes from almost seven hundred years in the past?"

Rather pleased to share the tale, as it seemed somehow normal and cast aside all the was horrifying and traumatizing—she'd friggin' time-traveled, for crying out loud!—Autumn happily related the entire incident, which was still a source of fodder for her three brothers.

"Okay, I went to a small, private school which had no budget for, well, for anything and in the third grade I was cast as a reindeer in the Christmas play. It was more a recital, each grade doing different holiday songs, but they called it a play. There were to be four reindeer—only four since it wasn't about that reindeer—and we would stay on the stage for the duration, as props in the background, even as other grades were taking the stage and belting out their show tunes. The Heffle triplets were chosen as the other three reindeer." God, how she hated those little brats, one whinier than the next. Melissa Heffle, who almost daily reminded someone that she was the oldest triplet, was particularly annoying. Autumn could still picture her buggy blue eyes and almost anemic pale skin, and how thin was her white-blonde hair. "All right, so the costumes were not provided by the school but were expected to be made by the parents. Well, that might have been fine except that I'd forgotten to give my mother the notice that had come well in advance of the play."

Charlotte flinched, possibly already seeing where this was going.

Autumn nodded. "Yep. Gave her the note that day after school, when there were about four hours until curtain up that evening. Naturally, my mother was in a tizzy, but she was not one to go down without a fight. It's actually pretty funny when I think back on it, watching her attempt to create a costume to make me a reindeer in so short a time. We made the rounds to three different craft stores and headed home—dinner was postponed and then my brothers were told to have cereal—and there, in the rec room of our basement, she proceeded to use spray adhesive in an attempt to attach faux fur to my dance leotard. My mother was a college math professor and amateur genealogist, and not a DIY-er." She recalled clearly that she'd had such a greater appreciation for her mother from that day onward, since instead of yelling at Autumn and telling her there was nothing to be done about it at that time—which would have been perfectly reasonable, Autumn understood now—she'd tackled the problem head-on. "As you might imagine, that didn't work," Autumn said to a very rapt Charlotte, "so she glued three bags of cotton balls to the leotard. Dad came out of his workroom in the basement, barely pausing but to note that I was going to look like a lamb, which then saw my mother stretching out the cotton balls so they weren't so round. That seemed to work, and Mom proceeded to spray paint the white cotton balls with what she thought was the perfect color, but was actually too dark. With no time to repaint, I'd been shoved into the costume though the paint hadn't really dried. Mind you, my three older brothers are half-watching all this from where they were gaming ten feet away. Now it's getting late, and Mom decided that high pigtails in my hair would serve nicely as antlers—I'm not making this up. And then, the show-stopping kicker: a tube of my mom's rarely used red lipstick was employed to redden my nose—as if that reindeer *was* in the play. Possibly, that was merely how my mother envisioned every reindeer."

Charlotte now had her hand over her mouth, partially horrified on Autumn's behalf but mostly, it seemed, trying to keep herself from bursting out laughing.

"Oh, it gets better," Autumn told her. "I had no browns shoes, boots, or sneakers but my brother, Sean, had a pair of brown dress shoes. Yeah. I thought it was a good idea, actually, even when I put them on and they were way too big. Oh, but no problem, there were extra cotton balls and Mom made those shoes fit. Honestly, at this point, even as my brothers' are laughing their asses off and my Dad has returned and is staring at me as if I look more like a three-headed sloth than a reindeer, I was thinking, *whew, Mom has really pulled this off*. She saved the day. But then we get to school, and I see the Heffle triplets. And I don't know if their mother is simply a DIY wizard or had a degree in costuming. She might have won an Oscar for her costume design. I might have only been eight, but it took me only half a second to realize I looked like an idiot. But truly I didn't realize how awful the costume was until I was on stage, standing next to the Heffle triplets, wearing hand-sewn costumes made entirely of fur save for the heads, which were custom made of paper mâché and plaster cloth and painted to lifelike perfection. My class recited that poem that starts, *'Twas the night before Christmas and all through the house*, by the way. You know?" Autumn grinned. "The one that mentions every reindeer *except* the one with the red nose? Meanwhile, every step I took loosened or completely dislodged one or more pieces of the paint-stiffened, cotton-ball-fur until I resembled—my brother, Adam's words—*the mangy, flea-ridden half-sister of Rudolph*."

Charlotte grabbed onto Autumn's hand and threw back her head, laughing so hard the sound echoed in the narrow stairwell. "Oh, my God. Autumn! That's hysterical. I mean, awful, but hysterical."

Autumn shrugged good-naturedly, her mood lightened a bit with that memory. "Anyway, not that your generously donated clothes should be likened to that infamous costume from the 2003 Christmas season, but just so you know how big an idiot I feel for being not only out of time, but spectacularly out of place."

Charlotte reined in her merriment. Though her eyes still shone with laughter, her smile faded. "But you survived that misadventure, did you not?"

"I did. But please don't say to me that you are classifying this—now—simply as a misadventure."

Charlotte offered her the gentle and wise smile of one who had been in the same boat at one time and had since learned to navigate well. "I suppose it depends on how you look at it. Adventure or misadventure is up to you."

Chapter Ten

"I simply dinna understand why ye never mentioned this to me," Marcus said.

He and Reid had ridden out from the keep with three units, mostly comprised of Nicholsons since the McInnes army had been drastically reduced. They were stopped upon a promontory of jagged stone, which overlooked the valley the locals called Glenverra, in the heart of the southeastern part of the McInnes demesne. While the lads meandered about, picking up on clues that the MacPhails may have lain in wait just here, Marcus questioned his long-time friend about that most fantastic and bewildering claim, first introduced by Reid himself, that Charlotte and now Autumn were not actually born of this time, but instead hailed from a world and era so far in the future as to be inconceivable.

"Do ye count it as fact?" Reid asked, lifting one brow, his attention pulled from the magnificent view, a lush expanse of rolling hills and valleys cloaked in a tapestry of vibrant greens and the occasional violet of the blooming thistle.

Marcus frowned. "Fact? Nae. Nae at all. Fancy, aye. Drivel, more probably. But nae fact."

"And that is why I did nae—could nae—tell ye," said Reid. "'Twas nuisance enough trying to comprehend for myself, coming to terms with it. I was nae going to introduce the wild theory to ye."

"Theory now?" Marcus challenged, frustrated by the varying terms and some notion that he was being played a fool. "Ye just said theory. Is it that or truth? Och, shite. Ye dinna believe it yerself, do ye?"

Reid's answer was short and meaningful. "But Charlotte does and so I must." He sighed then and gestured outward toward the stunning glen below them. "All our lives, we've heard the tales, of magic and mystery, any and all of them defying explanation. Ye yerself, ye've heard the whispers—have ye nae?—same as I, whispers o' time travelers walking among us, disguised as ordinary folk."

As Charlotte pretends to be, Marcus thought. Though he was loath to give in to persuasion merely because his friend subscribed to the lunacy, he was also reluctant to assert outright that Reid had gone daft. "Drinkin' too much of that guid whiskey ye bring in from Skye," Marcus asserted instead. "Time travel? 'Tis naught but a fairytale, something the bards spin to entertain us on feast days."

Reid shook his head, a glint of fervor in his eyes.

"Nae, Marcus. I've learned too much, too fantastic to be invented—"

"Learned from Charlotte? Invented by her?" Marcus challenged, forcing Reid to look within and ask if he only wanted to believe because he loved her. If time travel were not real, then Reid would have to realize and acknowledge that his wife was either possessed by demons or simply mad.

Possibly Reid sensed Marcus's judgment. "How else would ye explain it? Charlotte and now Autumn appearing out o' thin air? Dressed as they were? Speaking strange tongues? With so much knowledge about what comes?"

Marcus shrugged. "Mayhap they wander from distant lands or—ye have to consider—they are only mad," he finally said. "It is too fantastical, too far-fetched to be true."

"Charlotte is nae mad," Reid said hotly. "She's nae witless, nae a fool, and nae possessed of a wobbly mind." He sighed then and said in a softer tone, with much less vehemence, "Keep an open mind, Marcus. The world's a mysterious place, and the Highlands themselves hide secrets deeper than any loch. Whether time travel is real or nae, there's still more to the world than meets the eye."

The debate was left unresolved as they were approached by Osgar, with a report on the findings about this site.

This morning as Marcus had made his way through the keep and into the bailey and then up onto the battlements, he'd encountered again an array of injuries, found in one man and the next, each telling its own grim story. Osgar had not escaped the fight unscathed but sat upon his horse beside Marcus now, his left hand swelled to nearly twice its size but firm upon the reins. He bore a gash across his brow, since sewn closed but still looking angry, and had walked earlier, Marcus had noticed yesterday and today, with a noticeable limp.

At the inclination of Marcus's head, Osgar said, "A great deal of activity here. 'Twas nae only a passage but a resting place. Ye see the prints and the tracks. And we found their fire, buried, and food scraps, along with enough impressions in the earth to suggest they stayed the night here, ere they ambushed us yesterday."

His jaw clamped, Marcus acknowledged this with a nod.

"Darrie was a trap then?" Osgar concluded.

"Aye," he said. He'd already explained his suspicion of this to Reid, that the MacPhails had used their attack on Darrie to lure the McInnes from Balla Àrd. Both clans had erred, Marcus in his assumption that the fires that had moved them from the keep had only been that and not an attack, and the MacPhails in their supposition that the fracas at Darrie would have brought out the entire McInnes force.

Seamus MacPhail, if he wanted a battle—and surely he did—knew he couldn't possibly hope to lay a fruitful siege at Balla Àrd. The elevation of the keep, and the McInnes's ability to recognize a coming attack and defend from higher ground, had kept her relatively safe over the centuries. The physical barrier of the moat and the close proximity of the loch presented another challenge to any potential attacker. The size of Balla Àrd alone, with its massive curtain wall, which could easily hold hundreds of soldiers, was another deterrent to a besieger. Unless there came an army numbered in the thousands, archers on the wall could easily pick off any attempting to come close.

"But we will nae wait on another such attempt?" Osgar asked. "We will offend now, and nae sit back with naught to do but defend?"

Marcus nodded again and at the same time, Reid reminded both he and Osgar, "Of course, that's what MacPhail is hoping."

"'Tis a long time coming," Marcus stated, agitated once more. "'Tis nae more only rustling and thieving and all their countless maddening jabs over the years. MacPhail is getting closer to death himself, wants the dispute ended here and now, wants to assure his kin the land he desires but has nae right to, ere he slithers down to hell. I am prepared to send him on his way."

Osgar appeared coldly pleased to hear this. "I'll get the lads back to the keep, laird," he said. "We've the burials to arrange."

When Osgar left, Reid turned his horse away from the breathtaking view beyond the cliff and asked of Marcus, "And what will ye do with yer time-traveling lass while yer occupied with yer vengeance?"

Resenting the implication that Autumn Winters was his responsibility, Marcus wheeled his destrier around as well and walked his horse alongside Reid's. "'Tis nae mine she is." Much less so, in fact, if indeed there was any truth to her claim. She belonged not to him, not even to this time. He turned a bold glance onto his friend. "Mayhap I'll leave her in the capable and similarly century-hopping hands of yer beloved Charlotte, since I ken ye'll want to be at my side. Ye never did meet a fight ye dinna like."

***

"I promise you," Charlotte said, "Balla Àrd is not normally such a tomb."

Autumn made no response, not sure why Charlotte might think Autumn was judging the medieval castle presently, and by the somber air that hung all about, the reason being quite obvious and wholly justified.

"This will be a first for me," Charlotte continued quietly, her eyes lowered to their work. "Plenty of funerals have I attended in the last two years, but never have I seen or known of one large ceremony for so many."

Autumn wiped away at yet another tear that slid down her cheek and stoically cast her gray eyes around the courtyard, where she, Charlotte, and that sweet girl, Lorain, were busy shrouding bodies. Prior to today, Autumn had never touched a dead body. Not even at the wake of her grandfather, whom she'd adored and had wept over profusely when she was twelve, had she had any desire to put her hand on the cold, flaccid flesh of the dead. Today, she had no choice since Charlotte had essentially volunteered them for the task. And if the last three days weren't a fine how-do-you-do from medieval Scotland, today certainly made up for it.

The process was not so much elaborate as it was heart wrenching.

"Of course," Charlotte was saying now, "we might have done this in the hall or in a smaller chamber upstairs, but there are simply too many." She lowered her voice further to add, "It's best done out of doors anyway. Those still within the hospital ward that was the hall don't want or need to be surrounded by....well, the smell."

Autumn nodded bleakly.

In the courtyard, near a no-frills water well, a long and narrow wooden board had been set up on three saw horses. Able-bodied men and boys had already begun to make stacks of bodies against the wall of the castle by the time Autumn and Charlotte had arrived. One by one, a body was lifted onto the counter, where Charlotte, Lorain, and Autumn would wash the face and hands of the deceased with water and then anoint him with perfumed oil before each soldier was wrapped in what Lorain called, and Charlotte had translated, as a winding sheet. The shrouds were long rectangles made of simple white linen and were folded over each body, top to bottom, before a second one was used sideways, wrapped mummy-style as Autumn considered it, snugly from head to toe. When finished, the shrouded body was placed on a wooden cart that Charlotte had said would be used to convey the dead to their final resting place.

Breakfast, which had been hours ago by now, consisting of the fourteenth century's equivalent to oatmeal—far inferior to what Autumn was accustomed to—and more carbs in the form of bannocks, which Charlotte explained were fried bread cakes made from coarse oats, and then plenty of cheese, all threatened to resume their existence at Balla Àrd as Autumn struggled to keep it all down in her stomach.

Her legs ached from standing basically in one spot for so long; her shoulder throbbed with soreness, the ache seeming worse even than yesterday; Autumn was unaccustomed to wearing so many layers on what seemed a very mild day, and with the sun beating down on her, had started to overheat and perspire; and she was continually the recipient of keen regard from almost everyone she saw, not all of the attention appearing to be kind. Still, she suffered little over any of these matters. The task at hand, however, was likely to see her lose her mind.

Charlotte was beyond sweet but seemed to be one of those people who didn't so much appreciate long stretches of silence. She talked often, regularly, her voice always respectfully low, but then so much so that it became easy for Autumn to tune her out. To keep herself from going off the deep end, Autumn desperately needed to focus inward, to fill her mind with thoughts and images that hadn't anything to do with the work before her or the other tragedy. She fought silently and forcibly to make the quality of her thoughts pleasant. She focused on her breathing while internally humming a purposefully slow melody and paired that with images of her nieces and nephews. Snapshots of memories drifted across her mind's eye, recalling lazy summer Sundays at her parents' house, the air alive with excited chatter of little voices, three girls and four boys under the age of ten. Her secret favorite, Lily, always managed to get her hands on the chocolate chip cookies first, her blue eyes dancing with delight. Autumn recalled the impromptu talent show the kids had put on only a month ago, their faces beaming with enthusiasm as they sang off-key renditions of their favorite songs. Josh, the oldest of the grandchildren, had performed silly magic tricks; Sarah, at eight, had wowed one and all by acting out a scene from her favorite superhero movie, employing three different voices. Autumn had eagerly been part of their attentive audience, clapping and cheering with genuine joy, even when Josh's tricks hadn't quite gone as planned. As the memories flooded her, Autumn felt a warmth deep in her chest, a feeling of contentment and gratitude for the precious moments she'd shared with her family.

She thought of Jordan as well. She'd spent three years with him. He'd been such a huge part of her life. Considering what occupied her now, Autumn wondered what she wouldn't give to have the current road bump in their relationship be her greatest problem. Rising panic allowed her to generously downplay the truth of the matter of their relationship, and what his indifferent abandonment actually signified.

As quickly as peace and joy came to her, so then did it leave. She was swiftly overwhelmed with a sudden dread, imagining that she might never see them again—any of her family. The tune she'd hummed flew out of her head, and she began to breathe erratically, which drowned out all other noise. She was flushed with more heat, certain her brow dripped with sweat and that her cheeks must be a feverish red, and then her belly recoiled.

Autumn laid one hand over her stomach and one over her mouth, backing away from the dead body on the table, away from Lorain, next to whom she'd stood. The last thing she wanted to do was hurl her breakfast all over the poor boy being wrapped for burial just now. She whirled around, ignoring Charlotte's gasp. But she moved too quickly and was seized by a violent dizziness, wobbling precariously just as she realized movement at the gate, which she now faced. But she saw only blurry images, maybe riders entering the yard, while the sound of hoofbeats reverberated harshly in her head. Before coming to this century, she'd never fainted once in all her life but believed just then that she was about to. Her legs gave out and her eyes shuttered, the lids falling slowly, closing out the fuzzy yard. Charlotte called her name, but her voice was much deeper, bizarrely masculine, ringing in Autumn's ears as she fell to the ground, rousing a cloud of dust.

***

Marcus leapt from the saddle almost as soon as he cleared the gate, his gaze taking in the somber scene only a split second before he saw Autumn turn away from the boards and begin to teeter. He called her name, alerting many to her impending faint. The hurried stamp of his boots on the cobblestones mingled with the growing cacophony of concerned murmurs from others in the bailey, including Charlotte's cry of, "Oh, shit."

He didn't reach her in time, though, and yet she didn't so much crash to the ground as float downward, gently, as if she were made of liquid and poured slowly from a pitcher. He did reach her before Charlotte did, as she had to run all the way around the boards.

Anxiety etched furrows into his rugged features as he knelt beside Autumn's crumpled form. Marcus brushed a lock of unruly hair from her ghostly pale face. With his calloused fingers, he touched her cheek, and said her name again, this time much softer.

"Autumn." For reasons which would be questioned harshly later, Marcus stroked his finger down the velvet smoothness of her cheek. "Autumn? Can ye hear me?" Though his voice was mild, his gaze was severe, searching her bonny face for any sign of consciousness. It became clear in the next second that she wore no cosmetics today; though her eyes were rimmed in dark circles, they were no longer caked with powdery effects. The faintest spatter of freckles was visible across the bridge of her nose and her high cheekbones emphasized the triangular shape of her face.

Charlotte fell to her knees at Autumn's side, opposite Marcus.

"She fainted," she said uselessly. "She just turned around and...and fell." Worry was evidenced in the crease in her brow, furrowed so deeply as to present a vertical line above her nose, and her lips twisted into an anxious line. "Autumn? Christ, look how white she is—oh, her eyelids are moving."

Indeed, the delicate veils of Autumn's eyes fluttered. She groaned softly, sluggishly regaining her senses, blinking several times as she came to. Within a moment, she'd fixed her gaze on Charlotte first and then Marcus, her gray eyes lingering on him as a faint blush colored her cheeks.

Her chin quivered and in the next moment, she shifted her gaze again to Charlotte. "I want to go home," she whimpered. "I don't want to be here."

Marcus scowled crossly, despising immediately what her fragility stirred in him, a surge of protectiveness that made him want to shield her from the world's harshness and see that her desire was met.

"Of course not. All right," Charlotte cooed, almost nonsensically, as someone does when they don't know how to comfort or console a person. She was, however, wise enough to turn it around, effectively changing the subject, distracting Autumn from her grief. "I shouldn't have asked you to do this. What was I thinking? I'm so sorry, Autumn. Here, sit up. Marcus, help me. Lorain, go get a glass of water please."

While Charlotte tugged at Autumn's hands, Marcus slid an arm under her back, encountering plenty of her hair, and propelling her upward just as Charlotte tugged. A shadow fell over the three of them. Marcus recognized Reid's booted feet standing next to Charlotte.

"Easy, lass," Marcus murmured, hardly able to recognize the tender quality of his voice. Provoked by this, he cleared his throat and removed his arm from around her as soon as she was sitting upright.

"I'm so sorry, Autumn," Charlotte repeated, exchanging a worried glance with Marcus. "That was unconscionable of me, to put you to work out here in this heat and at this task. I don't know what I was thinking. Well, I do. I was thinking to keep you busy, you know, so that you might avoid thinking of...that other issue. You should go inside and—"

"I'm fine," interrupted Autumn, her voice contradicting her words, sounding as weak and unsteady as she looked.

She took a deep breath, her chest rising and falling with the slow effort.

Though it hadn't escaped his awareness that she was garbed more appropriately today, more so than she had been yesterday and the day before, he only noticed just now that her feet were still bare. He realized he'd taken note of her feet and toes once before, but then in the midst and the aftermath of the MacPhail ambush, hadn't time to examine the curiosity they presented, being that her toenails were oddly covered in a shimmery red paint, much like her fingernails.

"I don't want to go inside," Autumn said, drawing Marcus's gaze back to her. "It's too stifling in there."

She put her hands on the cobbles, meaning to stand.

Marcus moved up onto one knee and positioned one hand under her arm from the front while he put his other hand on her back, assisting her to her feet as he stood as well.

"Yes, I guess it is a little oppressive in there," Charlotte said, standing fairly close yet, her hands held up in front of her as if she expected Autumn might wobble or fall again. "Maybe a walk, away from...from this," Charlotte suggested. "That's probably what you need. Marcus, take her outside the gate," Charlotte irked him by suggesting. "A long dose of fresh air will suit her perfectly right now."

Marcus ground his teeth together. There were a million things that needed his attention, not least of which was completing the chore from which Autumn now needed relief. He was the laird with many things waiting on moments of his time, and not a nursemaid,. A large-scale burial and the necessary accompanying feast needed to be managed and his most serious want of action against the MacPhails could not long be relegated to the back of his mind.

A quick glance at Reid showed that eejit hardly expending any effort to hide a smirk over what his bossy wee wife was promoting.

"I don't need...I'm all right," Autumn protested weakly. "I'm embarrassed, but not ill."

While she stared at her evidently borrowed and ill-fitting skirts, brushing her hands downward from her lean waist, Marcus stared at her. Her blonde hair was tied in a knot at her nape, but strands had come loose and hung delicately around her pale face. Her gray eyes barely met his, but he saw that they were neither bright nor brimming with resolve. She was awash in sentiment—sorrow, dread, and fear—and Marcus realized that he was not unaffected by her emotions.

"A nice long walk is precisely what you need," Charlotte maintained. "Go. Marcus, offer her your arm."

He was not the only one now glaring at Charlotte, but sensed the same response from Autumn next to him, felt the stiffening of her body beneath his hands. And yet, Charlotte was correct, he supposed, that having her senses cleansed of the foulness of her chore and what it represented, might be a balm to Autumn's weary soul just now, but he could not in good conscience allow her to wander outside the walls without proper escort.

"Aye, c'mon, lass," he urged mildly, unwilling to see Autumn suffer further. "Like as nae, Charlotte will nae cease until ye abide by her wishes."

"She won't," Charlotte reinforced with mock sternness.

Autumn didn't quite look at him, but shifted her face a bit in his direction and gave a shaky nod.

Marcus repositioned his hand, wrapping his fingers lightly around her upper arm, and led her toward the rear of the bailey, meaning to take her outside the postern gate where there was ample solitude to be found.

"Honestly, I'm fine," she insisted after only a few steps.

Her posture was rigid, but he could not say if that was an attempt by her to control any weakness or if his touch made her so. He removed his hand altogether and they walked side by side around the keep, past the declining kitchen garden, where blooms and leaves a month ago had been ripe in summer's glory but now were waning and wilting with the coming of autumn.

He tipped his head at Wilfrid, high on the wall overhead, who lifted one arm in acknowledgement, the limb entirely wrapped in gauzy linen, having withstood the puncture of a stitching needle more than a hundred times by his telling, to bind the gaping sword slice he'd sustained.

Marcus unlocked and pushed open the postern gate and stepped through first, waiting for Autumn to follow before he closed the door behind them. There was only a narrow lane on this side of the curtain wall, wide enough for two persons walking abreast or a small, wheeled cart. It meandered crookedly through the rocky landscape and tall grass, rising and dipping for a hundred yards before it declined somewhat sharply and then leveled out as it entered the village.

Autumn paused and her mouth opened as she gazed over the village, turning Marcus's gaze upon the cluster of thatched cottages with plumes of woodsmoke rising from each of them. Nestled among the hills and bordered on one side by the loch, Balla

Àrd's village lay snugly in the shadow of the keep. A small stream, fed by the loch, cut the village nearly in half and could be forded at three different locations throughout the village by way of the wooden bridges that spanned it. The old stone church with its tall bell tower sat to the far left, once the greater social and spiritual center than Balla Àrd's hall but deprived of a priest now for more than a decade when the last one had died only three days after interring Marcus's mother into the ground. Beyond the village, cultivated fields, divided by low stone fences and often hedgerows, were dotted with cottars about their work. The grazing fields and pastures to the north were populated now with cattle and bleating sheep and beyond, the hills climbed into the sky.

Autumn drew in a deep breath. A sidelong glance showed that her color had already improved, the ghostly pallor replaced by a healthy rosy flush.

"This way," Marcus said, moving down along the twisting pathway, deciding to take the one that veered off toward the east so that they might walk undisturbed along the shore of the loch. He hoped she was robust enough to partake of a swift walk. He intended to spend a quarter hour with her and no more, and then deliver Autumn Winters, safe and refreshed, to Charlotte so that he might get on with his day and the countless tasks that required his full and eager devotion.

Chapter Eleven

Autumn followed Marcus along the winding path. The scene below was beautiful, charming and rustic, but disconcerting at the same time, being yet another indication that she was not in the twenty-first century. Not that it wasn't possible that any remote area of the Highlands such as this could be home to an ancient, inhabited, and working village, but this, coupled with what she'd seen and heard over the last two days rather supported its authenticity.

She was mortified by the fact that she'd fainted and had wanted to call out Charlotte for forcing her upon Marcus. A few darting glances at him had shown that he'd looked as if he'd rather have relived that battle yesterday than stroll around with Autumn. But then she did feel immediately returned to herself, almost the second they'd walked through that small man-sized gate at the back of the castle's wall.

Marcus did not follow the trail straight to the charming village but deviated toward an even narrower path, which suited their single file march and brought them to the fringes of the lake. He paused there, waiting for Autumn to move forward until they could walk side-by-side alongside the deep blue water. He kept one hand sitting on the top of his sword as they strolled, already a familiar habit of his. Autumn wondered how heavy the weapon was, finding it curious that it made not any sound at all as he strode along.

A bit nervous, she rubbed her hands on her skirts, recalling then how filthy they were.

"Pardon me," she said, skirting to the right. "I just want to wash my hands." She walked to where the land met the lake and crouched, dipping her hands into the cool water, scouring them roughly against each other. She stood and shook out her hands, drying them on a lower section of the surcote as she turned around to rejoin Marcus.

Autumn jumped, surprised to find that he followed her the few yards from the path. "Oh, Jeez. Um, I'm sorry for my faintheartedness back there. I know Charlotte kind of forced this on you, but you don't have to stay with me. I'm sure you've got plenty to do with...with everything. I just needed a few minutes away from..." she glanced back up at the backside of the castle, sighing when recalled to what transpired in there now and had for the last few hours. "I just needed a few minutes," she said with more clarity and more self-assurance.

Marcus did not pounce on her gracious release from duty. In fact, he didn't particularly look to be in any hurry to part company with her. Instead, his gaze fixed on her with an intensity that hinted at a deep curiosity.

Autumn imagined it would take her quite some time, certainly more than two days, to become accustomed to his manner, the way he often brooded so thoughtfully when he looked at her. Right now, though she dropped the gathering of the skirt she'd used to dry her hands, she kept them buried in the folds, worrying the fabric while he studied her so diligently, his striking, brown-eyed gaze moving slowly over all the parts of her face.

"Apologies to ye, lass," he finally said, "for being made to take on that most difficult task of swaddling the dead."

"Please don't apologize," Autumn was quick to say. Nervously she folded her arms over her chest, which reminded her of the ache in her shoulder, but felt compulsory, as if she might protect herself from the invasion of his searching gaze. In the next moment, she dropped her hands again. She had nothing to hide and hence, nothing to fear. "Charlotte was correct in her thinking. I mean, what else would I have done today?"

He made a sound that might have been one of agreement and stepped forward, passing Autumn, going closer to the lake. When she did not immediately join him, he turned only his head and remarked, "From where comes your name? Autumn Winters can nae be real, unless in your time there is more significance put to the seasons."

She smiled softly, believing she had at one point wondered when he would get around to asking just this. She'd learned that people might well be curious about her name but might only wish to avoid being labeled rude and often, it wasn't until she knew people for some time or better that they inquired about the origins of Autumn Winters. Eventually, though, they did get around to asking.

Autumn took a few steps forward, closer to him and the water. "No, I don't suppose you guys take such liberties with first names, using seasons and colors, and flowers and gemstones, and whatever else you want."

"But...Autumn Winters?" He questioned with a wee bit of hesitation, slanting her a sideways glance.

She laughed outright at this. "Honestly, my parents aren't flakes," she promised him. "Just the opposite in fact. My mother assures me she truly did love the sound of it, and really did believe the novelty of it would only ever be admired and not mocked."

"Mocked?"

"Um...derided, made fun of, I guess is the best way to interpret that."

"Were ye? Derided?"

"Oh, sure. More so when I was a kid, of course. Kids can be so blatantly mean, right?"

"And Charlotte? That is an acceptable name in the future?"

Autumn tilted her head and frowned with a bit of wonder. "Surely you've heard of the name Charlotte? There was a Queen Charlotte, of course, but I'm sure the name didn't originate in the eighteenth century with her." At his blank look and slight shake of his head. "Or maybe it did. It sounds very British, very old. I guess I just assumed it might have been around for...well, in this time."

"If ye are from the future—" he said next, putting a hearty emphasis on *if*, "—why do ye smile when I begin with those words?"

"Because I think it's curious that if I were to start a sentence in the same vein, I would begin with, *If this* really *is the fourteenth century*."

His next frown carved deep furrows in the rugged landscape of his face. "Do ye nae even believe it yourself?"

Autumn lifted her shoulders, shrugging very slowly so that they stayed raised for a few seconds. "It's just...the very idea goes against everything I know. Where I come from—which by the way, is so much better than saying, *in the future*, which simply sounds too preposterous—we know so much, about earth, about space and the planets, all the oceans, about the body down to the molecular level, and I can't believe we can know in modern times everything we do but not know about this, about time-travel. Like, there's no evidence of it. At all. Period. Ever. And trust me, if there had been, if there was, the world would know about it. It's really hard to keep secrets or hide things in my time."

He pondered this, seemed to really chew on her words and his thoughts about them.

The detail of his brow was unchanged; his frown remained. "*All* the oceans?"

Autumn hesitated, transfixed by his gaze. He'd shifted just a bit, facing her, his eyes now awash in sunshine. The vivid brown of his eyes sat in sharp contrast to the thick fringe of jet-black lashes and his ebony brows, which he used regularly to startling effect. It hadn't escaped her notice before, but it was put into actual words in her brain just now: his gaze was utterly mesmerizing. In the sunlight, his eyes glinted like gorgeous amber gems, effortlessly drawing her in with an irresistible allure. She wasn't sure it was intentional—why would he do that?—but there was a captivating sensuality in his gaze, a natural confidence that was first, very sexy, and next, spoke volumes even as there was silence between them just now. She wasn't sure what to take away from the long look—if anything; he *was* a most broody man—but still, her heart raced and her senses tingled with emotion, as if there were actual chemistry between them.

Unnerved by the magnetic intensity of his stare, Autumn blinked and looked away. Completely flustered, she cleared her throat, trying to pick up the thread of their conversation.

A small and wobbly smile creased her lips when she was able to face him again. "Yes, there are four oceans nowadays." She then rolled her eyes at how she'd misspoken. "I mean, there were always four—well, maybe not in the Jurassic era or before that. But, yes, there are four oceans. But I don't think you guys know about all of them now, do you?"

"Twice now, ye've said *ye guys*," he remarked, lifting his hand off the hilt of his sword to scratch at the opposite cheek.

"Have I?" She asked, fleetingly distracted by his bare arm, and the way his muscles flexed so enticingly with only that slight movement. Christ, but he was really handsome, so effortlessly virile that he made rubbing his jaw look breathtakingly sensual. Impertinently, Autumn thought he was probably fabulous in bed. Unless, as a general practice and because sex was possibly used only for procreation in this time, men in the middle ages employed more of a wham, bam, thank you ma'am technique. No, she decided charitably. Marcus would never do that, she somehow believed. When she realized where her wayward thoughts had gone *this* time, her cheeks flooded with color, heat rising everywhere. "It's a c-collective term," she stammered, "in this instance meaning you and everyone else in this time."

Her deep blush did not go unnoticed.

"Ye are nae well," he said. "Will ye faint again?" He closed the distance between them, putting his hand on her arm once more. "Autumn?"

Sadly, or unfortunately for Autumn, his protective nature was also very sexy.

"I'm fine. I promise," she said. Before she realized what she was doing or how it might be received, she took one step to the right, away from him. At the same time, she put her hand on his and pushed it away.

She swallowed down her unease, wondering why and how she'd been transformed into a stuttering, besotted teenager. She was better than that. She was a strong and modern professional woman. She absolutely did not fawn over or geek out over a hot guy. *Get a grip, Autumn.*

"Ye are afraid of me?" His question came loaded with mountains of disapproval.

This jerked her gaze back to him. It was incredibly easy to refute that suspicion with the truth. "I am not. Not at all." Oh, but she kind of wished she was. She wished she could relegate him to the role of villain in the present drama of her life. She might still secretly find him hotter than hell, but she wouldn't allow herself to be rendered witless by her fascination with a bad guy. Or maybe she would. She was known to have the occasional fixation with a hot baddie of cinema with amazing allure.

He slanted her an incisive look that said he didn't believe her but made no more of it. Instead he returned to what he had attempted to ask earlier. "But if ye *are* from the future, what do ye ken about the past?"

"Do you mean, like, about this century?" Autumn countered, pleased with the innocuous purpose. "And in this country? In Scotland?"

"Aye."

"I studied journalism and media studies, with a minor in English lit. I was never keen on history. I know of the war in which you are currently embroiled, and I know that Robert Bruce will become king but I'm not sure on the timing and aside from that—oh, shit," she said, her eyes widening, her brows lifting in horror with the same degree as Marcus's brows dropped in apparent shock. Autumn clapped her hand over her mouth and said through her fingers, "I don't think I was supposed to tell you that."

"Robert Bruce?" He repeated, a savage disbelief deepening his tone.

"Yes," Autumn squeaked, lowering her hand. "Eventually."

"Does he ken this?" Marcus wanted to know, the question spat with great skepticism.

Autumn opened her mouth but was clueless as to how to answer him. And then she burst out laughing, lost in the absurdity of his question. Helplessly, she lifted her hands, her laughter growing.

She knew exactly when Marcus understood how ridiculous his question was, by the way his expression softened, as the torrential downpour of his shock and awe faded to a drizzle of realization. Briefly, he compressed his mouth, as if burning now with anger for his foolishness before his features eased even more and a bemused smile tugged the corners of his gorgeous mouth.

He said sheepishly, "Like as nae, ye did nae meet him with him or speak to him about this."

"I did not," Autumn answered, her laughter fading, captivated now by how much more handsome Marcus was when he wasn't glowering. The smile infected his gaze, warming the depths of his brown eyes, and his posture became more relaxed. She caught a glimpse of perfectly aligned white teeth and found herself smiling now at his smile and the effect it had on him. "Maybe you should speak to him about it," she suggested, made a bit breathless by the magnetism of his smile.

"The Bruce is in England just now," said Marcus, putting his hand to the back of his neck while he gave his attention to the ground, boyishly and charmingly awkward, "by my understanding."

"Oh, that's right," Autumn said, revived, feeling like she was returned to equal footing with him. "He did kind of switch sides a bit, didn't he? Or...doesn't he?"

Marcus lifted his probing brown eyes to her. "Does he still? Again?"

Autumn nodded solemnly, knowing the answer was very important to him.

"Soon?" He asked, raising one brow in hopeful anticipation.

"I think so."

Marcus nodded.

Autumn appreciated very much that he did not dismiss her remorse at revealing even this much to him, and that he didn't pressure her for more details. Little good it would have done him anyway; aside from a very famous movie about this time period in this country, she knew or recalled very little of Scottish history.

Marcus gave her another of those probing, thoughtful looks, as if he were looking for something in her gaze to back up her claim. He straightened and half-turned, looking up at the castle before meeting Autumn's gaze again.

"Ye are nae unwell, though? But recovered from your faint?"

"I am. Thank you. This was very helpful." She swung her arms a bit, her fingers curled. "I should let you get back though. You probably have a million things you need to do."

"Aye." But he didn't move.

Autumn blinked. "Um, Charlotte said there is a big feast after the funerals." This emerged more as a question than a statement. What, exactly, was there to celebrate?

"Aye. 'Tis necessary, for those lost and those that remain," he explained. "We commemorate their lives and their sacrifice and dinna ponder only their deaths."

"How do you guys...I mean, how do you, all of you—as a community, a society—recover from so great a loss?"

"We dinna recover," he said with gravity. "We only carry on."

"Will revenge be part of carrying on?" She didn't take him for someone to let a crime go unpunished. And she wouldn't fault him for whatever hell he was likely profoundly capable of and would no doubt bring to the MacPhails.

"Vengeance is required," he said matter-of-factly.

"And there is none but you to bring it?" She was sure they didn't have police as an organization and protective force in this time, but didn't they have courts or some similar system where a person or clan could seek justice?

"None but me," he confirmed. "Aye, but the Nicholson is here and will nae want to be dismissed, though the cause is nae his." He sighed then and continued, "And yet I hesitate to include him. I dinna want Reid to lose men to my fight."

Ah, a conscientious warrior hero, she mused.

Marcus chewed the inside of his cheek a bit, subjecting Autumn to another one of his slow and thoughtful perusals.

"And what of ye?"

"Me? I have no idea. And frankly," she said, "I find that my predicament, while huge in my mind, pales in comparison to what's going on here at Balla Àrd. But I'm open to suggestions if you have any." She smiled cheekily at him. "What do you know about time travel?"

He grinned gorgeously in response. "Only a wee bit, and learned but recently as to be of little use to ye."

She hadn't truly expected any other answer. "Yeah, I don't know even where to begin. But....but maybe if the Nicholsons do leave—Charlotte said their house was a few hours away—maybe I should or could go with them. If they would have me, that is.

She's not in the same boat as me but at least we set sail from the same port, if you know what I mean."

At this, he narrowed his eyes once more, looking for the space of a second as if he might oppose this idea. But then he lost all his recent ease, which stood him taller, and threw a wistful look up at the castle, saying, "Doubtless a guid plan."

***

They went their separate ways once returned to the castle's yard. With a curt nod of his head, Marcus slipped inside the back of the house while Autumn made her way to the front, where Lorain was nowhere to be found and Charlotte was gathering what remained of the huge stack of linens, the unused ones. Autumn saw that all the bodies had been shrouded and the movable funeral bier was turned around, facing the gate. She guessed that horses would be attached to it when it was time to lead the funeral procession.

"Oh, there you are," said Charlotte when she saw Autumn. "Do you feel better? Your color certainly looks better."

"I'm good, thank you," said Autumn and took some of the cloths from Charlotte.

"We have just enough time to get cleaned up," Charlotte noted, turning and tracing steps Autumn had just taken, going around to the back of the house, "before they begin the procession out to the old church yard. Lorain went in to arrange fresh water in our chambers."

All bright light was left outside as they entered the castle. A confining corridor led them past several doors or wide archways, one of which opened into what was the kitchen where Charlotte and Autumn had quietly had their breakfast earlier. The scent of woodsmoke, grease, and cooking meat assaulted them as they passed. With her hip, Charlotte shoved open the next door, which appeared to be a large linen closet, with trunks lining the bottom half of the wall while shelves filled with a multitude of fabrics, in every hue of white and ivory, were hung haphazardly about the top half. They left the unused cloths there and Charlotte was on the move again, twisting and turning through the sparsely lit hallway until they reached a spiral staircase made of stone.

While Autumn wondered what she might wear to a funeral—her outfit wasn't noticeably dirty, but she was sure it must be infused with the woeful odor of death—Charlotte offered some relief from this worry as they climbed the stairs.

"They don't dress fancy for funerals the way we do," she said. "So we'll just wash up and go as we are. I asked Lorain if she might have or know of shoes you could borrow, but she didn't leave me with much hope that she could find any. But please don't fret about it. I'm sure you won't be the only barefooted person there."

They parted on the second floor, with Charlotte promising, "I'll come and get you when we're ready to go, probably in about half an hour."

Inside the chamber she'd been lent, Autumn leaned her back against the door and sighed, wondering if she would enjoy a day in this century if she could experience one that wasn't shocking, deadly, or morose. Maybe just one day without a constant and exhausting adrenaline charge.

Almost immediately, she felt awful for being so selfish. Seventeen men lay dead, cloaked in linen, their faces never to be seen again, laying one atop another in the extra wide cart that had been built only this morning to convey them all at once to their graves. True, her own circumstance was as astonishing as it was harrowing, but she lived yet, was breathing still, while they were not.

Shaking herself free from the self-serving dismay, Autumn pushed herself away from the door and began to ready herself for the funeral, making herself as presentable as possible.

As promised, Charlotte knocked on her door at what Autumn judged to be just about the thirty minute mark. Autumn was surprised that her husband was not with her and questioned this.

"Today I am merely a wife," Charlotte explained, with nary a hint of hostility. "The soldiers, led by their chiefs, will do this together—will *need* to do this as one unit. You and I and those who don't lift swords will only be mournful onlookers."

And so it was.

As Charlotte had said, people of this time did not dress for the occasion. Thus, the courtyard, when they arrived, teemed with soldiers and peasants garbed in what looked like their everyday clothes—and Charlotte was also correct, that Autumn was not the only person not wearing shoes. It wasn't an impeccably silent crowd that gathered and waited, but the mood was grim, the air heavy with a somber quality, and all conversations were low and muted. Even children and smaller babies seemed to understand the grimness of what was to come and not a cry or whine could be heard.

After only a short moment waiting in the midst of the quiet throng, Autumn realized that all those within the gates— soldiers, peasants, and household servants—were McInnes people and none of them were mounted, and that just outside the gates, the dozens and dozens of Nicholson soldiers waited, mounted and still, little noise heard but the occasional whinny of a horse or jangle of a harness.

And just as she wondered what they might be waiting for, the door to the keep opened and Marcus walked out into the yard. Before he disappeared into the throng, Autumn saw that he was dressed differently. Under his leather jerkin he wore a long sleeve loose fitting shirt of linen, and over the jerkin his wool plaid was pleated and draped over one shoulder, crossing his chest and secured inside his leather belt. His face was clean shaven and his hair slightly damp, suggesting he'd showered since she'd left him less than an hour ago.

As he crossed the bailey, the McInnes folk parted as if he were Moses. His stride was unhurried even as his gait was purposeful. He did not bow his head with any solemnity but held his chin high, accepting the acknowledgement of many persons as he passed. Standing several rows of people back from him, Autumn's lips parted as she watched. He managed to look at the same time both properly dignified as necessary for the task ahead but then so resolute, a steely determination darkening his brown eyes. Though she barely knew him, she guessed the resolve etched upon his rugged features was both intentional and then not. Likely he meant to walk tall and proud, as he did, to demonstrate to his people that though the tragedy was great, their resolve should be greater. Unintentional though, or rather instinctive, because Autumn had a certain suspicion that Marcus McInnes by his very nature bowed to no man and could not be broken by misfortune; he did not and would not yield, he would find solace in his revenge, the very idea of which likely painted his demeanor with steadfastness just now.

As he walked alongside the bier with bodies piled so high as to be taller than his impressive height, his jaw tightened. He positioned himself in front of the four massive horses that had been hitched to the sorrowful wagon and started walking toward the gate and then through and over the drawbridge.

There was no driver for the overlarge cart, but two men stood on each side, handling the bridles of the horses. Slowly, prodded by these men, the team of four followed the laird outside of Balla Àrd. The mourners followed in their wake, several soft keening cries heard now as family, loved ones, and friends walked them home.

Charlotte threaded her arm through Autumn's, and they found themselves somewhere in the middle of the sad parade. Men she recognized—Osgar, a gingerly walking Gibbon, the kid Lewin, and the guy with only one hand—walked in front of them. Autumn peeked inquisitively at the Nicholsons on horseback who stood as sentinels on either side of the gravel lane, some bowing their heads as the dead were walked by, paying homage to their brethren. At the end of their line, furthest from the wall of the castle, sat Reid Nicholson, who moved his horse when Marcus came abreast, walking his horse into the line of mourners, one full length behind Marcus.

The funeral procession did not stay long on the main road, such as it was, but followed a path equally well-traveled to the right, which rose over a gentle knoll and then dipped and went straight through a thicket of trees, emerging to the west of the village, where they turned right once more and approached the stone chapel Autumn had spied earlier.

The march took more than fifteen minutes, due in part to the respectful pace set and then for the number of people included in the rite. Marcus waited, facing the crowd now, his feet shoulder-width apart, one hand on his sword, his gaze lowered.

When they were gathered fully around the bier, Marcus lifted his gaze from the ground and addressed them. As he spoke, he looked not at those saddened and weeping, but at the shrouded bodies of the men under his command. He used a strong voice though it was dulled by pain and did not read from a prayer book but seemed to devise the eulogy as he went.

Chapter Twelve

The kid named Lewin, who wound up standing directly beside Autumn when they assembled closely in the small churchyard, gave her a shy and grim smile as a greeting, and then must have read her distress in the parting of her lips, when Marcus began to speak in that unfamiliar language, and she couldn't understand a word of it.

Lewin leaned close and graciously whispered a translation near her ear.

"Kin and kindred, he says," Lewin interpreted quietly, "we join here today under the darkness of grief, our hearts heavy with the burden of loss. We stand united to honor the memories of those we have lost. In this time of sorrow, when the winds of adversity blow cold and harsh, we will find solace in one another and draw strength from the bonds that tie us together."

Lewin caught up while Marcus paused.

Autumn listened intently to Lewin's generous translation but kept her gaze on Marcus. A muscle ticked in his cheek as he pursed his lips with a wave of grief that he managed to power through.

"So they fought together and died together, so, too, they will be interred together," Lewin repeated in English when Marcus continued. "Our loved ones, who now rest with our ancestors, were brave and valiant souls, warriors who faced danger with unwavering courage. They fought not only for each of us but for the very ideals and values that define us. As they join our forebears in the great hall of eternity, we remember their sacrifices and the legacy they leave behind."

Marcus drew in a deep breath and exhaled, moving his brown eyes away from the fallen soldiers and over the heads of the mourners as he carried on.

"Let us take a moment to reflect on the lives that have touched ours, the laughter, the tears, the shared triumphs, and the moments of quiet understanding. Each departed soul has left an indelible mark on our hearts and on the tapestry of our McInnes history."

Another pause followed this.

Autumn's heart broke for Marcus. His jaw flexed harshly with an effort to maintain his stoic demeanor. The laird must always be in control, she imagined.

Her nose and throat burned, and her eyes watered with heartache.

"As we mourn," Lewin resumed when Marcus did, "let us also remember that grief, though heavy, can bind us closer together. In our unity, we find strength. In our shared memories, we find comfort. And in the face of adversity, we find resolve. We shall honor our fallen with the promise that their sacrifices will not be in vain. We shall persevere, rebuilding what has been lost, and we shall continue to uphold the traditions and values that define the McInnes. Brighter hence the honor—'tis the McInnes motto," Lewin explained this last part.

"*Clarior hinc honos*," repeated the mourners.

"Let us offer our prayers," Marcus, and thus Lewin, went on, "not only for the departed but for each other, that we may find the courage to face the challenges that lie ahead. Let us stand together, as our ancestors did before us, and let the memory of our loved ones inspire us to carry on their legacy with honor and dignity. Our fallen shall forever be in our hearts, guiding us as we march forward. May they find eternal rest, and may we find the strength to honor their memory in everything we do."

Marcus nodded, indicating he had finished, and moved a few paces to his left.

It was just then that Autumn realized that there was a hole dug in the earth. Her eyes widened and her heart constricted at the size of it.

Lewin bowed his head briefly at Autumn and darted away through the crowd, going to assist with the moving of bodies.

Tears rolled down Autumn's cheeks now as each shrouded man was removed from the cart and laid into the hollow earth, set into the waiting hands of the men standing in the vast depression.

Charlotte clutched tightly at Autumn's arm. Without looking, Autumn covered and squeezed Charlotte's hand.

"It's so awful," whispered Charlotte brokenly. "So heart wrenching."

Autumn's misty gaze found Marcus again. Reid had dismounted and stood at his side, his pose similar to Marcus's, feet braced apart, hands now behind their backs, rigidly unmoving as they followed with severe gazes the journey of each body.

Despite the wretched sadness of it all, Autumn thought it all spectacularly done. The inquisitive reporter in Autumn was attentive to all the sad faces surrounding her and greatly moved by the humble spectacle.

Marcus had been amazing. She was a public speaker—literally, that was her livelihood—and she was sure she would have faltered over so grim a ceremony, and without a teleprompter or script to guide her.

She'd interviewed her fair share of the military, and police officers, fire fighters, and other first responders. She'd seen it time and time again; they had no choice but to master the ability to compartmentalize their emotions, to rise above the want to lie down and cry, to give up, to be wrecked permanently by tragedy, focusing instead on dutifulness and deliberation. Usually they did so with an even greater dedication to their profession, to Autumn's knowledge. And so she supposed Marcus would, as he'd said, seek his vengeance, and maybe that was what was needed to survive this. He would dedicate himself to vengeance.

Autumn wondered how much of himself he would lose in the process.

***

Marcus sat cheerlessly at the head table, looking out onto the diminished McInnes population of Balla Àrd. The meal, though plentiful and well-presented, had been consumed in near silence. Likely the hall would remain gloomy until the whiskey started to deliver its effects.

One might never guess that all of yesterday and as recently as this morning, the keep's hall had been crowded yet with the dead and dying. Small was the household staff at Balla Àrd but great was their industry on this day. The living wounded had been removed to the third floor dormitory, once a chamber that housed numerous servants, which now only kept cast-off furniture and moth-eaten linens. The dead were now gone. The table boards and stone floor had been scrubbed with lye, its biting odor lingering but preferable to the scent it had overcome.

He could or would do no more on this day and so planned to get good and blootered. He'd specifically ordered that the reserved whiskey be served, knowing that ordinary ale or watery wine would do little for the misery universally felt.

Aside from that, and the offer and hope of salvation by way of vengeance, Marcus wasn't sure what more he could do for them. He pushed away the platter before him, the idea of food, of eating, being more unpalatable than the food itself.

At his side, Reid reminded him in a low voice, "So long as ye sit sullen and morose, so too will they."

"Ye suggest I shrug off death and lead the dancing?" Marcus clipped. "Mayhap ye would suppose I was capable of plucking a tune on the lute."

"Nae more than I," Reid said, impervious to Marcus's sullenness. "I dinna tell ye anything ye dinna ken already. Grieve. Rage. Plot. Do all that, but on the morrow. Ye said yourself, tonight was to celebrate their sacrifice, but this, now, seems only an ugly extension of the graveside rite."

Marcus nodded, knowing his friend was right. With a grumbled curse, he stood and left the table, stepping off the platform. He walked over to where the widow Margaret sat, the closest in proximity to the head table of any grieving kin of the ones they buried today. She had always been frail in appearance but endowed with infinite fortitude, Marcus thought, having given up to God already a husband and three weans. Only one more remained now that they buried her lad, Fergus, today.

"Margaret," he said in their native tongue as he knelt on one knee at her side, "Fergus fought with honor, riding into the fight with righteousness singing in his breast. He will be remembered as a McInnes hero. We share in your grief."

"And will ye avenge my Fergus, Laird?" Asked the woman.

"'Tis my vow to ye and all others," he swore. "I will nae rest until vengeance is ours."

Margaret nodded her head with the aplomb of a queen, acknowledging his pledge.

He moved onto the young Isobel Fraser, who held her infant daughter in her arms and stared at Marcus with hard eyes. Tears stained her cheeks as she watched the laird approach.

"Isobel, William's sacrifice will not be in vain," he said of her husband's death. "And we, all of us, will ensure that you and your child are always and ever cared for."

The young widow nodded tightly, unable to speak. Her dark eyes shone with pain.

Next, Marcus found old Anghus, once a warrior himself, long ago deprived of his left eye and yesterday, his only son. "Anghus, your son fought valiantly at my side, a testament to the strength inherited from you. His spirit will live on in the hearts of all who knew him."

He lingered long at Anghus's side, who was eager to talk at length about his lad, Niall. Marcus listened patiently to stories he'd heard already, ones he'd likely hear again and again.

A chuckle from the head table hastened Marcus's gaze there. Gibbon, who'd sat at Marcus's left during the meal, was now reclined in his chair and talking across Marcus's empty chair to Reid. 'Twas no disrespect in his laughter, but indeed Marcus wondered if there were some added volume to it, as if Gibbon, like Reid, thought the hall should not resemble a crypt any more or longer than it had.

Having turned toward the head table, though with his ear still bent to Anghus's speech, Marcus let his gaze settle on Autumn. Though he had been focused and attentive to his role earlier, presiding over the funerals, Autumn had not entirely eluded his awareness. She had revived herself once more, or more so after her faint and subsequent respite with him. She wore the same kirtle he'd found her in earlier but appeared to have brushed the linen scrupulously, the russet fabric appearing nearly spotless. She'd twisted her hair in a knot at her nape, the result being that she looked older than when her hair was loose. No less exquisite, he decided, only more womanly and less waifish, less vulnerable.

He was visited by the memory of her laughter of today. Her laughter had been as a melody dancing through the air, a delicate cascade of tinkling bells that had filled him with an uncommon warmth. She and her laugh had been infectious, incredibly sweet, had made him believe or recall for that small space of time that there was beauty to be found in the mad world.

He was, in truth and not only at this moment, revisited by many parts of their interlude together.

Robert Bruce? King?

'Twas not entirely implausible. The Bruce had been one of the thirteen contenders for the crown before that war had started. It had been that dilemma, naming the next king, which had kick-started the war with England.

But could it truly be real? And to happen soon? Might they one day know peace with the Bruce as king, and all the greedy and fighting English banished from their land? Marcus thought he might question Reid about this. Would Charlotte be in possession of the same knowledge? Would Charlotte and Autumn's supposed knowledge of this time, as seen from another, match well enough to convince him—anyone—that they had indeed traveled through time?

While Anghus continued giving voice to his memories, scarcely did Marcus attempt to prevent his thoughts from being overrun by Autumn or attempt to remove his studious gaze from her person. He wondered presently what she made of all this commotion: the ambush, the aftermath, the hall as hospital, the shrouding of bodies, the sorrowful funerals. And that, all of it, on top of her first trauma, allegedly traveling through time.

She sat now at the high table, three places removed from Marcus's seat, on Charlotte's right.

Eadric sat on the other side of Autumn. Eadric was serious-minded, normally distrustful of outsiders and their agendas, and not one to have his head turned only by beauty. And yet he and Autumn had been regularly engrossed in quiet conversation for most of the meal, as they were still. This was curious to Marcus; though Eadric's English was reasonable, his ability or desire to speak at length to any person was uncertain.

Eventually, Marcus was compelled to wrench his regard away from Autumn. He offered more words of condolence to Anghus and moved on to the next grieving person. The din inside the hall increased, people losing their glumness. The tanner, Colm and his daughter, Ailean, moved up to the minstrels' gallery, and soon the sound of the lute and the crwth drifted out and over the hall. They played neither a melancholy nor a festive tune, but for just now a wee background noise of a middling tempo. No one would be expected to simply rise and sing or rise and dance. First they would have to feel the music, would need to grow accustomed to its presence, and would likely need that first person to make a move toward advancing the grief to festivity.

***

"Wait. What?" Autumn asked Eadric. "You were the one who stitched me up?" She was astounded, and not only because they'd been having a nice conversation almost since dinner began and he'd yet to divulge this very significant piece of information, but also because he didn't look like he was skilled in such regard or frankly, disposed to performing life-saving measures for strangers.

Eadric was thin and toned, not any taller than Autumn, with sharp features. His cheeks and jaw were angular, his nose thin and pointy. The lines of his mouth were drawn hard, his lips thin. And, like Marcus and Reid Nicholson and so many of the soldiers of this time, he wore what seemed to be a natural and perpetual scowl. In other words, he looked mean as hell, like he would've been more liable to stomp on her injured shoulder sooner than sew it up. But then maybe the existence of his noticeable limp, which had caught Autumn's distracted attention at some point yesterday and then again today, had made him disposed to extending sympathy and succor where needed, he possibly understanding more than some or most how far even the smallest service might go. Also, he'd since proven as her dinner companion far nicer than his façade suggested, but still the news surprised her.

"Aye, I did," he answered.

Autumn laughed, which brought a question to Eadric's light blue eyes.

"I'm not laughing at you," she told him. "I'm laughing at myself over the embarrassing fact that it never occurred to me to wonder who had done it. I don't know...I don't know what I thought, or who I thought had sewn me up. Oh, wait. I do think I remember Marcus mentioning your name," she just recalled.

And I'll wager my last farthing ye tear open Eadric's bonny stitches ere the cock crows at sunrise, Marcus had said when she'd wanted to leave their camp that first night. "Well, thank you, Eadric."

Some reporter I am, Autumn thought, but then allowed herself forgiveness, given that there had been other pressing issues that required more of her overwhelmed attention.

She liked Eadric very much, and not only because he'd relieved her anxiety during dinner by engaging her in what had, at first, only been minimal and stilted conversation, but since had expanded to what she was sure was genuine friendliness. He was relatively pleasant, even as she could see very well that he was somewhat puzzled by her, and that several of his seemingly polite, get-to-know-you questions were really more intended to figure her out, and possibly to find out if she posed any danger to the McInnes. But overall he was very kind.

Still, she was slightly taken aback by what he next brought up.

"Ye are nae longer wearing all the paint as ye were then," he said. "'Tis guid."

Autumn frowned, puzzled. "Paint?"

Eadric lifted his hand and swirled it around in front of his face. "Covering yer face. Laid with so heavy a hand as to make ye nearly unknown when we saw ye again."

Autumn grinned, knowing her make-up had in no way been overdone at the time she'd been shot with an arrow, when she'd first encountered Eadric. Had she just come straight out of the make-up chair at the studio, now that, that likely would have seemed to this medieval man like heavy-handed artistry.

A wee hesitation preceded her response, wondering what might be acceptable to him and yet not raise any red flags, alerting him to the fact that she wasn't exactly what she pretended to be. Per Charlotte's whispered instruction during their arm-in-arm walk from the church yard to the hall, Autumn was only to suggest in a vague manner that her travel had been interrupted, that she'd been forcibly separated from her kin, with whom she hoped to soon be reunited.

"Just say you're from the lowlands," Charlotte had advised. "That's a completely different breed of people, mostly unknown to these Highlanders."

That was nearly verbatim what she'd said to Eadric when he'd very casually inquired about her.

Charlotte had further advised, as Marcus had suggested the other day, "Whatever you do, do not say a word about the truth of your story."

Presently, Autumn responded to Eadric's remarks about her make-up.

"It's not vanity so much as it is familiarity," she told him. "I'm just used to wearing it. Although, I do think I look better when I have make-up on." Otherwise, she thought her skin too pale, her freckles more distracting than cute, and her eyes too wide and large in her face.

"I dinna ken so."

"Oh, thank you, Eadric." That was very sweet, possibly the nicest thing anyone had said to her in the fourteenth century.

"Ye were a whore at one time, I gather," Eadric then shocked her by saying. "Or still are."

Autumn gaped at him. The shocks just kept on coming. The only saving grace presently was that she didn't detect any judgment attached to his assumption. She was torn between being grossly offended and hugely entertained. The latter won out and she let out a low peal of laughter. "No, Eadric," she said after a moment, "I am not a whore. Are they the only people who paint their faces?"

"Far as I ken." He shrugged, apparently unperturbed by any offense he might have given.

Since Eadric had asked about her personal grooming, Autumn believed it might be fair game to inquire about his limp, which seemed no more or less intrusive than his question. She half-expected—and half-feared—she might find the answer had something to do with another gruesome battle.

"Have you always lived at Balla Àrd, Eadric?" She conceived as an opening. "Were you born here?"

"Nae, lass," he said. "Born at Briarcliff, I was, which as ye ken sits regally upon the sea in Skye."

She did not *ken*, but she was learning.

"You are...am I right in assuming since you sit at the laird's table, you are highly regarded? Would you be, like, a lieutenant or something comparable?"

"Aye, the laird's lieutenant, one of them. Gibb is our cap'n, as ye ken. Osgar, Aelred, Wilfrid—that auld bastard, pardon, lass—we're the next in line in regard to position."

"But what brought you from Skye to Balla Àrd?" She presumed to have risen to lieutenant, he must have been here a while.

"Naught but a seething hatred," he answered so casually one might have thought he'd said, *Ah, a spell of good weather brought me to the mainland.*

"Oh. I see." Actually, no, she didn't. "Hatred for whom? Or what?"

His face twisted with annoyance, but Autumn thought not so much with her as with the object of his hatred, and maybe her, a little bit, for forcing him to recall it.

"My own dear brother."

"Really?"

"Firstborn I am and always will be," he said, with a new harshness in his tone. "But they dinna suffer gimps out on Skye, ye ken, and I was forsaken as heir in favor of a lad nae half my age, because he was whole."

"You *are* whole, though," Autumn stated, heat creeping into her voice, in defense of Eadric.

"A gimp is nae whole, lass," he said dismissively.

"That is obviously a matter of opinion," she said, "and it makes me question the wisdom of those who subscribe to that hideous one."

"Ye're a fierce one, aye?" Eadric decided right then, studying Autumn intently once more.

"If you say so," she allowed, and then demurred a bit, "and only when I'm not quivering with fear or fainting—twice now, I guess—with an all-around weakness."

"Bah," scoffed Eadric. "'Tis only... I dinna ken the English word, but ye speak of things scarcely able to control, of the body. But yer heart, yer mind—aye, ye're a fierce one."

Autumn decided she liked Eadric more and more, with every minute spent in his company.

"So how did you come by your limp, Eadric? Is it a trophy from the war?"

He grinned at this. "Would be admirable, would it nae? Nae, lass. 'Tis nae great tale. I was merely born this way."

No less admirable, Autumn decided, for what he'd withstood—banishment, it seemed—because of it. Before she could tell him this, his attention was called by the man sitting on his other side.

Pondering his easy explanation, the phrase *born this way* somehow skittered through her head. What a strange thing to come to her now. Autumn's mouth turned up in a bittersweet smile. If she'd been at home, with her parents or brothers, even her sisters-in-law or any of her nieces and nephews, she might have belted out at least one line of that Lady Gaga song as it struck her. The kids would have laughed, might have joined in. If so, it wouldn't have been the first time someone had broken into song and the rest of the family had joined in, and the house rang with shrill screaming, each trying to be louder than the next.

Idly, her mind engaged, she ran her finger down the side of the dull silver tankard in front of her, which held a generous, possibly hazardous amount of whiskey. The whiskey, she was pretty sure, was the equivalent of a potent, kick-your-ass moonshine, something similar to what her brothers sometimes home-brewed for different occasions.

Autumn let her mind wander and dwell in thoughts of her family.

Good God, but did they even know she was missing yet? How could they? She wondered. Her mother might be a bit surprised that she'd not had a text for days, but would she yet be concerned? Alarmed?

Not for the first time, Autumn worried that she might never see them again.

Jordan's image came to mind. Was he worried? Would he know? Would he care?

A heart wrenching and unbidden thought nearly broke her: *I thought I'd have more time with them.*

She picked up the tankard and sipped the potent whiskey, just now requiring something to wet her parched throat and maybe a bit more, something to dull the ache inside her at the very idea of never seeing her family again.

No, don't do that, she scolded herself. *I will get home. I will not be stuck here forever, will not spend the rest of my life without them.* Her family was everything to her.

She gulped down the sudden tightness in her throat and in her chest, though was unable to draw more than only shallow breaths, panic hovering.

And while Eadric's attention was yet drawn to the man at his side, another McInnes soldier, Autumn suddenly was tickled by a peculiar sensation that she was being watched. She lifted her gaze and scanned the room, going breathless when she saw Marcus standing near the center of the hall, with his head bent toward a slim and elderly woman, who stood at his side, holding a bit of his sleeve between her gnarled, pinched fingers while she tilted her face up as she talked.

Marcus nodded at whatever the woman was saying, but his gaze was unswerving, locked on Autumn.

It was as unsettling as it was invigorating. He didn't politely remove his gaze, didn't give one hundred percent of his attention to the old woman. No, he paralyzed Autumn with the intensity of his stare until her cheeks flooded with heat and surely a bright color. She was unable to either blink or look away, attempting instead to interpret his searing stare. She didn't read anger, but then there wasn't anything casual about his regard. It was simply steady and willful, causing Autumn's pulse to race. Time was marked by the rhythm of her slow inhales and exhales until she was, thankfully, addressed again by Eadric, and forced to wrench her gaze away from the extraordinary figure of Marcus McInnes.

Good God, smolder much?

The low background music gradually increased in tempo. Aside from the whiskey, ale and wine flowed as well. People left their tables, moving about and mingling. Children, released from their parents' sides, began to run around the hall. A bit of dancing commenced, begun by a trio of young girls performing what appeared to be a choreographed number, which was really lovely, their steps slow and well-synchronized to each other and the haunting tune that accompanied them. Only a few songs later, more and more people began to dance so that the gathering now resembled more a rowdy banquet or wedding.

When Reid Nicholson abandoned the head table, gathering with a huddled group of soldiers, Charlotte coerced Autumn from her chair and they walked about the hall, making polite conversation with the peasants of Balla Àrd, those who remained seated still.

At any given time throughout the evening, Autumn thought she felt Marcus's silent and brooding regard. Sometimes she might be visited by a prickling sensation and guessed he watched her again. More than once she turned and found Marcus staring at her with a blazing thoroughness that didn't alarm her so much as it baffled and exhilarated her.

Autumn had happily managed to elude the dancing all evening, having no interest in looking like a fool in the center of the hall, not quite sure she could manage some of the complex steps executed by sometimes as many as twenty or thirty people at once.

But then she wasn't sure she could withstand Charlotte's cajoling much longer.

"I'm like you," Charlotte said. "I would never put myself out there like that. I don't know the steps and I'm not sure even a proper tutor could make magic from my two left feet."

Autumn grinned at this.

"But you're here now," Charlotte said, her eyes lighting up. "And I haven't danced in years—God, I miss a good, old fashioned twenty-first century wedding! Dance with me, Autumn. We can keep to the fringes and look silly together."

Autumn tried, she really did, to get out of it. In the back of her mind, she imagined Marcus watching her dance and cringed at the very idea.

But then Charlotte would not take no for an answer and Autumn was prodded and pushed out onto the dance floor. As Charlotte had suggested, they did keep to the perimeter. Neither she nor Charlotte dared to even try emulating the steps of those closest but did their own thing. Autumn didn't lose her inhibition until she and the whiskey decided to let herself go, at Charlotte's insistence. She was quite sure she and Charlotte dancing by themselves rather looked like two girlfriends hanging out and gossiping on the dance floor at a wedding, having no particular style but moved by the music, which was felt under her feet. Autumn laughed, her comfort level improved, realizing Charlotte had only as much rhythm as Autumn, who had never thought herself a particularly good dancer. But God love her, Charlotte didn't seem to care, which helped tremendously. Soon enough, Autumn was relieved of the last of her reserve and let herself be free, moved half as much by the whiskey as she was by the music and the growing joyfulness all around.

Chapter Thirteen

He wasn't the only one watching her.

Hell, 'twas not only the male population watching her. And he wasn't deceived into thinking that Charlotte garnered even half the attention that Autumn did. Charlotte was pleasing to look upon, but she was the wife of the Nicholson. Several times in the last year, she'd visited Balla Àrd and so her status was known to all. None would dare to objective Charlotte and thereby incur the wrath of Reid by ogling her lewdly.

Autumn was not so much a spectacle for the fact that she and Charlotte danced by themselves and so differently than every other person in the hall, but she was indeed the object of much awareness —some of it lewd, Marcus had to imagine—for the *way* she moved.

She was neither flamboyant of movement or garbed in such a way to draw so much attention but the gentle swaying of her hips, the way she lifted her hands up and then slithered them downward—had she meant that to be as seductive as it was?—was staggering for how sensual it was. Her hands frequently traced invisible patterns in the air.

While Charlotte's dance was more energetic, more lively, Autumn swayed modestly, allowing the music to move her and not her enthusiasm. Her dance was unhurried, subtle, as a leaf blows in a calm breeze.

Her long blonde hair had some time ago begun to fall from the ties that bound it. Charlotte laughed when it began to fall, and then had helped to bring down the rest of it, plunging her hands into Autumn's hair and shaking out the length of it as she pulled it over Autumn's shoulders.

They talked frequently while they danced, sometimes about people, Marcus had to assume. Charlotte would lean forward and say something and then Autumn's gaze would swivel and settle on some unsuspecting person. Sometimes they giggled together, appearing much younger, unburdened; sometimes they shrugged; once, when Charlotte had sent Autumn's sparling gray eyes to the lad, Eoin, who struggled simultaneously with sobriety and gravity, it seemed, Autumn had cringed.

Marcus was mesmerized, scarcely able to tear his gaze from her, no more so than he had been earlier when he'd watched her talk with Eadric and had been captivated by her smile. Throughout the evening, his gaze regularly sought her out, he being entranced even by lesser things, simply the way her mouth moved around her words. He'd known what havoc he'd introduced to her with the smoldering weight of his stare, had noted the initial furious blush that had colored her cheeks, but for the life of him, he'd been unable to offer respite by removing his hungry gaze.

He was eventually ensconced within a group of men, Reid, Gibbon, and Eadric included. He didn't miss how unwaveringly Reid watched his wife and didn't for one minute think that his friend's tight jaw or the tic of a muscle near his cheek represented fury of any kind; Reid was as enthralled with Charlotte as Marcus was with Autumn. But the circle of men and their garrulous conversation did often force Marcus to forsake his vigilant observing of Autumn.

However, at one point, as Marcus realized that he and Reid were watching Charlotte and Autumn mayhap a wee bit more—or more fervently—than any other person in the hall, he was compelled to discuss this with his friend.

"Is that part of the attraction?" Marcus quietly dared to ask Reid, who slanted a furious glare at his friend. Marcus brushed off Reid's instant expectation that his dander should be lifted. "I only mean because they—she, I mean, Charlotte—is nae like anyone ye've ever met, so different than what and who we ken in...in this time." He sent his regard to Autumn, swaying hypnotically with the music. "Almost as if she's something rare, to be treasured?"

He met Reid's contemplative stare and held himself very still. Possibly, he'd just revealed quite a bit.

Reid didn't pounce on Marcus's unintended disclosure.

"Aye, I was smitten with Charlotte—almost from the start, she'll tell ye," Reid said, an uncommon grin easing his normally fierce expression. "She'd also tell ye, she puts on her pants one leg at a time, same as everyone else." When Marcus lifted a skeptical brow, Reid only shrugged. "Truth is, she's nae so different from anyone in our time, or what is possible of any person in any time. She's fierce and loyal and owns a heart bigger than most, somehow manages to make me laugh," he said and then smirked a bit. "Aye, and more often she irks me and tests me beyond reason but then," he sighed, "it's all in how she makes me feel. Aye, I was as surprised as ye look now. And yet I say to ye, friend, whatever I believed of myself before Charlotte—and ye ken I'm an arrogant bastard, so there was a guid bit of conceit—I am ten-times more worthy in her eyes and thus in my want to be so." He shrugged again, as if that should explain everything.

Reid then lifted his goblet and saluted Marcus. "May the gods favor ye with exactly the same."

When the night grew old and the gathering began to thin, due in part to several people actually falling down drunk, left to lay where they fell, and Reid announced that he would collect his wife and they would seek their bed, Marcus decided that it would behoove him to remove Autumn from the hall as well. Exhaustion dictated that his day was also done, but he knew he would not leave Autumn to her own devices among the revelers. The occupants and the carousing would only become more raucous, less civilized, as the night grew older still.

He and Reid approached Charlotte and Autumn. Their dance slowed. Charlotte beamed at her husband, leaning into his side as Reid put his arm around her.

"Sweet Jesus, I'm exhausted," Charlotte said, "but God, I needed that."

"Perfect time to retire," Reid asserted.

"Mm," Charlotte agreed against his chest.

Standing closer to Autumn than he had all evening, Marcus once more subjected her to yet another silent and stark perusal. She positively glowed. Slightly breathless, her chest rising and falling, her neck and forehead glistened with a delicate sheen of perspiration. The soft overhead candlelight caressed her, seeming to cast a warm, ethereal aura about her.

"You don't have to call it a night, though," Charlotte said to Autumn. "Marcus is here, you can dance with him."

Marcus ignored yet another attempt by Charlotte at manipulation. Truly, he didn't need her meddling, no matter how well-intentioned. He could—and would— advance his connection with Autumn without any help from Charlotte. He'd been thinking of only that all evening.

Autumn's shimmering gray eyes took on an air of expectation, even as she said, "I'm rather tired as well."

"It is late," Marcus said. "I will take ye up."

Charlotte and Autumn exchanged a hug while Marcus paused, turning to set down his tankard.

A high-pitched whoop from Charlotte spun him back around, just in time to see Reid scoop up his wife in his arms and make his way through what remained of the crowd, taking the stairs at the end of the hall two at a time to the cheers of those below.

Marcus and Autumn grinned, their gazes set upon the couple for a moment before they faced each other again.

"I'll nae swing ye over my shoulder," he told her, hardly allowing his lips to curve.

She smiled again, a wee cheekily now. "What a shame," she said before she followed the path Reid had taken.

Marcus lifted a brow and immediately stepped into her shadow.

***

What a shame?

Oh, my God. Why had I said that?

Hopefully, he would read nothing into her very inappropriate comment.

Autumn's brow crinkled. Or maybe...did she want him to?

They climbed the stairs single file, neither saying a word. Though she was dog-tired, she was rather sorry the night had to end. But then she was harassed by a sense of guilt, for having fun in the first place on such an occasion, and then being deflated by the end of that good time.

She blew out a restless breath at the top of the stairs and turned left, toward the room she'd been given. At the door, she turned and faced Marcus, wondering how to politely tell him thank you for the first good time she'd had in the fourteenth century, a sentiment that seemed very misplaced tonight. She glanced down at her bare feet, dirty once more despite the thorough scrubbing she'd given them just before the funeral.

Lifting her gaze, she met Marcus's striking brown eyes, which were rendered nearly black by the lack of light up here, but still gleamed, now with some unfathomable shimmer.

"I hate to say it was a lovely party," Autumn said awkwardly, "but I do feel as if it was a constructive alternative to solitary grief for everyone. At least for tonight. "

"As it is meant to be," Marcus allowed, directing his response to her lips.

A dawning of understanding evolved. The *unfathomable shimmer* of his burning gaze was hence defined.

He was thinking about kissing her, she realized. Possibly, that had been what had stirred him to stalk her with his magnetic gaze most of the night.

The air and the moment were pregnant with anticipation, with something that seemed to have been building for days now and certainly throughout this evening. Her heart fluttered with a mixture of nervousness and desire. Autumn swallowed convulsively, needing to decide here and now, right this moment, if she really wanted Marcus to kiss her. If she wanted to be kissed by him. Her internal answer was both immediate and forceful: *God, yes!*

She wasn't only reading too much into his frequent and sometimes fiery tracking of her tonight or the way he regarded her now, as if he needed only one word or sign from her before he might pounce as he wished to do. Though he'd yet to move, she absolutely knew she wasn't wrong about this, about him and his intent right now.

But Christ, was it really a good idea? Wasn't her plate crowded enough with everything piled onto it over the last few days? Did she really need to further complicate her situation by possibly having her knees buckled by Marcus McInnes's kiss? Oh, she had no doubt he could do that and more. Something told her his smoldering sensuality was not only for show.

Almost unconsciously, as if her body were way ahead of the debate in her brain, Autumn lifted her hand, reaching for him. When she realized what she'd done, she curled her fingers into a fist and dropped her hand back to her side.

And then her pulse escalated as finally Marcus took a step closer, his eyes dark with desire. She could feel the heat of his body drawing near, and she nervously licked her lips. The anticipation was almost unbearable as she watched him reach out to gently tuck a stray strand of her blonde hair behind her ear. The touch sent a shiver down her spine, and her breath caught in her throat.

"You kent I would kiss ye tonight, did ye nae?" he whispered, his voice low and husky.

She nodded, but said nothing, so afraid her voice wouldn't work, even as her brain answered, *I hoped you would.*

With that, Marcus cupped her cheek with his hand, his thumb tracing the delicate curve of her jaw. His gaze fell again to her lips, and he leaned in, their breaths mingling in the sweet, charged air. He brought his lips down to meet hers. The kiss began gently, a soft and searching exploration of each other's mouths, a tantalizingly slow, searing kiss. The world around them faded away, leaving only the sensation of the kiss and the thundering beat of their hearts.

Autumn's hands found their way to Marcus's broad shoulders, and she pulled him closer, deepening the kiss. His tongue teased at her lips, and she willingly parted them, allowing him access. Their tongues danced together with needful rhythm, with desire and longing that had been building for days now.

Marcus's hands encircled her waist, drawing her nearer to his chest, until there was no space left between them.

Their mouths moved together with a heated urgency, driven by their desire and whatever was this thing between them, that soul-reaching yet nebulous connection. He tasted of oaky sweetness, hints of the earthy whiskey discernable. Somehow, his kiss and taste seemed familiar to her, yet another tease of that mysterious bond between them. Autumn found him absolutely delicious.

Time seemed to stand still as they lost themselves in each other, the world around them fading to insignificance. The music and laughter from the hall became a distant echo, drowned out by the pulsing cadence of their own heartbeats.

Marcus's hands roamed down Autumn's back, leaving trails of fire in their wake, while her fingers explored the sculpted contours of his shoulders and chest. Every touch, each sigh, every shared breath amplified her craving, igniting a fire that had burned since their eyes had first locked tonight. Maybe even before that. She shoved her fingers into the hair at the back of his head. His hair was soft, his body hard.

When his hand slid upward and covered her breast, her body sighed with delight, but her brain clapped its hands for attention. With a strangled cry, Autumn broke the glorious kiss she had no business rejoicing in.

Why! Why at this moment was she compelled to think of Jordan when in truth she'd barely thought of him at all over the last few days. Just this evening, she'd nearly wept as she was so happily assailed by memories and images of her family. A picture of Jordan, the very thought of him, had only come to her after the fact. So why now?

Autumn dropped her forehead against Marcus's square jaw.

Marcus's voice was a low, sensual growl as he murmured, "Dinna ask me to stop."

"I-I can't do this," she said, hating herself for taking the high road where Jordan was concerned, when he didn't deserve it. Her shoulders slumped. She raised her gaze to Marcus, almost wishing he would kiss her anyway.

"Ye bade me stop and now ye shed tears."

Lifting her hand off his shoulder, she ran her fingers over her right eye. "Because I...I want you to kiss me...but I—."

"Ye enjoyed my kiss," he said, more an accusation than a guess.

A slow and sad smile came to her, entertained by his alpha maleness, more than a little seduced by it as well. "Yes, Marcus. Very much. Too much, in fact. But that's a problem. I...I am not free to be kissing another man."

"Another man?" He questioned fiercely.

And she could see very clearly when the truth dawned on him by the deeper crinkling of his brow.

"In yer time, ye are wed."

"Not wed. Not married, but dating someone," she explained glumly. "With someone. Or I was."

"Ye are or ye are nae," he said, his voice raspy as he demanded clarification. His hands slid away from her.

"I don't know," she cried, bemoaning the loss of his touch. "It's complicated. But then that's not so surprising given how everything has been turned upside down in the last few days."

His eyes now burned with a ferocity that scorched her. "But why did ye let me kiss ye at all?"

"Because you…Christ, Marcus, you're not easy to resist."

Such blatant praise did not puff up his chest with manly pride. Marcus didn't suffer any insecurities, she somehow knew. While he possibly didn't think about it regularly, he didn't need her to tell him how magnetic and irresistible he was. He was completely comfortable in his own skin, acted on pure raw physical desire, his actions governed by craving and the magnetism already known between them.

He sighed and took one step backward, his hand finding the hilt of his sword. His knuckles were nearly white.

"I will nae be the cause of your dishonor."

"I kind of want you to be," Autumn said, rather whiny, somewhat hopeful, and with a bit of mockery directed at herself, for wishing someone else would force her or compel her to behave badly.

Marcus's eyes widened before he barked out a laugh, the sound short and gruff, as if it surprised him as well.

"So ye are a fair and noble lass, but ye clearly wish ye were nae," was his brusque appraisal of her statement.

Autumn shrugged helplessly. "That about sums it up." At least where he was concerned.

The lines of his jaw, always strong and defined, became more pronounced, setting his mouth into a firm, unyielding line. A moment ago, that same gorgeous mouth had kissed her nearly insensible.

She was super pissed at Jordan for having put her in this position in the first place, or more pertinently, for coming to mind now, in this moment, when she'd managed to think of hardly him at all in two days.

Almost unconsciously, she leaned forward, moving one foot toward Marcus.

"Nae," he said, the furrows returning to their regular home over and between his eyes.

The rejection was harsh and stung bitterly. Autumn clenched her teeth, wanting now only to escape.

Possibly he read her abject misery. He softened the blow, with what she supposed was Marcus McInnes's attempt at lightness. "I'll nae have ye break my heart."

Autumn tilted her head at him, narrowing her eyes quizzically. Something lingered and lived behind the sudden coolness of his gaze. His nostrils flared while he fought to keep it tamped down.

Autumn's lips parted. "Ah, but I can't, can I? It's already broken, isn't it?"

***

What the hell is wrong with me? Autumn wondered disparagingly as she lay in bed a little later, staring at the midnight gray ceiling.

Her brain was on a mission to torment her, replaying the kiss and her rejection and then his, over and over again until she was ready to cry. And she wasn't entirely sure she wasn't about to throw up.

Ah, hell. What was one more sleepless night?

She wanted to blame Jordan for denying her what surely would have been one of the greatest nights of her life, if she'd let things develop and progress to where they'd so magnificently been headed. She wanted to blame Jordan for coming to mind then. For the last hour, since she'd so slowly closed that door to Marcus, she'd tried to make sense of it.

She didn't really think she was—or wanted to be—still dating Jordan. She was angry at herself for letting Jordan come between them. Jordan had his chance, plenty of chances in fact and plenty of time, and he'd blown it. She owed him nothing.

But Autumn knew there was more to it, why she'd put an end to their kiss. And only a small part of it had anything to do with the fact that she hadn't showered in days and hadn't properly brushed her teeth.

Truth was, she'd been paralyzed by a huge dose of fear. It had nothing to do with Marcus himself. She didn't fear him. But she feared his power over her. Whatever was the strange and pulsating bond between them, that she'd felt almost since the beginning, she had some suspicion that it would only grow stronger if she slept with him.

She wanted to go home. She needed to go home.

She wanted and needed to *believe* that, to keep that in front of everything else.

So there was some fear, maybe better categorized as dread, that with each reluctant and rusty smile worn by Marcus, with each smoldering stare, with every touch and any subsequent kiss, Marcus—possibly without realizing it—would chip away at her resolve, would slowly reel her in. She simply couldn't let that happen; she had to go home. Autumn was torn up inside at the very idea of her family mourning her, never knowing what happened to her if she didn't make it home. She didn't want to get comfortable here, didn't want to crave Marcus's touch, to want or need him more than anything and anyone else.

And yet, despite the brevity of their acquaintance—but possibly aided by the hypnotizing kiss—she saw that as a strong possibility as far as outcomes went.

But oh, to give up the chance to sleep with Marcus? When he clearly wanted to do more than only kiss her? Was she strong enough to do that?

Her mind worked overtime, trying to come up with some way it could be possible, that she could know more of the sweet torment and virile passion of his kiss without her heart becoming engaged,

Bereft of ideas, Autumn asked herself, as she sometimes did, what her mother would do or say.

"People think they have all the time in the world," had been the last bit of solicited advice that her mother had given her. That had been last week, after Jordan had made Autumn feel as if getting engaged was not that important to him.

She'd hesitantly brought up the issue with her mother. At one point in their discussion, Autumn had defended Jordan to her mother, saying that she mostly loved how thoughtful were all his decisions, how much maturity it showed to not leap ahead in any regard but always step cautiously. Maybe he just needed a bit more time, she'd suggested to her mother.

Her mother had tried hard not to roll her eyes, had even been minimally successful. Her mother liked Jordan, or she used to, but even the ever-patient Donna Winters had started to lose her patience with Jordan's foot-dragging.

"People think they have all the time in the world," her mother had said. "We have but one life, and only a set number of days. How will you—and Jordan for that matter—use them most wisely?"

So that's what finally convinced her that she should have slept with Marcus. She might only have a certain number of days in this time, in his company.

People think they have all the time in the world, she mused again. She'd thought that very thing only this evening, when thinking about her family. *I thought I would have more time with them. I didn't see an end in sight.*

Should she ever get back to her time, would she wish for one more day with Marcus? Would she kick herself for not exploring that impulsive force of desire that burned between them?

Possibly. Still, she might wish she could be more sure that she wouldn't develop feelings for him and thus be torn between the future and the past.

Hm, she thought with a lethargic humor, *I could ask him if that could be a prerequisite to any sex we might have.*

Autumn's eyes opened and widened dramatically.

I could ask him that.

Chapter Fourteen

As she had yesterday, Charlotte knocked on the bedroom door early in the morning. Autumn was thankful for this, that Charlotte thought of her. If left to her own devices, Autumn wasn't sure where she might go first upon leaving the room or what she might do. Sadly, though, Charlotte did not come bearing gifts as she had yesterday morning, not a fresh set of clothes or the basin and cloth that Autumn was looking forward to, to clean her face.

Charlotte explained the lack straightaway. "I've managed to put together an outfit for you," she said. "That woman, Fiona, with the frizzy red hair—remember we talked to her last night? She is as tall as you and I gave her a few coins for a shift and kirtle, and a pair of shoes. Don't get excited, though," she cautioned, wrinkling her nose. "The shoes might have you wanting to be barefoot again."

"Charlotte, you didn't have to do that," Autumn objected, in awe of Charlotte's generosity. "Pay for clothes for me. Obviously, I have no money to pay you back."

Charlotte waved her hand dismissively. "It's not a problem. I'm happy to do it. Anyway, I am in dire want of a bath and I'm assuming you'd like one as well. But I wanted to help in the kitchens for a while and with the clean-up in the hall, so do you mind waiting until this afternoon to get good and gloriously clean?" She lifted brows, tempting Autumn with, "I have a fabulous honey and lavender scented soap."

"I'd wait even longer," Autumn assured her. "That sounds like all my dreams come true."

Charlottes tossed at saucy smirk at Autumn, turning her shoulder in as she questioned, "All your dreams? Really? Not any of them are reserved for Marcus?"

"No," she lied automatically, wondering why she did but then pressed on about what had irked her somewhat last night. "And will you please stop so flagrantly trying to force us together? *Marcus is here, you can dance with him*," she said, using a generic, high-pitched voice to repeat Charlotte's words of last night.

Unashamed, Charlotte shrugged, her grin unchanged. "C'mon, I know you saw or were aware of the numerous longing glances he sent your way last night. Hell, even the hair on the back of *my* neck stood up. That was a lot of scorching heat sent across the hall. I'm amazed you weren't turned to dust by some of his looks."

Autumn did not pretend she hadn't been aware of them. Her shoulders sagged even as she became nearly giddy as she confessed to Charlotte, "I did notice them, so then I wasn't too surprised when he..." she paused, enjoying tremendously how Charlotte's green eyes widened with anticipation, "when he kissed me."

Charlotte fisted her hand and pumped it into the air above her head. "Yes! I knew it. Oh, my God, tell me everything."

"I just did," Autumn said, knowing she'd just lied again—*he kissed me* in no way conveyed the magnitude of the act, not the irresistible finesse of his kiss or her tremendous reaction to it, or the way the memory so happily lingered with her—but wanting to ask something of Charlotte instead. "But, I don't really know what to make of it. I mean, does he make a habit of it, rousing a woman to senselessness with his smoldering looks and then a knee-weakening kiss? Am I simply fresh meat in this time period? At Balla Àrd? That I seem interesting or more likely, an easy target?"

"Are you asking me if he's a player? A man-slut?"

Autumn snorted out a laugh at Charlotte's phrasing. But, well... "Yes. I am."

"I don't think he is," Charlotte said, all serious again. "I've known him for two years now. Granted I've only met him a handful of times, but I've never seen him with another woman. I had an idea in my head, when I realized I was in the fourteenth century, of men in charge rather doing what they wanted with the female servants, you know, having their way with them, a different woman every night—some of them by force— that kind of thing. But honestly, I've seen little evidence of that kind of behavior. Now it could be only because Reid and Marcus are really good guys. They put honor above almost everything else. They might be killers—by necessity, as you've learned—but they never go looking for a fight and they would kill to protect and serve an innocent or naïve or crushed person. I've seen it."

Autumn wasn't sure that answered her question. She tried a different tactic.

"But you did mention that Marcus was engaged—betrothed, I mean. Several times, you said."

"He was and I don't know all the particulars, but I do know that whatever happened, he was or is kind of soured on women, so I think it's fabulous that he's obviously not soured on you." She clapped her hands over her mouth, her eyes sparkling with joy.

Autumn wasn't sure if Charlotte's mien might be described as schoolgirl-ish, or if it leaned toward proud mother.

They might have discussed the kiss more but there came from below a loud crash that at first startled and then froze Charlotte and Autumn in place, until they realized the yelling that came immediately after was only someone—a woman—reprimanding someone else for creating the bang. Thus provoked from the bedchamber, Autumn and Charlotte made their way downstairs.

Autumn had hoped today, supposing it might only be a normal day inside a keep in the fourteenth century—no war, no ambush, no hastily made ER in the hall, no funerals—that she might have been presented an opportunity to question Charlotte about two matters that, behind from Marcus's kiss at the fore, had been churning at the back of her brain: Megan West and how Autumn might get home. Sadly, they were kept relatively busy all day and often in the company of others, so that she did not get a chance to bring up these subjects.

When it was, by Autumn's estimation, around midafternoon, and the hall was returned to its pre-hospital, pre-war funeral banquet state, Charlotte wiped the back of her hand across her brow and said to Autumn, "I think it's bath time. I'm whipped. But I should warn you: a bath, certainly here at Balla Àrd—is a good thing, bad thing kind of thing."

Tilting her head quizzically at Charlotte, Autumn wondered, "How so?"

"Okay, there is a bathroom, if you will. But it's not like our bathrooms, obviously. Though there are bathtubs, there is no running water. And we could have them filled, the tubs, or we could simply do it ourselves, but—hear me out—I would much rather take a bath in the loch."

Autumn's brows shot up into her forehead, but she said nothing, willing to hear Charlotte's reasoning.

"Reid says I'm fussy," she explained, "which may be true, but Autumn, I'm funny about where I sit my butt. It's not like they're scouring these tubs after each use, if you know what I mean, and these ones here at Balla Àrd are made of wood and that, to me, is beyond gross, just thinking about every imaginable bodily fluid having been absorbed by that wood."

Autumn was, by now, cringing herself.

"At home, at Kingswood, we have copper tubs and they are scrubbed regularly, but here—and I love Balla Ard, don't get me wrong—but ew, I don't know who's been chafing their arse on that wood. So, do you mind using the loch as our bathtub?"

Autumn laughed. "Well, you've totally turned me off taking a bath in these medieval tubs, so no, I guess I don't mind. But Charlotte, it's the middle of the day."

Not unexpectedly, Charlotte batted away Autumn's concern with a wave of her hand.

"It's a pretty big lake, you make have noticed, and Reid will make sure we have privacy."

"Where is he, by the way? Him and Marcus?"

"On the training field," Charlotte answered flippantly, "practicing sword thrusts or whatever they do out there for six to eight hours a day. Although today, the training field will likely serve as an operations room. I know they're plotting their revenge, formulating an attack on the MacPhails."

Autumn had not forgotten about that.

"Charlotte, don't you worry about Reid? I mean, like fear for his life? I witnessed the entire fight the other day—that ambush. I could never have conceived of so much violence."

"Oh, God. Every day. All the time. And it doesn't really help that I know how proficient Reid is, how masterful he is with a sword, or mace, or pike. But then, I know *who* he is. He's fearless but not reckless. He fights smart, I just know it. But then, more relevant to my infinite fear, it's who he is. If he didn't fight, because he feared death or even because I did, he would...well, he would simply wither and die. He would have no purpose and frankly, he wouldn't be the man I love."

"That doesn't make it easy for you to live with, though," Autumn guessed.

"Not at all, but don't tell him that. I really do try to keep my nagging and massive worry from him. I can't have him worried about me, worrying about him, and not be able to fight for the distraction of that."

Charlotte found a young kid and asked him to fetch Reid from the training field for her, and then she and Autumn visited the bedchamber that Reid and Charlotte shared. There they collected the aforementioned scented soap, and towels and cloths made of linen, a comb that looked as if it were made of bone, and a change of clothes for both of them.

"Grab that stack there, "Charlotte said to Autumn about a pile of cloths sitting on a small three-legged stool near the fire.

Next, they strolled outside the keep, which lived today under an overcast sky. They waited only a few minutes for Reid to come riding into the yard.

"You didn't think I would send for you, did you?" Charlotte asked her husband. "You were so sure I'd be careless and go have my bath without waiting for your escort."

"Aye. I was all set to have to tan yer hide for disobeying."

Charlotte surprised Autumn by teasing her husband, "Oh, you and your kinky promises."

Reid Nicholson, who to Autumn's mind looked on any given day, at any given hour, as if he might have just committed murder or was contemplating it—his mien was that severe—was softened by a grin and then made nearly handsome by the wink he sent his wife.

***

He didn't often second guess himself. But it had been by his command that only two units were called to attend the fires in Darrie that day. He fought every moment since with the certainty that if he had assembled a larger force, possibly seventeen men wouldn't have died.

It didn't help now that Gibbon had concurred with his estimation then, had raised no ruckus to ride for Darrie with more men. No relief from guilt was known simply because another had concurred with his plan. Marcus was the laird; the decisions and the subsequent outcomes, good or bad, were solely on him to assume either pride or blame.

And he wasn't feeling particularly uncertain, but he did want to exercise greater caution with the news he'd just been given so that he sought out Reid now, wanting to confer with him about what the scouts had discovered. Though he'd only been with Reid an hour ago, he was forced to search all throughout the keep and yard until the stable lad, John, his scrawny arms hanging over the side of a stall, wondered if the laird was searching for the Nicholson.

When Marcus nodded, the lad informed him in their own tongue, "Might be found yet at the loch, near the bathing spot, with his bride and the other one with the spun gold hair."

Marcus scowled at him. "Spun gold hair?" His scowl didn't last though, a grin eventually coming. For the brilliance of it, Autumn's hair might well be likened to spun gold. "And what do you know of spun gold?"

The lad shrugged. "Naught. But mam said that's what it was." He lifted his hands and let them fall back down. "Mam said all the witches wore crowns of gold."

Marcus's grin faded. It should not have come as any surprise. Though she'd made some progress assimilating with Balla Àrd's people, and though Charlotte was not so different than her, plenty of Marcus's men had seen Autumn that first day, and surely had bandied about tales of that initial encounter, when she'd looked like anything but one of them. People generally feared that which they did not know, that which didn't resemble them so favorably in all their wretched despair.

John's màthair, a disruptive and cantankerous woman, was indeed a person of abject misery, most of it self-generated.

"Tell your màthair to seek me out on the morrow," he asked of John. He would nip this bud ere it bloomed.

Marcus mounted his destrier, which had been tethered loosely near the stables and rode out to find Reid. He expected that Reid had likely accompanied Charlotte and Autumn outside the gates rather than leave their safety to chance, or just as bad, in Reid's mind, Marcus was sure, in the hands of any other. He rode along the flattened grass path alongside the loch, the trail curving about as did the loch. Five minutes later, he followed the trail as it skirted further away from the loch, forced to do so by the thick grove of trees that closely flanked the water's edge. He slowed when he spied Reid, dismounted and unmoving, laying upon the ground with his arms under his head.

"*Jesu*, some protection ye are," he said lightly as he came upon him, and his shadow fell over him.

"Ye ken I sleep with one eye open," Reid said. "I saw ye approach."

"They are actually bathing?" Marcus asked, assuming that to be the reason that Charlotte was allowed out of sight of her husband, but likely more in deference to Autumn.

"Aye, follow the sound of the giggling," Reid said dryly.

Marcus smirked. "More than last night, mayhap?"

"Thereabouts."

As if on cue, a very charming, very feminine peal of laughter floated to them from beyond the trees.

"Was more of a screech at first," Reid commented, "when they met with the frigid water."

"They've grown accustomed to it, it seems," Marcus said as he dismounted.

Reid sat up, leaving his long legs stretched out. "What brings ye away from the training?"

"Osgar and Wilfrid just returned," Marcus told him. "They're nae on the move, the MacPhails, but the scouts stumbled across—at a fair distance—a marching unit, twenty-six foot soldiers. They went out and have nae returned. Osgar and Wilfrid trialed them for almost eight miles by their reckoning. And there they stopped, the MacPhails, Osgar estimates about five miles east of where they ambushed us, within a quarter mile of the River Lochy."

Reid's brow furrowed. "Still on MacPhail land."

"Aye, but designing something," was Marcus's guess.

"Aye. I want to see for myself but dinna want to be caught unawares again, would want a force of one hundred, no less."

"But ye dinna want to leave Balla Àrd vulnerable," Reid guessed.

Marcus sensed Reid was making calculations in his head, same as Marcus had in the last half hour.

"I dinna. But if you're willing to assist, we have the numbers. With the wall closed behind us as we investigate, we dinna need more than a few dozen here. There are always the tunnels as a means of escape if trouble came to the keep."

Reid stood finally, just as the chatter between Charlotte and Autumn grew closer. Their baths, apparently, were done.

"Ye want to do this today?"

Marcus shook his head, keeping one eye on the trees, filled with a wee anticipation to see Autumn. "Nae enough hours of daylight to guide us. At dawn's light, I'll want to go," he'd already decided.

Reid nodded his agreement. "We'll discuss it more after last meal."

That was set aside as either Charlotte or Autumn squealed with fright and both of them burst from the cover of the trees at once. Marcus and Reid leapt forward, expecting trouble though unable to imagine its source.

Autumn's cheeks were pale, and her lips tinted just a wee blue, like as not an effect of the crisp water. Her hair was long and loose, hanging over one shoulder, drenching the fabric of her kirtle. Marcus was a wee entranced by its color, not the bright and shiny spun gold he'd grown accustomed to, but a deeper, vibrant honey color.

The ladies were brought up short by the sight of Marcus and Reid drawing their swords, but their alarm only lasted a moment before they glanced at each other and dissolved into laughter.

"A spider," Charlotte managed to inform them through her giggling. "The sword might be overkill."

"Although he was huge—the spider, that is," Autumn added. But her initial easy chuckle had faded as she stood still now, with her hands folded over her chest, several garments or fabrics held in her arms. She stared somewhat awkwardly at Marcus, but he didn't know if her blush was caused by his unexpected presence or by either her bath or the fright of their encounter with an apparently gigantic spider.

"Oh, but I'm glad you're here, Marcus," Charlotte said. "I was hoping to stop by the village and Elspeth's cottage to see about her son's wound. Would you mind seeing Autumn back to the keep?"

Even Reid rolled his eyes at yet another instance of Charlotte's blatant manipulation.

Charlotte walked to her husband's steed, slapping down her own stack of garments, blithely unaware of her husband's reaction, or that of Autumn, who bit her lip and appeared less enthusiastic about the idea than outright opposed to it.

Marcus bristled at Charlotte's meddling but did not refute it. He'd meant to seek out Autumn at some point today.

"Oh, shoot," Autumn said then. "I left Fiona's shoes at the lake." She held up her finger to Marcus, ostensibly asking him to wait a moment and dashed off into the trees again.

"All right," called Charlotte breezily, pulling herself up onto Reid's big destrier. "I'll see you back at the keep, Autumn."

Reid sent Marcus a broad grin and climbed up into the saddle behind Charlotte, turning the horse toward the village, either to give credence to Charlotte's stated mission or because it actually had been her plan to check in on the lad, Patrick. Though Patrick had survived the MacPhail ambush, he'd suffered a grievous injury to his right arm, which would likely prevent him from ever wielding a sword again.

Left standing by himself, Marcus shook his head and pursued Autumn through the trees. He might take advantage of the total seclusion of this area of the loch to have a private word with her.

When the trees thinned again and gave way to a small clearing, which was little more than a narrow stretch of loamy beach where the loch water lapped slowly against the gentle shore, he found Autumn just turning from where she'd picked up a pair of shoes, which were apparently Fiona's.

She came again to a quick stop, filled with what seemed to be another sudden awareness. They were alone now. They hadn't the buffer of Charlotte and Reid to moderate and soften their first meeting since their kiss.

She read his intent, that he was in no hurry to vacate the area, and only waited.

Inexplicably, while he briefly studied her lips, he was visited by the memory of how her mouth had been painted red when he'd met her. He liked this version so much better, actually adored the shape and color of her natural lips. Swift was the leap to a recollection of how they'd felt pressed against his, how very potent had been her kiss.

"Marcus?"

He blinked, recovering himself. "I meant to inquire," he said, "how it can be possible that ye dinna ken the state of your relationship with a man in your time."

Autumn dropped her arms, though she didn't release any of the items in her hands, including the shoes. But it did reveal that she had donned fresh clothing, a newly borrowed shift and kirtle, he would imagine, both bland in color. But then she didn't need vibrant hues to highlight her beauty.

When she didn't answer directly, Marcus thought he could almost imagine the workings of her brain as she stared at him. She might believe that his query just now suggested that he'd been thinking about their kiss, mayhap even lamenting the reason it had been stopped. She would be correct in her thinking, if that were the case.

Autumn tipped her head to one side and offered him a thoughtful stare before she said, "I don't know the answer will make any difference. Although I'm pretty sure I've squared that away in my head. I am not with Jordan."

Marcus didn't want to question what possibly benefitted him, but then he didn't want anything standing in his way or coming back to bite him.

"Some might say that's fairly convenient," he challenged lightly, "given that it disagrees with what was revealed last night."

"That's fair," Autumn said. "I-I'm not sure if it was simply because I haven't kissed or been kissed by anyone but him in the last three years—I don't know why I thought of him at that moment—but it did kind of, well, no it didn't kill the mood, but it made me feel," she paused, shrugged and finished in a small voice, "icky. But that was misplaced, what I felt then. And that was unfair to me. And you."

"But you ken you betrayed him?"

"No," she said with confidence, staring boldly at Marcus. "I didn't betray him. He betrayed me. But I don't want to talk about Jordan, Marcus. I'm sorry that I let him...come between us last night."

While he stared at her, considering what his next question should be, Autumn shocked him by admitting, her chin held high, "I want you to kiss me again, Marcus. But I want you to know that no matter what happens, my number one priority is getting home, back to my time. So I don't want to be...hampered by emotion. I just need to tell you that there is and will be no emotion. I can't sleep with you and then want more and be enslaved by your touch or something very medieval like that, and have my heart engaged. I have to know I am free and clear to go home whenever I want."

"Autumn, I dinna comprehend but half of your words, or what ye are trying to convey. Mayhap you should tell me what my response should be."

Her shoulders sagged. "Are you confused?" She bit her lip and fidgeted with the neckline of her kirtle.

"Admittedly, yes."

"All right, I want to sleep with you. I think that's what was about to happen last night, but I will still want to go home. I won't want to stay here in the fourteenth century just because I slept with you."

He was fairly certain he understood what she referred to, but wished for there to be no misunderstanding, especially since he absolutely wanted to *sleep with her*, if it meant what he imagined it did, which strangely had little to do with sleep.

"Sleep with ye?"

"Oh, um, I don't know what they call sex here, I mean now." She flopped her hand out helplessly, the one that held her borrowed shoes. "Hook up? Go all the way? Shag? No, that's a British term, I think. Make love? No, it can't be that. That's what I'm trying to avoid."

"I ken I understand now," he said. "And you want this with me?" Last night, she wasn't sure.

Autumn nodded, her mouth pressed tightly together.

The only thing that kept him silent and unmoving at that moment was wondering if he would, if he should, sleep with her right here at the loch. 'Twas conveniently secluded and he wouldn't have to wait until nightfall to find her in her bedchamber.

"Marcus? You kissed me last night and I assumed..." she began when his slow response made her fret. "Oh, well, this is embarrassing. Do you not want to...?"

His brows lowered severely. He stepped closer and lifted a finger between them to make his point as he said, "Last night, *ye* asked *me* to stop. Ye are the one who dinna ken aye or nae. I ken what I wanted when I kissed ye, Autumn. And when I kiss ye again—and I will—I'll ken then as well, what I want and the why of it."

Her eyes gradually widened with each word he spoke, with the growing intensity in his voice. "Damn," Autumn breathed, "for as simple and straightforward as that was, that was powerfully seductive. It was ten times more powerful, more seductive than any hundred words Jor—than anyone else has ever said to express desire to me."

He did not say aloud that maybe his desire for her was ten times greater than any other's. But he thought it.

"Marcus, I want you to seduce me," Autumn continued, a breathlessness creeping into her voice. "Honestly, I want you to ravish the hell out of me. But not unless we swear that we won't...develop feelings."

As she struggled increasingly with even respiration, so Marcus struggled with control of his anger at this extraordinary criterion.

He wasn't sure what Autumn saw or read in his stark visage, but she hurried out with, "Yeah, I know, little chance of you falling in love with me, right?" Her tone left no doubt about her feelings or what she thought about that possibility of that. "I'm not from this time. I don't speak the language. Obviously, we have nothing in common. I will never rest until I find a way to get home. Knee-knocking kiss aside, you spend a lot of time glowering at me, so I'm pretty sure you don't even like me." Her eyes widened with a spark when another thought occurred to her. "Oh, and my being from the future makes you suspicious—rightfully so. I don't blame you. Hard to get around that, right? You probably think I'm a sorceress or something like that."

Through gritted teeth, becoming incensed by her offensive prattle, he asked, "And ye dinna like me? Nae at all?"

Autumn twisted her face with mock distaste. "What's to like? I mean, sure, you're probably the most beautiful man I've ever seen. But that's simply genetics." She lowered her gaze to his bare arms. "And apparently a lot of training and exercise with the sword. Possibly the clean eating helps." She shook herself then and locked her gaze on his. "But really, I hardly know you at all. I'm not sure I want to. You're kind of moody, you hardly ever smile. And, hello, we literally just met, so there's that. It's not like over two days we could have developed feelings for each other."

And he understood perfectly and exactly what she was saying and why.

She wanted to protect herself.

"I see."

"And Marcus, that's what's perfect about it, right? It can simply be...well, call it whatever you want—an experiment, physical release, curiosity, whatever. It's fine so long as there's no emotions involved."

"No emotions," he mused.

"Right," she readily agreed. "I don't have any feeling for you. You don't have any feelings for me. It's perfect." She smiled with satisfaction. "There. I've just made it so that we can...um, kiss some more."

The dark slashes of his brows slanted downward.

And suddenly, his own plans were rather treading water until he considered what might be the consequences of *going all the way* with Autumn. Not for him. There would be few consequences. His heart was hard, was walled off to emotion, and had been for years. But for Autumn and her soft heart and her desire to go home, what would it mean?

Gruffly, Marcus turned his back to her, thinking the honorable thing to do would be to walk away. Mayhap *run away* should be considered. His heart was indeed hard—battered and scarred and weary—but damn, if he weren't sure that Autumn had somehow managed to knock beguilingly at the gate behind which it was locked.

Neither said a word for a long moment. The only sound heard was a small splash in the loch and the gently lapping waves rolling in.

"Marcus?" Autumn finally said behind him, closer than where he'd left her. "Do you...ever get the sense that—this is going to sound crazy, I know—but do you ever feel like us meeting wasn't simply...an accident? Do you feel it, too? That something exists between us? That might have been there even before we met? Not emotions, not feelings. I'm not talking about love or anything. But...actually, I can't even say that I felt as if I knew you because I didn't—I was terrified of you in the very beginning, of course—but I felt...I don't know, like there was some unspoken connection between us. I can't explain it, can't even describe it. It was simply a feeling I had. Even when I left you that first night, I had this sense in the back of my head that we would meet again. It's weird, I know. Actually, forget I brought it up at—"

She stopped speaking when Marcus turned around. His features were contorted in a savage grimace—bluidy hell, he hadn't imagined it!—while Autumn's eyes slowly widened.

"You felt it, too?" She guessed, a bit of awe coloring her words, making them whisper. "I can see it in your eyes."

He clenched his teeth.

A noisy breath escaped her, half cry, half laugh.

"Honestly, I thought I was only imagining—

He interrupted her small and anxious chatter by taking her face in his hands and crashing his mouth down on hers.

Chapter Fifteen

Her hands emptied themselves, her used clothing and Fiona's shoes falling to the ground. Her heart soared with relief and delight. And a need so powerful she marveled that she'd never noticed its absence with Jordan.

Though his lips were soft, Marcus's kiss was demanding. It was hungry and fierce, a collision of desire and yearning that sent shivers down Autumn's spine.

Marcus slid his hands from her face into her hair, tangling his fingers in the silken strands. Autumn wound her arms around his neck, pulling him closer, wanting to feel him pressed against her. The kiss deepened, becoming a dance of tongues and sighs. Today, he tasted like the honey ale consumed so liberally in this era, and, she thought whimsically, like a promise of tomorrow. His very essence, all this chiseled male flesh, intoxicated her senses.

Marcus's hands moved down her shoulders and arms to her waist, pulling her flush against him. The hard lines of his body connecting with hers sent shivers down her spine. His fingers trailed up her back, sending sparks of pleasure wherever they touched.

Their kiss grew even more heated, their breaths coming in ragged gasps as they lost themselves in each other. Desire flamed, building enthusiastically between her legs, aching and insistent. She wanted Marcus with a fierceness that consumed her, and she was exhilarated by his eagerness to demonstrate he felt the same.

Autumn's hands roamed over Marcus's chest, moaning when she encountered his leather jerkin and not only his strong body. She longed to feel more of him, to explore every inch of his body.

She found the laces of his jerkin and began to undo them, her fingers fumbling in their fervent haste.

Marcus broke their kiss just then, shrugging out of the leather vest. He rested his forehead against hers as he did so, pushing at her while they caught their breath. "Lass," he rasped, his breath hot on her face, "say to me ye dinna need a feather mattress and closed door, nor taper snuffed."

"I need you, Marcus," she answered. "Kissing me, touching me. I need more of this."

"Now?" he asked.

"Right now," Autumn said, breathless, meeting his glistening brown eyes. "Oh," she moaned. "But are you up for this? Your shoulder? Your thigh?"

"Both would protest if I were to stop," he assured her. "Every part of me would gripe and object if I dinna pursue this with ye."

He claimed her mouth again, his eyes languidly drifting closed. Autumn opened for him needfully, taking his tongue, giving her own. She closed her eyes and sank into him, only her hands between them, glorying in the hardness of his chest, scrunching up the linen of his tunic in her frenzy. With each kiss, every stroke of tongue and lick of lips, the world around them faded more into obscurity, until they heard and felt and knew only each other and the force of their passion.

She slid one hand downward. She questioned only briefly why she was so brazen, why she'd taken the initiative. The answer was obvious: she wanted him. She'd never known such need, such fantastic yearning for anything, for anyone, in all her life. His breeches were made of a heavier linen and there, where her hand meets and cups his erection, there is heat. Autumn moved her palm up and down and it was she who groaned in response, made to tingle with anticipation at the size and stiffness of him.

And then, as if his kiss had started a fire and her hand at his crotch had just added kindling, they began to throw off their clothes, lips and tongues attached and then parting as needed to remove her kirtle and his tunic, and for those few seconds when he cursed and had to take time to loosen and then toe off his boots. And then they stood facing each other, Marcus so magnificently bare-chested that Autumn nearly whimpered in appreciation.

He was, quite simply, a masterpiece, a work of art, a chiseled sculpture of power and might, so ridiculously beautiful. Each muscle was defined with precision and purpose. The top half of his chest was covered in short black hair, liberally enough that the word *hunky* sprang to mind, as if he were a cover model from the '70s or '80s. His flesh was often kissed by the sun, and even now, under a dreary sky, it gleamed with bronzed vitality. Even his scars did not—could not—detract from his glory. Autumn catalogued them, those badges of honor, short and long jagged lines, some pale, some stark white, some thin and others not. The newest ones, acquired only two days ago, were red and angry, several sewn with small stitches, the top of one arm still wrapped in a linen bandage. She knew no pity for how many scars he owned, but felt pride instead, for how brave he was, and because he kept on fighting.

Marcus closed the small space between them and placed his hands on Autumn, slowly, with near reverence, settling his fingers on her hips. Her chest rose and fell with ardent expectation. He began to bunch up the fabric of her shift, collecting and gathering the length of it and then lifting it over her head. He tossed it aside without looking, his gaze riveted to her body in a way that set her pulse racing and brought a blush to each part of her stroked by the raw and powerful worship of his gaze. Autumn was electrified by the admiration of his slow examination and was not disturbed at all that her nipples tightened for him. She was simply too undone by his stare. She believed she was pretty. She considered herself quite photogenic and was grateful for that. But never in her life had she been made to feel beautiful. Not until now.

Marcus parted his lips as he lifted his eyes to hers, his gaze filled with a luminous passion, and something else, which if given enough time to investigate, might have been discovered to be some accusation, as if he suspected her of keeping secrets from him, as if he were disappointed that she hadn't told him that he would very much like what he saw when she was naked.

Mechanically, Autumn smiled at him, a little in love with his bold appreciation.

His gaze did not leave her, and his expression did not change as he doffed his breeches, pushing them down and away, pulling his feet from them. Autumn had but a glimpse of his penis, wonderfully tall and erect, nestled within a patch of glossy black hair set over powerfully thick and long thighs, one protected by another bandage, before he approached her again.

Her mouth watered. The clenching between her legs was wholly involuntary.

Marcus lifted his hand and traced the remnants of the wound near her shoulder with the tip of his forefinger. Whisper soft, he ran his finger around the outline of the raised and puckered skin. Earlier, she and Charlotte had inspected it, deciding it looked well enough to be submerged during her bath. They'd judged it healed sufficiently that she did not apply a fresh bandage when her bath was done. Charlotte had said Autumn's few stitches should probably be removed in another day or two.

"A warrior, ye are," he said. "Or have been made."

Slowly, transfixed by his regard, Autumn shook her head. "I am not a warrior, Marcus. This is nothing but me being in the wrong place at the wrong time. You, though, and your wounds, old and new, large and small...you are a remarkable warrior king," she declared generously, believing it to be true.

He dropped his hand and regarded her with a speculative gaze.

"Are ye now in the wrong place at the wrong time?" He asked.

She shook her head again, a slow inviting smile coming. "Absolutely not."

He placed his hands on her sides again, above her hips, his fingers sliding almost under her arms while his thumbs sat just at the side of her breasts, moving slowly back and forth. To her great dismay, he pursued nothing else with her breasts. He used his hands to draw her closer again, their bare chests meeting for the first time. This drew a ragged gasp from Autumn, for how solid and warm was his flesh against her suddenly aching nipples.

He brought his mouth down on hers again, their kiss enlivened by their nakedness. Marcus backed her up as he kissed her, his strong fingers digging into her hips to move her, while his tongue explored deep and hungrily inside her mouth.

Sex was not new to Autumn. Sex with a good-looking guy was not new to her, either. But this was Marcus, a man so far above and beyond merely good-looking, a man unknown to her before three days ago, and this was the fourteenth century, and so naturally a part of her wondered if she was merely dreaming.

No, she decided, it wasn't a dream. Had it a been a dream, she wouldn't have been able to feel the exact and scorching heat of his kiss or the passion in his hands as he trailed them around her back and down over her ass. If it were a dream, it would have been hazy, the way her body responded to his touch. In a dream, she would not experience emotions such as this, wouldn't have felt that she burned with yearning. This was real and Autumn thanked God, or Fate, whoever had brought them together. She felt everything. Her senses were on fire. Marcus smelled of leather with a faint sandalwood note. He was hard and strong, his chest, his hands, his cock, but his kiss was sensual, decadent.

If she were dreaming, she was pretty sure she wouldn't have known the absolute and breathtaking beauty of the first time Marcus touched her nipples, grazing the pads of his thumbs roughly over the hardened pebbles. Her core tightened again, at the surface and all the way to her center, aching for him, to have him inside her. When he lowered his face to her breasts, she threaded her fingers in his hair. His clever teeth plucked at her nipple while his hand squeezed and lifted the whole tit. He used his tongue on the peak while his teeth held her nipple to his mouth.

Autumn whispered his name—a dream in itself, to sigh his name while he did these things to her—and withdrew her hands from his hair to grasp at his lean hips, pulling his erection against her.

Marcus groaned in response, the guttural quality of that sound seeming as a mating call to Autumn.

The kiss was broken but the fire between them continued to burn, even as Marcus turned, bent, and arranged a few pieces of their discarded clothing into a pallet of sorts upon the clay earth. When he faced her again, four hands reached out simultaneously with need. Marcus gently laid her down on the makeshift bed, their eyes locked in silent communication, a heated exchange signifying a want, an expectation of ecstasy. Autumn opened her arms to him.

He returned to her mouth, kissing her with renewed fervor, gliding his tongue over her lips as he moved his hand lower, across her smooth abdomen and between her legs. Immediately, his fingers were claimed by heat and then moistness as he glided them over her lips and further, to the center of her. She lifted her hips, granting him greater access, oblivious to the unforgiving ground and the crisp air.

They groaned together, against each other's mouth, at this touch. Autumn's groan evolved into a moan of pleasure when he opened her and pushed one finger inside her. His hand and fingers massaged her with expertise. Every inch of her body trembled with need and want. He teased her, coaxed her, flowing and ebbing, again and again until Autumn clasped her fingers around his wrist. He fought against her hand, until she managed to push his away.

"I don't want to come yet," she told him. "I want to come when you're inside me."

His dark eyes searched her face until she pulled him to her and kissed him,

Autumn grazed her hands over the corded muscles of his neck and shoulders and ran them down his muscular arms. She wedged one hand between them, wanting so badly to touch him again, more. Her fingers met with the compelling proof of his desire, and she closed her fingers around the velvety hard length of him. Autumn stroked with a tender frenzy, and he hardened further in her hand, imbuing Autumn with a sense of power when before now, she believed she had none.

A ragged curse was squeezed from between his clenched teeth. "*Jesu*, lass." He lifted his face to Autumn and kissed her senseless once more. "Tell me ye want me inside ye," was commanded against her lips.

Marcus made love as he went about every other thing in his life, with dedicated intensity. Autumn was definitely in love with that.

"Yes, Marcus. God, how I want you."

His hand abandoned her breast. The other was drawn away from between her legs. Marcus rose and shifted and settled his magnificent body over her. With a sigh of complete and ridiculously happy surrender, Autumn opened her legs to allow his to nestle between. His cock seemed to have a life of its own, straining against her. He pushed it down between her legs, teasing her as he stroked it against her folds.

"I want ye wet, lass," he breathed. "I want to drive hard inside ye."

"Christ. Yes. Please, Marcus," she whimpered needfully in response. Her eyes were closed, her back arched. Her voice was wispy, had no volume to it at all. She answered further by lifting her hips and squeezing his shaft between her legs, riding him from below. She needed him inside her, more than life or breath just now. She craved that ultimate connection with him, holding him within.

Heat radiated from his body, enveloping her. His hair fell over his face as he watched her, and she quivered with pleasure.

"Enough, Marcus," she begged. "Come inside me."

He growled, lifted his hips, and stared deep into her eyes as he sank deeply into her as if he'd done so a thousand times before. Their bodies became one, a perfect fit, as if they were two halves of a whole, destined to be united just like this. He withdrew and plunged forward slowly, and locked his gaze with her, his elbows on the ground on either side of her. Even as he continued to push in and out, filling her with so much heat and sensation, he lowered his head and kissed her, tenderly now, as if with gratefulness. When he lifted his head, taking his mouth from her, the fire between them continued to burn. Their eyes met again, a silent exchange of desire. Autumn saw only pleasure in his gaze.

And then the muscles of his arms bulged as he straightened and lifted his upper body from her. He paused but a moment before some purpose overtook him, and he reared back. Autumn bent her knees at his side at the same moment he pushed her legs up with his hands at her shins. He thrust again, harder, and again, filling her more deeply and more completely than she ever imagined possible. It felt as if her insides did not expand to welcome him but contracted to keep him. Autumn unraveled inside, her senses were inundated with all of him—his hot body; the way his shaft filled her, claimed her; the ferocity of his features; the hissed breaths as paradise beckoned. She clawed at his shoulders and panted, raising her hips higher and quicker, to reach that tantalizing finale.

This—right now with Marcus—was perfection. Every glorious bit of it.

Their bodies rocked together in perfect synchrony, faster and closer until she cried out with her release, her orgasm engulfing her. Liquid fire coursed through her veins.

She convulsed around him, whispering his name, her legs turned to jelly so that she had to fight to keep up with him.

"Come with me, Marcus," she pleaded. "God, it feels so good."

He grunted and stole her breath with a searing kiss just as he thrust rigidly once, twice, and then stabbed at her a third time. Marcus stiffened, and groaned, "Bluidy hell," against her lips before he sagged against her. His face dropped next to hers, cheek to cheek.

Lazily, Autumn wrapped her arms around him. Neither moved for a long time. Neither spoke. No words were needed. Autumn could not imagine words that could adequately, properly describe what she'd just experienced. It was more than pleasure, more than titillation and a climax. Now they were truly connected, she imagined, as she'd somehow sensed they were meant to be, as had been inevitable maybe.

At length and with energy Autumn knew she didn't possess right now, he swept an arm under her and scooted her upward on their bed of clothes. When he collapsed this time, it was only his head and hair falling on her chest.

Autumn scratched the skin of his shoulder, meeting with more than one old scar. While he remained unmoving for another few minutes, she traced the jagged pattern of one particular scar on his back, just below his right shoulder. She closed her eyes and followed the lines of it over and over until she was sure she could draw it from memory, likening it somewhat to the shape of a boomerang. Or the letter L, laid on its side.

Finally, Marcus lifted his face to her and promptly astonished her and warmed her heart with the next words he uttered.

"I want to sleep with ye at night," he said, his voice low, the rumble of it felt all along her still-trembling body. "This night and the next, many more. I want ye to lay your fingers upon me as ye have, upon my scars, and trace patterns until I find this same peace again."

Autumn's eyes watered and her nose burned.

Possibly those were the most poignant, the most profound words ever spoken to her. He hadn't said he wanted to get naked every night, have sex in a hundred different positions, or screw her until she was bow-legged. He'd found peace in her arms, and he wanted more of that.

Solemnly, she nodded.

She cupped his cheeks and pulled him to her kiss.

***

For quite some time, more than only a few months, maybe for more than even a few years, he rather expected that he would die. More sooner than later if he had to guess. He could envision no future beyond days or weeks, or the coming harvest, or the next season. The odds were simply—and tremendously—stacked against him. He would die by the hand of a MacPhail or more probably by way of the English, since individual fights in the war far outnumbered the times he'd directly lifted his sword against the MacPhails.

Thus, he feared that even if Autumn did want to stay, though she'd made it very clear that she did not, he had little to offer her. Though he had no idea how it might be accomplished, he reluctantly acknowledged that it was in her best interests to return to her own time. He wasn't ready to let her go, not now, not yet, but he thought eventually—soon—he should do what he could to help her make that journey. However, the fact that he could not conceive of a way to make that happen for her, short of summoning a bevy of witches—and even on that he would no doubt prove inept—did not give him leave to put the matter aside indefinitely.

But it didn't have to be today, he decided, glancing sideways down the head table to where Autumn was once again seated between Charlotte and Eadric at last meal. He'd thought about having her sit next to him. He wanted her close, within reach of his hand. Their coupling was only hours old. Satiation had been fleeting; he wanted more, would never *not* desire her, having been so amazed by the strength of her passion. No sweeter dream would ever come to him greater than the sound of his name being sighed from her lips as she'd found her release.

He was made to feel young, much younger than his actual years, by the coy glances Autumn kept sneaking at him. Twice, Charlotte had noticed them and had turned a pleased and knowing gaze in his direction. Those from Charlotte he pretended not to notice. Those tantalizing ones from Autumn he would seek retribution for later. 'Twas not fair that she should taunt him all through supper, causing him to twist and wince with occasional discomfort for the hitch in his breeches.

Still, he managed to put forth a laird-ly demeanor, wearing his customary scowl whenever he gazed out over the assembly. Let them believe he was still contemplating revenge against the MacPhails—he was, and he would—but for a wee bit, he didn't mind smiling behind the façade, as joyful as he'd ever been. 'Twould be as fleeting as had been the force and effects of his own climax, this happiness, he was sure. He was bound to die, not intended to know many years beyond what he claimed now. 'Twas simply the way it would be, he'd imagined for some time.

And she was bound to go. She was strong-willed, determined to get home, spoke of a large and loving family that would mourn her if she stayed gone. Marcus had no idea how to measure the value of that—a large and loving family— having little by which to compare it. His family had been fractured, gone one by one, so long now that Marcus couldn't remember the last time they were all together. Had they ever been?

He did not escort Autumn up the stairs when the meal was done or follow directly when she departed the hall. He didn't mind if Reid and Charlotte knew of their liaison but presumed that Autumn would rather the general population of Balla Àrd did not label her a leman or jade if they should learn what they'd done this afternoon or what he planned to do with her tonight.

Thirty minutes after Autumn left the hall, Marcus quietly opened the door to her bedchamber.

He found her standing near the lone window, her back to the chamber. She turned her head, but her arms and hands remained perched on the inclined slope of the window sill.

There was an insolent tilt to her head and though a smile was discerned in the dim golden light, she said to him, "Very impolite of you to make me wait half an hour."

Marcus stepped inside and closed the door behind him, leaning against it. "And now ye will withhold your favors from me?"

Autumn laughed, the sound low but rich. She pivoted fully from the window but did not move away from it.

"Favors is it?" She asked, her hands behind her.

She was dressed in only her shift. Her hair was loose and fell like a gilded curtain over her shoulders.

Marcus shrugged, pleased to simply look upon her. "Seemed as a favor to me, to have given yourself so freely."

She laughed again, this time with a bit of mockery he soon understood was directed at herself.

"Given myself? No, Marcus, I took." She stepped away from the window and walked with tormenting slowness toward him. "I was greedy. Hungry. Eager. I took, I grabbed, and I seized." She stopped directly in front of him, her bare feet nearly touching the tip of his boots, so close he had only to lift his hand to pull her near.

Before he could, Autumn leaned into him, melting splendidly against him.

She tipped her face up to his at the same time she boldly rubbed her hand downward. His body twitched to life. Autumn maneuvered her hand under his tunic and inside the waistband of his breeches.

"Do you mind if I take more?" Her languid voice dripped with seduction.

"I am pleased to be at your mercy," he said, enjoying her sweet game.

Her lips curved languidly while her eyes glittered with sensual purpose. "I was hoping you would say that."

And she went to her knees before him.

Marcus exhaled roughly and dropped his head back against the door.

Jesu, but he might well die by her hand—or mouth—he thought as his heart hammered inside his chest.

Chapter Sixteen

Delicately, Autumn traced her fingers over the scar on the back of his shoulder, reading his history. A tranquil warmth unfurled inside him, soothing his soul. The softness of her touch upon the rugged landscape of his back was somehow a comforting contrast, as if the tenderness of her caress would or could diminish the horrific story connected to the scar, to that particular one or any of the others.

Though he knew dawn approached, Marcus didn't open his eyes. He wasn't ready yet to relinquish her touch. He remained as he was, on his stomach, with his arms under his head, his face angled in her direction.

He hadn't slept well, despite how gloriously exhausted he'd been after hours spent gaining all that exquisite carnal knowledge of Autumn. She'd worn many emotions since he'd met her, but certainly her initial fear or that quiet primness she sometimes adopted, or how moved she'd been by the funeral, hadn't really prepared him for how passionate she would prove as a bedmate. Even the manner in which she'd danced didn't fully infuse him with any expectation that she would be so excellently bold and fearless in his arms.

Despite a desire to do so, he could not remain abed all day with Autumn. After some time, in which she seemed not to tire of her cathartic caressing any more than he did, Marcus opened his eyes.

She was there, right in front of him, propped up on her elbow. Her shoulder was bare above the sheet, which was trapped under her arm and covered her breasts. Her hair floated around her, charmingly disheveled, a large portion of it laying between them, some of it upon the arm that was bent under his head.

"Methinks you've been awake for longer than only a moment," she greeted him, a teasing glint in her gray eyes.

He didn't move. "Aye."

"You were afraid if you opened your eyes, I would stop." She tapped her finger twice and then resumed her small strokes over his scar.

"Nae afraid." He feared nothing, he believed. "But I was pleased to be indulged a while longer."

"Only fair," she conceded, explaining, "since you indulged me so superbly last night. Twice."

Marcus grinned. He had played the generous lover, had been thrilled to do so, had reaped benefits beyond his imagining. He raised himself onto his elbows and leaned to the left at the same time Autumn slanted herself toward him. Their lips met in a lingering kiss.

"You're making it very hard for me to disavow any appreciation of the fourteenth century, by the way," she told him.

"You would rather ken a constant aversion to it?"

"Well, sort of. I wasn't trying to hate it," she qualified, and winced a bit, "but then I hadn't seen too much to love."

"To whom should we speak about your unfortunate welcome?"

"I guess I bring my complaints to you." At the arching of his brow, she said, "I mean you are the laird, the local authority, the most powerful man in all of...?" She raised a brow at him, expecting him to provide the answer.

"Balla Àrd," he replied promptly, with a wee self-deprecation.

"Hm, I guess I'll have to register my grievances to someone higher up the food chain."

"Nae," he countered, "ye just admitted you now have a wee appreciation for this time."

"Wee is only a little." She sighed dramatically, tilting her head back. "Ah, if only there was someone—anyone—who could give me *more* reasons to appreciate the Middle Ages."

Marcus sat up, swinging his legs over the side of the bed, which sadly saw her hand slide down and away from his back. He glanced over his shoulder at her. "Nae anyone, but me," he said to her. "And ye will have to wait until tonight. I will supply motives aplenty."

Autumn smiled with beguiling satisfaction.

He yawned, considering the wee playful exchange, unable to recall another time in his life when he'd been so uselessly idle with another person and to such pleasing effect, or, indeed, if he'd ever before engaged in bedchamber banter with any woman he'd lain with.

"I lied to you," she said behind him, the mischievous tone now absent from her voice.

Marcus swung his gaze round to her, his heart skipping a beat.

"I do like you," she expounded. "And you were right, I inserted that ridiculous prerequisite—that this should only be physical—essentially to give myself license to do something I knew was only going to cause me...trouble."

His response to this came first as a constricting in his chest, relief known that her confessed fib was only this, and then a rare sense of joy for the content of the lie. But he didn't let himself smile, didn't show any reaction at all. *Trouble*, he had to imagine, might be similar to what was his, an irksome premonition that Autumn Winters was made in such a way as to have the potential to crack his shell.

His limited previous experience with females—those whose company was not attained by the exchange of coin—all of which had ended poorly, harshly, meant that he guarded himself well. Trouble, then, would likely start with him lowering his walls. While he didn't fear vulnerability, he did naturally have a trust issue with Autumn. In spite of Charlotte and Reid's supporting testimony, Marcus still could not embrace the idea that time travel was possible, which meant that part of him believed she did lie.

And yet, his greatest reluctance to inviting *trouble* stemmed from his rather firm belief that he would not live long enough to know joy, and that he had not sufficient time to relish a bond with someone who was not critical to what he was compelled to do while he lived, fight for just causes. The weight of duty, the fragility of life, the fear of loss all combined to make him least likely to wish for a bond with another, certainly not one who might possibly be from another time.

"'Tis nae allowed, lass," he said mildly, his disquiet disguised as indifference. "Ye made the rules."

At her crestfallen expression, which he could not long suffer, he stood from the bed and playfully smacked her gorgeous bottom. "Get up, wench," he said lightly. "The day waits for nae one."

He began to dress, glancing out the window, now gray with the dawn. Autumn was quiet behind him.

To fill the awkward silence, he informed her, "We plan to move ere the sun rises."

"Where are you going? Who is *we*?"

"The Nicholson and I will lead a large contingent to where the MacPhails have intriguingly made camp, upon their own land, but well removed from their keep."

As he pulled on his breeches, he heard a swift whisper of noise, Autumn sitting up, he imagined.

"To fight?" She asked, her voice laced with a deep concern. "Marcus, are you going to war? Now? And you're just telling me this now, as you're getting ready to leave?"

The part of him that was self-directed and self-reliant, that kept himself closed off to others, imagined that he owed her neither apology nor explanation. The other part of him, that element that emerged in her presence, most prominently when she was in his arms, sought to appease her.

"I dinna expect a fight," he said, which was partly true, "though we will go prepared for such. 'Twould nae be war, at any rate, even if a battle should arise."

He turned, pulling his tunic over his head, and found Autumn gaping at him. She was indeed sitting up, holding the soft cotton sheet in front of her, atop her breasts.

"You're taking your entire army, though? Right?" She asked. "And all the Nicholson force?"

"Nae all," he said as he sat at the foot of the bed and dug his feet into his boots. "I canna leave Balla Àrd unprotected."

"Yes, you can. You should," she suggested hastily. "We'll be fine. Take everyone. Take all the soldiers and all the arrows or weapons, whatever. Oh, God. Why couldn't I have brought a gun instead of a stupid camera?"

"Dinna speak with emotion, lass," Marcus said softly, reminding her of her own expectations of what should be allowed to happen between them. "It has nae place in this, per your own instruction."

Her mouth twisted with frustration. Her hand fisted where it held the sheet. "Right. Of course."

His boot laces tied, Marcus rose and fetched his belt and sword, fastening that to his hips. He would stop off at his chamber, where he'd left his leather breastplate.

"'Tis nae but a scouting expedition," he said dismissively as he approached her on the bed.

She held herself rigidly, either tormented by dread or because she disliked his glibness.

"But ye should still send me off with a kiss," he prompted as he bent over her, putting his fists on the feather mattress on either side of her.

And whatever had thinned her beautiful lips and stiffened her back dissipated. Autumn's shoulders drooped downward, and her eyes glistened more with worry for him than frustration at him. She lifted her face and her hands and laid her palms against his cheeks, the sheet sliding down her breasts when she let it go.

"I'm not sure if I do like you anymore," she said. "But will you please be super careful and make sure you come back to m—to Balla Àrd today?"

Marcus kissed her nose. "I promised to give ye reasons aplenty to adore this century. I have nae plans to nae return."

"Thank you," she said, but was only mildly appeased it seemed.

When she opened her mouth again, Marcus covered it with his own, giving her a slow and tantalizing kiss. His lips were persuasive, the pressure meant to be reassuring. It was but a moment before Autumn relaxed, distracted as had been his intent. Soon enough, Marcus, too, was lost, the sweet kiss quickly becoming intoxicating, until he nearly forgot his objective.

Breaking away abruptly, Marcus pressed one more parting kiss to her lips and turned toward the door, clenching his jaw against the sight of her wickedly alluring breasts and their hardened peaks. 'Twas not easy to walk away from her, but he did, closing the door softly behind him.

Ten minutes later, in the wispy fog that floated about the bailey, Marcus, mounted upon his destrier with Gibbon at his side, discussed with his captain how they would approach the odd MacPhail camp.

"From the sky, would suit my preferences," Gibbon said. "In lieu of that, we are left with little choice but only two sides."

"East and south?" Marcus guessed.

"Aye. And I dinna want to leave only those wounded as the house guard," Gibbon went on, "so we will have in the lines some of those sliced up nae but a few days ago. But we'll disperse them evenly, east and south, in those units, and keep them back of the line."

"And that is where ye will be," Marcus instructed, in consideration of Gibbon's injury, from which Marcus knew Gibbon was not fully recovered.

"I'll nae be made to—" Gibbon began to protest.

Firmly, Marcus, interjected, "Then ye may remain here." While Gibbon snarled silently at Marcus for giving him no choice, Marcus reminded him with false cheeriness, "There will be other fights. Ye'll be able to redden your sword again."

Reid walked his horse away from the stables and toward Marcus just as Gibbon moved off a bit to inquire of Lewin why he wasn't wearing his helm.

"Are ye wearing the same clothing as yesterday?" Reid asked directly, wearing a smirk that Marcus felt compelled to smack off his face.

But he said nothing, only shot his friend an annoyed glare.

"It matters nae to me," Reid said, unwilling to let it go, still wearing that maddening grin. "Aye, but Charlotte will be pleased."

"If ye hadn't so ably come at so impeccable a time," Marcus said, "if you had nae saved us from total ruin, I might be asking ye when you plan to depart Balla Àrd."

"And yet I did," said Reid smugly, "and so ye will nae so easily be rid of me."

"Mayhap I will disturb Charlotte," Marcus remarked, "incur her wrath in some manner that would hasten your leave taking."

"I would suggest," Reid replied, all good humor gone, "if ye value your hide at all, that ye make nae attempt to dismay my bride."

Marcus returned Reid's glower, suggesting to his friend that surely, he knew him better than that.

Not long after, Marcus and Reid led the combined army from the gates of Balla Àrd. They rode out in a two-man formation so that it was several minutes before all had cleared the gate and the doors could be secured, the portcullis lowered. While they moved at first with some swiftness, there was no opportunity for any reasonably voiced conversation. Within a few miles of the target, however, when they slowed their march to a walk, and before they split into two groups, Marcus said to Reid, "If anything should happen to me, today or at any time—when it does," he said, reflecting his internal belief, "I need ye to assure that Balla Àrd survives. Petition the Bruce," he instructed. "Autumn claims he will be our king one day. Take Balla Àrd for the Nicholsons."

Reid swung his head around sharply. He stared hard at Marcus, as if coming to grips with something, before he said, "Charlotte said the same. About Robert Bruce."

They stared at each other, each reaching separate but similar conclusions about what this meant, to have this told by two different people. Neither dared to suggest that either Charlotte or Autumn might have lied.

"*Jesu*," Marcus breathed. He wasn't sure he had believed it, but to have it all but validated by another. "Petition the Bruce," he repeated, coming back to the matter at hand, "now in preparation, or when the time comes. Make Balla Àrd yours."

"And what of yer lass?" Reid asked.

"Aye," Marcus said, nodding tightly, "assume responsibility for her as well. Charlotte would nae have it any other way, I might guess."

"Dinna get dead," Reid commanded gruffly. "I dinna ken I can manage more than Charlotte."

Marcus was made to grin. "She does keep ye on your toes, does she nae?"

Reid's lips curved again, this time with a serene satisfaction. "She does. And though I want to, I can find nae fault with the arrangement."

Marcus chuckled, wondering if he might possibly, presently, understand his friend and his statement as he might not have been able to do even so recently as a week ago.

***

"So you rode all the way out there and…and nothing?" Autumn asked very late that same night, looking for details to be added to the sparse ones he had given her an hour ago.

Marcus and Reid and their combined army had only returned then, well after midnight. Though she'd managed to keep the heaviest worry at bay throughout the day, in Charlotte's company and industriously moving from one chore to the next, what had seemed achievable during the day had become more difficult in the darkened hours, after she and Charlotte had said good night and had each closed the doors to their private bedchambers.

Charlotte had left her with some hope before she'd said good night. "If anything untoward *had* happened, we would have known by now. They are not that far removed from Balla Àrd. Same as happened at the beginning of the week, if they had been ambushed or outnumbered, someone—at least *one* person—would have made it back to the keep to warn of that trouble. My guess is they're camping themselves, keeping watch, or they've set up some perimeter around the MacPhail fortress."

Presently, Autumn's hand was linked with Marcus's, their fingers entwined as they lay in her bed, naked and sated after their lovemaking. Their sex tonight had been wild with need, with no sense that there would be any lessening of desire anytime soon. When he was inside her, he was hers completely as she'd yet to feel at any other time. Her orgasm had left her weak and drained, and she felt she hadn't yet recuperated fully.

She snuggled against him, her head in the crook of his shoulder. Her hand was linked with his, their fingers entwined. Autumn found herself captivated by his hands and not only for what magic they worked on her body. She was struck by the size and strength of it, yet equally entranced by the gentleness, the soft finesse of his every touch.

"They were nae only unseen, but little evidence could be found to say they stayed at all where Osgar had spied them," Marcus said. He paused to yawn before he continued "Because we could make nae sense of it, we decided to explore further. A risk, aye, going deeper into MacPhail territory, but I ken they are up to nae guid."

"Well, I can't say I'm not happy about it," Autumn said. "Not running into them, I mean."

"The fight will come," Marcus stated emphatically, with something more than only expectation. "'Tis inevitable and thus, today only delayed what must come."

The fight will come. How remarkable that he was able to utter these words so casually, as if he only reminded her that rain, eventually, would fall. How was it possible to be so desensitized that speaking about an event that very possibly might cause death could be mentioned with so much calmness?

"And you would have it done sooner rather than later," she supposed.

"Aye. I want it settled. Would have been more agreeable to beget revenge in that regard, upon an open field today, the MacPhails being the ones outnumbered and overrun this time. It would have made the siege of their keep more likely to succeed."

Every bit of post-orgasm lethargy left her. "You are going to lay siege to their castle?"

"Aye. But that will need a few more days of planning," said Marcus, scratching idly at his chest where her hand was not, yawning again. "A few more days to have all those wounded at the hand of the MacPhails made healthier by time, so that they might exact their own vengeance. Moreover, I've charged the carpenters to construct two siege engines. I expect another few days to wait on those machines."

"Line up your ducks," Autumn remarked absently, terribly distracted now, again, by his want of vengeance and her fear for him.

"My ducks?"

"Oh, it's just a saying. Like, get everything in order. My brother says that a lot." And Sean never said, *Get your ducks in a row*, but always the other way, as she just had.

"Ye said ye have a large family, so ye must have more than only a brother."

She nodded against his chest. "I have three brothers. And they are all married, so I have three sisters-in law. Between my three brothers and their wives, there are seven children, so I am an aunt many times over. And of course I have my parents."

"What kind of men are your brothers?"

"Well, first and foremost," she said, pleased to expound on this subject and abandon the distressing talk of war, "as their little sister, and with nine years between the youngest brother and me, my opinion of them might be skewed. They were, growing up, sometimes awful." She felt him stiffen. "Not like that, whatever you're thinking now. Just typical big brothers. They loved to torment me—all in good fun, they loved to say. My father assures me it was good practice, to ready me for the world. If I could handle their constant brotherly bullying, my father thought, I could handle anything."

"And so ye manage to survive in a century far removed from your own, thrive almost, and any gratitude for this should be given to these brothers?"

"Hah. Absolutely not. Anyway, as adults, they are really great. Of course, they still can be annoying, but I really do adore them. They are all solid citizens, if you will. Adam is a doctor—that's like a healer here and now, but much more advanced. Michael works for my dad's company, which I'm sorry, you would never understand in a million years of me trying to explain it. And Sean, he's closest to me in age, he and his wife own a restaurant, which is um, I don't know what to compare it to. Oh, it's like an inn. They have inns here, right? And they serve food? Well, a restaurant is like an inn, it serves food—except their inn doesn't have rooms—chambers, I mean. They don't have people staying overnight."

"And your father? He is a guid man?"

Autumn nodded, bringing an image of her father to mind. "He is the best. I might be biased, of course. But my father is smart and funny and the king of dad jokes. The jokes are awful, mind you, but the way he delivers them almost with giddy delight, is seriously, the cutest thing I've ever seen." Her heart ached then, thinking of her father. She fought down a rising wave of panic and then was happy that Marcus asked more questions to divert her.

"And ye are nae wed?" He pursued. "And ye live at home and manage the keep with your màthair and these wives of your brothers?"

"What? Oh, okay, no." She turned around in his arms, propping herself up against his chest, one arm thrown across him. "It doesn't work like that anymore. I have a career. A job. I go to work every day."

Marcus's expression was nonplussed.

"And everyone lives in their own house. Or, at least, my family does. Most families do. Michael and Amy have their own house. Adam and Melanie have their place. I have my own loft, which is like a small house, one of many in a large building."

"Ye live alone? But who defends ye?"

"No one defends me. It's different in the future." How had those three words become so easy to say? *In the future.*

"And what is this career to which you go to every day?"

Autumn considered how to dumb down her job description. If he didn't know TV and likely had no idea what a newspaper was, the precursor to news stations and channels, how could she make him understand what a journalist or reporter did?

"I am a reporter for the local news, which means I tell the people what is happening all around them, good, bad, and ugly. The news, in general, whether written or broadcasted, informs people about politics, the weather, crime, sports—all sorts of things." She gave her answer some thought, only able to add, "Honestly, Marcus, again I can't even conceive of a way to break it down to make you understand. And that's not at all because I don't think you're intelligent enough, but only because so much had happened—there are so many inventions—between now and then, over the next seven hundred years, that it likely won't mean anything to you. Suffice it to say, I'm the town crier."

"Frankly, lass, the more ye speak about your time, the more improbable it seems."

Autumn laughed. "Oh, but just wait until I start telling you about planes, trains, and automobiles. And that's probably nothing compared to telephones, TV, and the internet. Your head would explode."

Marcus was horrified. "Heads explode in the future?"

A bark of laughter burst from her. "Good Lord, no. I just mean you would be amazed, overwhelmed."

While the hand beneath her scratched idly at her back, Marcus proposed, "Name one thing, lass, one thing from the future that would, if seen by me, drop my jaw with awe."

She liked very much how engaged he was, that he showed such a genuine interest in her family, and now with this, maybe even her time.

"I guess I would name an airplane. There are probably greater things to strike awe in your heart, but I think I can properly describe an airplane that it might make sense to you."

"And what is an airplane?"

"All right, bear with me. Think about how an eagle soars across the sky."

"Aye."

"So we know that things can fly. Well, in the future they've created a machine that flies."

"An arrow flies, lass," he reminded her.

"Yes it does. But this machine, the airplane, is massive. It flies across the sky, can cross oceans and mountains and entire countries in only hours. But the kicker, see, is that airplanes can carry people."

As expected, Marcus frowned, with some combination of disbelief and suspicion, as if he might suppose she was making it up.

"It's true," Autumn said. "Some planes are smaller and can hold just a few people. Then there are huge planes that can fly hundreds. When I came to Scotland, I flew on a plane with more than two hundred passengers."

Marcus remained dubious. But though he looked as if he might have questions about an airplane, he asked nothing.

Autumn looked down at his furry chest, scraping the front of her hand over just the hair, the short black fur tickling her palm.

"When I was a kid," she said, "my best friend and I would lie on our backs in the grass and watch planes fly overhead. Some of them leave in their wake a, well, it's called a contrail, but it looks like a straight line, white cloud of dust. Kimmy and I would watch the planes go by and make up stories about who might be in those airplanes. We would plan trips of our own, flying all over the world. I had so many travel dreams when I was younger." A short laughed emerged. "Funny, I never imagined the fourteenth century as a destination."

"Hm," was all Marcus said.

Autumn chuckled softly, patting his chest. "Yeah, I get it. You'll need a moment to digest that one."

Whatever he did with that news about an airplane, Autumn was not to know. After a moment, he returned to the subject of her brothers.

"Your brothers—they are nae soldiers?"

"No. Not that we don't have soldiers in my time. Every country has a military force. But it's not like here, where ambush and attack are, apparently, daily possibilities, and if it happened, regular people, like these farmers here, would pick up a weapon and become a soldier." She wrinkled her nose, considering this. "Although, not that they wouldn't—regular people. If push came to shove, I guess. If something awful happened."

"Your brothers are honorable men?"

"I like to think so," was her initial response. She said next, "Actually, I know they are. They work hard, are faithful and loving and reliable. All three of them are good sons and good fathers."

A hint of a grin teased the corners of his sensual mouth. "But nae guid brothers from a sister's viewpoint?"

"No, they really are very good brothers...nowadays. Tell me about your family, Marcus."

"'Tis nae much to tell. My grandsire—Baltair he was—was more a father to me than my own." He paused, his thoughts wandering, maybe back in time. "When he passed, so too did much of life. My own sire was nae the man his father was but ye dinna want to hear about those sorry years, when he lived. When my sire fell under the sword at Dunbar, I did nae weep with sorrow but gratitude."

Autumn's heart ached for him even as she wondered if Marcus's scowling persona was only one he'd developed while his father had lived. It wasn't false—Marcus was a severe and savage man—but there was more to him than met the eye. She'd been wonderfully met by the tender and loving Marcus while in his arms.

"Tell me something about your grandfather," she said, "a memory or anecdote, maybe, that still makes you smile today."

A beautiful, boyish smile evolved. "My grandsire spent much of his time trying to convince me that he had fought with dragons in his youth."

Autumn smiled. "And did you believe him? Maybe when you were very young?"

"Like as nae, I did at one time. But as I ken on it now, I wonder why I never challenged him on it. He claimed that dragons breathed fire and were like wolves, powerful predators, but likened to the hawk as well, able to glide or soar across the sky, much like this airplane you speak of."

"And now," Autumn asked, "if you believe in time-travel, or at least entertain the possibility of it, does it follow that you now question whether dear old granddad might have been telling the truth about dragons?" Autumn was certainly considering it at the moment.

"Shite," he murmured, sounding disgruntled. "I wish ye had nae put that question in my head, lass."

"I'm sure it was all make believe." Autumn leaned up and kissed him, just a peck, feeling that she was beyond sleepy right now. She liked very much how he saw her coming and lifted his head off the pillow, meeting her kiss almost halfway. She then turned over, pushing her back and butt up against Marcus. "Snuggle me, Marcus. I'm so tired my eyes are crossed, but I want to feel your arms around me."

He obliged, shifting on the bed and fitting his hard body against her, wrapping his arm around her, cradling her with exquisite warmth and tenderness.

Marcus said, his breath fanning against her hair. "I dinna ken if this will work, lass, if sleep is the objective, and ye continue to wiggle your bottom as ye are."

A sleepy grin was roused. "I'm trying to get comfortable."

"And making me nae comfortable with your attempts."

She settled, relaxing in his embrace.

"Better?"

"Nae really," he said. He moved the arm that covered her, bringing it under her arm, and cupping her breast, the one that leaned against the mattress. And then he sighed. "Better now."

Autumn smiled.

Chapter Seventeen

"Charlotte, are you sure I should be doing this?" Autumn asked.

Charlotte raised her green eyes from her own project, leaning forward to steal a glance at Autumn's. She did not hide her grin upon seeing the mess Autumn had made of the tunic. She was supposed to be repairing the tunic by sewing but it looked as if a toddler had been given needle and thread and told to have at it. *Have at it* was something Autumn's mother might say to her grandkids on those occasions when she covered the kitchen table with paper and markers and kid-friendly paints and paint brushes.

"My needlework is only slightly better," Charlotte said with a shrug, "and only because I've had a couple of years to practice. Whenever I really botch up one of Reid's shirts, I just tell him that one is now part of his work clothes collection." She lifted her hands, expressing another thought, giving an indication that her remark hadn't been as effective as she might have hoped. "Of course, he reminded me that he doesn't have a separate wardrobe for different activities."

Autumn smiled. "Oh, there's not one set of clothes for lairding around the castle and another for when he's wielding a sword?"

"Nope. But just do the best you can," Charlotte suggested. "I want to get back to Elspeth's place and check on Patrick but I want to wait to see if this rain stops. And since I don't really want to be scrubbing floors on my hands and knees, though they need it here, I thought this would be a nice job to keep us busy. And dry."

Autumn glanced out the window at her right. They were presently ensconced in the charming window seat in a room on the second floor, far removed from the bedchambers, which Charlotte called the solar. The window and the seat were made of stone, which was cool beneath Autumn's butt, and were set deeply into an alcove. The seat part curved from the entrance of the alcove, narrowing as it reached the glassless opening of the tall and thin window so that Charlotte and Autumn, seated left and right, were almost knee to knee. With only a small fire in the hearth, the solar was dimly lit, but the light from the window, even on this dreary day, was sufficiently bright enough for their chore.

Even as her stitches in the ripped seam under one arm of the tunic were really untidy, Autumn ran her hand lovingly over the fabric. It belonged to Marcus, she knew, pulled from a basket of household items in need of mending, and which, according to Charlotte, was left unattended because of the previously mentioned business about Balla Àrd essentially being a bachelor pad. Even if Marcus hadn't been one of the few people who lived and slept inside the keep, she'd have known this shirt belonged to him. It was simply too large to properly fit another person and she'd noticed that most of his tunics were a light beige in color, with little variation. Possibly, she only imagined it, but she also thought she caught a hint of his scent, which was a curious mix of leather, straw, and man, a combination that was woody and earthy and very male—curious in that it should have been at most, nose-wrinkling or at the very least, so non-descript as to beckon little notice, but that which filled Autumn with an evocative sense of nostalgia, some bittersweet thing that saddened her. It was almost as if she knew she wanted to hold onto his scent, that she would need the memory of it to keep Marcus alive in her heart and mind when she was gone.

She added more stitches to finish closing the tear in the underarm and brought up something she'd been meaning for days to ask. "Charlotte, are you sure you've not heard of or met a woman named Megan West?"

"I'm sure." She pulled the needle through the tablecloth she was working on, mending one corner where the edge was frayed for several inches. "I've never met anyone—aside from you—from the future."

"But would you know a time-traveler if you—oh, I guess you would. Our speech is rather hard to miss." She chewed her lip. "Would you have any idea how I might even begin to search for her? Or any of the others that went missing? I'm beginning to think they're all here, which would be fantastic, if they were all alive, but then kind of terrifying, to know that people could just willy-nilly be moved through time." She tilted her head at Charlotte. "How did it happen for you?"

To her surprise, Charlotte dropped her hands and the cloth into her lap with just enough force that Autumn had the sense she really didn't want to talk about it.

"It was nothing spectacular or earth-shattering. I was hiking on one of the Ben Nevis trails and I met this woman there and we talked a bit. She said something strange to me and walked away and then," she paused, shrugging, her eyes on her sewing, "like, the air felt heavier. I thought it was because I was climbing. But then nothing was familiar and…and poof, I was in the fourteenth century. No fanfare, no mindboggling warping through dimensions, no bright lights or black holes. I was just…here."

Autumn's brow wrinkled as she stared at the top of Charlotte's head. "Why is this not more important to you, Charlotte? Why don't you have more curiosity about the most amazing thing to happen since...well, since forever?"

"Because I don't care about it," Charlotte shocked her by admitting, lifting her face, which showed a tightness suggesting annoyance. "I mean, I do. I'm thrilled that it happened. I have Reid. But I just don't want to tempt fate by constantly harping on it. That's sounds awful. I'm sorry. I just worry sometimes that the witch will be summoned by any mention of it, that she might come and—"

"Excuse me." Autumn blinked, her eyes going wide. "Witch?"

Charlotte's shoulders sagged. Briefly she closed her eyes, tipping her head back. "Yes," she said when she opened her eyes and looked at Autumn. "I'm not positive but I'm pretty sure that the woman I met on the trail was a witch. Or a sorceress or an enchantress—she was super pretty—or some mythical or magical being. There was just something not right about her."

"What did she say to you?"

"I made some crack about having underestimated my hiking skills, what I was capable of, and she gave me this weird smile and looked further up the trail, which climbed higher, and she said, *Go now, he's waiting for you.*"

Autumn gasped, her hand slapping over her mouth.

"Shit," Charlotte swore. "Did you meet a witch as well?"

Autumn wasn't sure why she felt suddenly like crying but thought maybe it was simply a manifestation of the overwhelming emotions attached to this crazy new twist.

She shook her head. "No. I met no one. But I heard—felt, actually—those words, or something very close to it. Charlotte, there wasn't a soul in sight, not anywhere around me, but I heard someone say, *He's coming for you*, right before I...before it happened. I *felt* the words inside. Goosebumps rose on my arms. And then...and then Marcus was the first person I saw." This last part, given with a bit of wonder, as that detail bumped around in her head with ideas like Fate and Destiny.

Autumn saw that Charlotte was shaking, seriously quivering with her upset. Her lips were pursed as she stared at Autumn.

"I don't want to talk about it, Autumn," she said, her voice breaking. "I'm sorry. I really am. But I can't—I'm just too afraid that I might be thrown back into the 21st century and that, well *that* terrifies me more than any war or any other terrible thing in this time."

"But I need help," Autumn pleaded. "I want to go home."

"Do you really want to?" Charlotte challenged weakly, very clearly hoping the answer was no. "I mean, now that you're...you know...with Marcus?"

That conversation had been their first one of yesterday, Charlotte almost springing upon Autumn to ask what had happened at the loch. Much to Charlotte's chagrin, Autumn had been stingy with her reply, reluctant to share what was so new and so precious to her at the moment.

However, she still wanted to go home. And she needed to do so now, as soon as possible, before she became further entwined with Marcus.

"I have to get home," she said, the broken sound of her voice a plea of its own. "I love my family. The longer I stay, the more Marcus and I...the more difficult it will be to leave." She'd known this would happen. This was exactly the consequence she'd fear most and had been trying to avoid.

Charlotte stood abruptly, setting aside the half-finished project of the tablecloth, rather carelessly leaving it in a rumpled heap upon the stone seat. She brushed down her skirts with nervous hands. "Let's go. I can't do this now. It's hardly raining. Let's go see Elspeth and Patrick."

Autumn understood, or she thought she did.

And they left the keep, stepping out into a light drizzle of rain, not more than a cold and bothersome mist. Autumn followed Charlotte as she marched with purpose, hands fisted, toward the village. As soon as they stepped foot outside the wall, six soldiers scrambled down from the battlements, falling into pace behind them, apparently with orders from either Marcus or Reid that they were not to be left unprotected.

At times Autumn almost had to skip to keep up with her, but she didn't protest the maddening pace or have to question the reason behind it.

And that's when she felt it, a change in the air that hadn't anything to do with the cloying drizzle. The change was palpable, as if Mother Nature herself held her breath in anticipation. It carried an otherworldly aura, an enchantment that entranced and unsettled Autumn at the same time. A prickling sensation danced along her skin. A few paces ahead of her, Charlotte seemed not to notice. Autumn glanced around but saw nothing out of the ordinary.

It was familiar and then not, being more pronounced than when first she'd met this delicate atmosphere that felt both weighty and weightless, as if the very essence of the world had shifted.

She was visited by hope and dread, understanding this might be it. Without even trying, she might move again through time, might get to go home. Oh, but her chest tightened at the very idea, knowing she would never see Marcus again.

And then, most odd, Autumn could very clearly hear her mother's voice—hear, not feel, as those other voices. It was very strange because her mother didn't seem to be calling out to her, wasn't begging her to come home or anything as dramatic as that. Her voice was simply there, in the air or in the wind, the quality of her voice known, recognized, even as the words, whatever she was saying, was not.

"Charlotte!" Autumn called out frantically, flustered by what was happening. She stared at her tingling hands, and tried to understand which emotion was more powerful: her desire to go home or her yearning to never leave Marcus's side.

And then, as quickly as it had risen, the feeling dissipated. The air returned to normal.

Charlotte turned around. "What?"

Autumn's heart raced. She lowered her hands. "Nothing."

***

He was buried deep inside her, the sensation unlike anything he'd ever been so fortunate to know. It was difficult to believe that she hadn't been made only for him. Across the chamber, the small fire hissed and then popped, the louder noise timed perfectly to Marcus's last thrust, when he touched her womb, and his release tore him apart at the same time Autumn cried out her rapture.

He collapsed, but kept his full weight off her. Panting still, he dropped his head into her hair, and whispered, "I kent only this all day long."

Breathlessly, Autumn teased him, "Shouldn't you have been prepping for war?"

"Like as nae," he quipped.

Slowly, he rolled to his side, wanting to behold her flushed body, pulsating with exertion and glistening with perspiration. Her hair lay around her head and shoulders like a golden cloud. The stubble on his jaw had scratched a red pattern all around her lips, down her neck, and across both breasts.

Autumn turned her face toward him, her eyes shining with liquid delight.

"I'll want to do that again," she said. "Soon, but not right now. Just let me catch my breath."

Marcus adored the strength of her desire, how potent was her passion.

Eventually, they rested in each other's arms, same as they had last night. They talked as they had then, in their hushed lover voices. Marcus hadn't known what he hadn't had, but found now that he enjoyed these conversations, that he looked forward to sharing his day with Autumn. He confessed that he *had* actually done more today than only think about laying with her, that he had surveyed the MacPhail perimeter again with Gibbon and Osgar and an entire unit while Reid had overseen the training of both armies. The siege engines advanced but were not yet ready. The fight with the MacPhails, which he hoped would end with this one, would wait another day or two.

"Charlotte and I went to see Elspeth, to check on her son."

Marcus's breath caught for half a heartbeat.

"I didn't know," Autumn said, her voice soft still, "and how or why would I? But I didn't know you had been engaged to Elspeth's sister."

Marcus exhaled. He wasn't sure this was an issue, or should be, or if Autumn were bothered by it or only curious.

"Aye. And how did that creep into conversation there?"

"It didn't," she answered. "Charlotte mentioned it after we left the cottage." Another few seconds passed before Autumn said, "Charlotte told me you've had several betrothals."

Charlotte should keep her bluidy mouth shut, was Marcus's most uncharitable thought just then. But he was only mildly perturbed. It wasn't anything he yearned to conceal, wasn't anything all of Balla Àrd didn't know about. Still, he wondered what Charlotte's agenda might have been. What purpose was there in telling Autumn?

"Aye."

"Don't be angry at Charlotte. I think I upset her today," she defended, "trying to talk about my trouble, which she doesn't want to talk about. At all. I think she was simply making conversation so that I couldn't introduce the subject again."

And silence again, until Marcus sighed and said, "I was, as she told ye, betrothed three times."

He waited for the obvious queries to follow.

When they did not, and though he felt no pressure then, he heard himself saying, "The first was arranged almost at birth. My grandsire arranged it with a child who was kin to the MacDougall. Ysabella, she was, and apparently she did nae grow into adulthood with any fervor in her heart to honor the pledge between the two families. She had developed a tendre for another, and when her father insisted she give up her love and went so far as to have the lad imprisoned and eventually hanged for— I have to imagine—a crime more supposed than real, the fair Ysabella died by her own hand, burying her dagger to the hilt in her own breast, rather than wed me."

"Jesus," Autumn cursed, with no small amount of heat. "That's...dramatic. Although, obviously, it wasn't about you but about losing her lover."

"Possibly," he conceded. "Next, in my twenty-first year, I was betrothed to Agnes of Nairn. She set out, apparently willingly, I was told, at the appointed time, for Balla Àrd from Skye. Upon the Inner Sound, her ship met with an unfavorable weather event that sunk the ship and drowned all aboard."

"Holy shit, that's awful."

He could almost feel Autumn's wince against his chest.

Wanting it all done and told, and put behind him—them—he went on. "Elspeth's sister was Miriam. I kent her all my life. A marriage was nae ever considered because of the betrothal to Ysabella."

"Said like that," Autumn interjected, "kind of makes me think you might have wished you weren't engaged to Ysabella and were free to pursue Miriam."

He detected a question in there, that she was not only putting forth her assumption.

She wasn't wrong.

He had never met Ysabella, but he did know Miriam. She'd been a brown-eyed beauty with a flirtatious smile, who enjoyed having a multitude of lads chasing her. She'd purposefully tempted and teased Marcus to the point he made a move to do something about it. At that moment, all her coy flirtation had ceased. She had no intention of being only his leman. She'd not live in the shadow of Balla Àrd while he housed and showered favor upon a wife in the castle itself.

"I could nae wed her, of course," he told Autumn now. "I was to be laird and she was a peasant. Her grandfather had been a slave to my great-grandsire. 'Twas nae permitted. I could nae break the betrothal."

"Did you...did you even try? Or want to?"

He had, but not with great fervor. "It dinna matter. I could nae break my pledge, nor that of my grandsire."

"I see. But then you did eventually betroth yourself to her, so I guess you got over the fact that she was a peasant?"

He didn't care overmuch for the way she had worded that, but took no issue with it.

"After Agnes was killed, the war came on," he said. "The class divide mattered less. I needed an heir if Balla Àrd was to survive."

"So what happened with that betrothal?"

Marcus sighed. "I kent she held it against me that I had chosen another over her, nae once but twice. I discovered she was laying with one of the archers, weeks after I had announced our betrothal." And that had been that. He hadn't needed or wanted either Miriam's tears or apology; certainly, he wished he could have avoided her falling to his feet and begging his forgiveness as she had done.

"So..." Autumn began, "you are three times unlucky in love and what do you—"

"'Twas nae love," he corrected firmly. It had been but fleeting, any notion at the time that his world was crumbling around him. How easily he'd been able to convince himself of that had confirmed that his love for Miriam had been more shallow than even he'd realized.

A second, and then two and three elapsed before Autumn asked, "Are you sure?"

He didn't feel he needed to respond to her doubt.

"It dinna matter. Miriam and her lover were banished, and I give the matter none of my time."

'Twas true, he rarely thought of Miriam. On the rare occasions she was recalled to mind, his thoughts were indifferent. More often, though, he did consider that a wife and bairns were simply not to be his.

Presently, he had to wonder how glad he was that none of those arrangements had come to fruition. If he had wed or been married now, what might have become of Autumn? Clearly not this, she laying naked in his arms. He wondered now if that had been Fate intervening on his behalf, with any or all of his ill-fated betrothals.

A gust of wind flapped the oil cloths covering the window and made the tiny flames of the fire dance.

Marcus rubbed his hand up and down Autumn's arm. Eventually, his eyes closed.

At length, Autumn was the one to break the long silence.

"I thought I might have left today."

Marcus's eyes shot open. His body tensed and he glanced down at the top of her head.

"Left?"

"Something very strange happened," she said, "as Charlotte and I were going to Elspeth's cottage. Not anything...seen, but I felt something in the air, same as I did that day I was brought here."

"And...?" He prompted impatiently, his pulse quickening.

"And nothing. I felt a strangeness in the air, and I thought I heard my mother's voice but now I'm not sure. And then...it was gone. Or done."

"But—" He didn't even know what to ask, or why his heart pounded the way it did.

"But what? Nothing happened. No one spoke to me. Not my mother or that other voice I felt last time—"

"Ye heard a voice then?" He asked, even as he did recall some mention of that.

"I *felt* the voice," she emphasized, "or the words, I guess, just before I was pulled through the portal the first time—"

"Portal? There's a gateway?"

"No. sorry. I just say that because that's how I think of it—wherever I slipped through time—as a portal, because that's what they call it in the movies—never mind. There is no doorway, if that's what you're asking."

His jaw clenched but that didn't stop him from probing, "But if there were a door, ye would have gone through it?"

Willingly? Easily? Without a backward glance?

Autumn failed to respond swiftly enough to suit him. He jerked upright and flipped her onto her back, trapping her beneath him.

"I'm nae ready to let ye go," he told her, putting forth a robust effort to sound more an imperious despot than a lovesick fool. He wasn't in love, of course. He simply hadn't had his fill of her yet.

"I mostly read true crime, and Agatha Christie, and only a smattering of romance," Autumn said, none of which made sense to Marcus, but apparently trying to make light of his confession.

"But I can almost see the words: *In that moment, they were lost to each other, two souls bound together in a steamy, timeless embrace*."

He thought she expected a grin to come, to match her own, the one that didn't reach her eyes. It was intentional, her making light of this, of his sudden earnestness and this situation.

"Are ye lost, lass?" He asked with all due gravity. "Do ye feel that way still?"

Autumn sobered slowly, perchance returned to what must surely be a frightening reality of being trapped in a century seven hundred years in the past.

"You have no idea." She said, a sadness softening her expression. 'Twas fleeting, though, as she painted on a languid smile, likely for his benefit. "It's fine, though. You are a great distraction until I find my way."

Marcus witnessed the moment regret entered her shimmering gaze, conceivably provoked by how his own eyes darkened at her careless words. He was a distraction?

"Marcus, I'm—I didn't mean—"

"'Tis nae offensive to me," he said, attempting to disguise the effect of the injury. Ruthlessly, he reminded her, "We agreed we would entwine only our bodies and nae our hearts."

A veil of dull sorrow clouded Autumn's gray eyes, as if his words were more painful than hers had been, as if she were disappointed that he'd struck back.

She ran her hand down his cheek. "I'd be lying if I said I didn't know what I was getting into."

And then, before his eyes, her trembling lips curved upward, forming a smile that was as mechanical as it was fragile. Beyond the resolve of that forced smile, her gaze remained haunted.

She turned into him, swaying her hips and thigh against the leg he'd thrown over her.

"Ye are attempting to manipulate me," he guessed, "to distract me at the very least, with your delectable body."

He would let her. Tomorrow was not promised to either him or her. These were but stolen moments, he'd been reminded, naught but a bittersweet indulgence that might at any moment be taken from him. He was under no impression that she, too, was not filled with awareness that this moment, all of their moments together, were but fragile occasions.

The melancholy remained in her gaze, but she aimed for lightness, asking with false modesty, "You think my body is delectable?"

Marcus frowned at her. "And now ye try to distract me with foolish questions."

Autumn grinned and walked two fingers up his broad back. "Is any of it working?"

"It's nae entirely fruitless," he admitted grumpily.

"Kiss me, Marcus," she begged, her voice weighted with longing, her eyes reflecting a poignant ache. "We can be distracted together."

Sometime later, he watched her sleep. In those quiet moments, when she was undisturbed, so still, he savored her as would have been unwise for him to do when she was awake. In slumber, her face retreated into utmost calm, which somehow rivaled the beauty of her sunniest smile. When she slept, and he held her, and he watched her, the world outside the air she breathed became small and so insignificant. Even the brutal demons of a mercurial Fate and the perplexity of time travel seemed to have been put to slumber.

He wasn't ready to say farewell to Autumn Winters.

Chapter Eighteen

She'd woken this morning feeling sick to her stomach. When she'd finally fallen asleep last night, she'd been in much the same condition. Autumn recognized it for what it was: dread. She needed to get out of here, away from the fourteenth century. Far away from the lengthening and strengthening grip on her heart.

Oh, but she'd significantly underestimated Marcus's ability to captivate and mesmerize her. In hindsight, only a week removed, she realized she shouldn't have. She'd been fascinated with him from the start. Idly, she gave some thought to the future, hers specifically and not only time. If she never found her way home, what might come? Would she stay with Marcus? Would she ever allow herself to love him? Or would she resist all her life, simply to avoid heartache because she would never stop yearning to go home? Would she become like Charlotte, trying so hard to forget, ignoring every mention and hope of the twenty-first century?

She was compelled to wonder if she might only exist in a terminal, uninspired paralysis, unable to go home but unwilling to commit fully to any sort of life here.

If she managed to somehow get home, would that be easier? Would forgetting Marcus be easier than living in this century with him, away from her family, and what seemed like real life? Would she discover, without him, what he'd truly meant to her? Good Lord, how could she ever explain this to her parents? She kept no secrets from them but this one was too fantastic not to share. But how *could* she share this with her parents, expecting they would—rightfully—think she'd finally gone off the deep end? They'd have her head examined. Their relationship would never recover. Everything they thought they believed about their only daughter would be tossed on its head.

This was just a dream, a non-reality—right? It had to be. How could she ever explain to another—one who hadn't experienced it—that it was real? She hadn't fully grasped it herself yet, not really. Part of her guessed she had only adapted, as little as she had, as a survival instinct. What she shared with these people here and now, Marcus and Charlotte most prominently, was borne of desperation, was it not?

She would share nothing with Charlotte today, apparently.

She'd waited this morning for Charlotte to come to her chamber as she most kindly had every other morning, but she did not. Autumn guessed she might still be upset over their discussion from yesterday. Charlotte had remained pinch-lipped throughout much of their visit with Elspeth. Autumn expected she understood about as well as she could, supposing that even after two years she might adopt the same protective-slash-resistant manner if ever someone wanted to talk about the future and how to get back. Well, she would if she allowed herself to fall in love with Marcus.

With Marcus gone from her chamber before the sun had risen and no knock on the door from Charlotte, Autumn was forced to make her own way. She tidied the bed, thankful for the weight and warmth of the blankets and the fur since the nights were cold. She was in desperate want of a bath but knew she wasn't brave enough to venture outside and down to the loch by herself and thus supposed she would have to show herself inside the kitchen and ask help of those women there. She dressed without any particular rush and left her chamber.

This would not be her first visit to the kitchen. In Charlotte's company, she had been there several times now. It was located on the ground floor, one long and narrow corridor removed from the hall, and was made of stone walls, one of which was entirely devoted to a huge fireplace with different compartments, including two different open fires over which kettles were always hung, and sections that served as ovens, one open and one with a wooden door that could be closed. Bellows, tongs, iron pokers, and a basket of peat sat haphazardly near the hearth. There were several different work stations, one long counter in the center of the room and others along the walls.

Autumn was pleasantly assaulted by the aroma of roasting meat—a large haunch of meat was being cooked, rotisserie-style over one of the fires—and baking bread while the scent of rosemary presented itself more subtly.

She was surprised to find the kid, Lewin, within the kitchen, and then equally curious when she realized he was, albeit very slowly, almost ineptly slicing cabbage at one counter. About as quickly as Autumn realized what he was doing, she understood why the sword-wearing soldier was helping with the meal prep. Lorain stood at the same counter, her cheeks a darling shade of pink as she worked, rather more adeptly, at chopping another head of cabbage into small pieces.

Autumn only paused a minute to contemplate the scene, but it was enough time that she realized Lewin did more talking than cutting. The blade in his hand moved with much less frequency as did his mouth. Immeasurably charmed by Lewin's attentiveness—he stared longingly at the top of Lorain's head when she wasn't shyly meeting his gaze—Autumn was smiling by the time she approached Ròs, the cook, the woman in charge.

Charlotte had informed Autumn that there was a strict hierarchy in the kitchen, with Ròs at the top and the scullions, kitchen maids, char boys, and apprentices all falling beneath her, and that if Autumn needed something, she should approach Ròs first, as it would be considered an unforgiveable slight if she were bypassed.

Ròs was short and thin with smooth olive skin, despite being well into her sixties by Autumn's estimation, with small, deep set eyes of blue. She wore a gown that swept over her ankles and a long apron that was surprisingly clean. Autumn had no idea about her hair, not even its color, since her head was covered by a woolen headscarf that she kept tied under her chin. She seemed, to Autumn's modern mind, a caricature of a Grimm character, so much so that Autumn wouldn't have been surprised if she ever found a little boy in a cage in the kitchen, being fattened up to make a stew. And yet, she'd been very pleasant the few times Autumn had met her.

Ròs's English was either rusty or incomplete, but Autumn eventually managed to convey her want of a bath, being quick to explain that she didn't expect someone else to have to do all the work, but could manage it herself if she were shown how. Per Charlotte's discourse of the other day, Autumn was prepared to have to scrub a full layer of grime and wood off a large wooden tub before she might mentally be able to enjoy it.

However, the bath was not to be. Ròs smacked her hand on her forehead, staring at Autumn as if she'd asked for a full banquet to accompany her bath. The cook threw out her arms, jabbing them at several points around the kitchen, likely to indicate how busy she was. More than one person inside the kitchen cringed and shrunk at the cook's robust response and Autumn was sorry to have wakened the sleeping beast, as it seemed she had done.

Autumn nodded quickly. "Okay, I get it," she said, when Ròs, previously so amiable, began to rant in her native tongue, the words rushed and practically hostile in tone. Autumn held up her hands in surrender and walked toward the door. "Sorry. Sorry. I'll figure it out myself."

She grumbled her way through the corridor. There was, or should have been anyway, a nicer way for Ròs to have refused her request.

"Lass!"

Autumn turned to find Lewin jogging toward her.

"Forgive me, lass," he said as he caught up to her. "I dinna ken your presence until Ròs began jawing at ye. What did ye need?"

No, she didn't suppose Lewin had noticed her entrance, with his regard so happily focused on Lorain.

Autumn waved her hand. "It's nothing. I was hoping to have a bath—and I would have fixed it myself—but I can wait."

"Ye can bathe in the loch," he said.

"Yes, I know. But I was under the impression I shouldn't be wandering outside the gate without a guard," she said. "But I don't want to take anyone away from their own duties." And she wasn't super comfortable with the idea of some unknown soldier standing watch while she got naked twenty feet away. Also, she didn't want to have Lewin playing babysitter to her. "Lewin, I don't want to take you away from Lorain," she said and grinned impudently, "and whatever you're trying to get going there." She arched her brow suggestively, kind of hoping he would spill the tea.

"My lass will still be there upon my return," he said confidently, appearing briefly older than his years. "The laird would nae take kindly to any discourtesy on my part, lass."

"Honestly, it can wait. I don't even have towels or soap or anything." Not even another change of clothes. "I'll find Charlotte and see what she can do for me."

"Come. I will take ye to the Nicholson's lady."

"Oh, do you know where Charlotte is?"

The kid shrugged. "Nae, but there are only so many places she can be."

"Thanks, Lewin," she conceded since he seemed so willing, eager almost, to help her. "That's very kind of you."

They walked outside, Lewin leading the way, and Autumn was a bit surprised to find so many soldiers milling about the inner enclosed courtyard. Each of them appeared at ease and so Autumn was not sent into any panic to find so many grouped together. Maybe they were on a break, or had no training planned for today. Because Lewin paid them no mind, Autumn didn't lend any wonder or worry to their casual gathering.

Eadric was among one of the small groups, hanging out near the well.

Lewin spoke before Autumn might have greeted Eadric properly. "Lass is looking for the Nicholson's lady."

Autumn smiled hello when Eadric inclined his head at her.

"Down to the village," Eadric said, "Just passed her on my way in. Aye, I'll walk with ye."

And so the three of them set out from the keep, using that same man door at the back of the castle as Marcus had once done. The wind was fierce here and Autumn regretted not tying back her hair, which now blew riotously across her face despite her best efforts to sweep it away.

Once outside that gate, Eadric led the way, tossing conversation over his shoulder. "And what do ye make of our bonny Balla Àrd, lass?"

"It's most impressive," she said, with genuine appreciation. "I can honestly say I've never seen anything quite like it. When was it built?

"'Twas in the early 12th century, lass, when the original wooden fortifications were raised upon the beinn," Eadric answered.

"The keep as ye ken it today did nae come about until a hundred years ago," Lewin added.

"And the curtain wall is nae more than fifty years auld," Eadric announced. "Has weathered many storms and sieges, to be sure, but has nae ever fallen."

More talk of war, Autumn mused, wondering if the constant battle to survive was simply the centerpiece of their lives. Was it all they knew? Could anyone in this time say they had seen or lived months or years or decades in peace?

"She stands as a magnificent testament to the resiliency of Scottish pride and patriotism," Autumn remarked, unconsciously assuming a reporter's cadence and speech and because she rather presumed Eadric and Lewin would expect more veneration from her.

They were not quite a hundred yards from the rear gate when Marcus appeared before them, further along the path, walking toward them, coming from the village. Gibbon and Osgar walked with him.

The view would never get old. All of Scotland, every bit that she'd seen—in any year—was breathtaking for its scenery. Marcus was breathtaking as well for his imposing figure, the chiseled work of art that was his face, and for his noble bearing and unwavering confidence. Autumn knew if she spent a thousand years with him, she would never *not* be in awe of him.

The two parties met at almost exactly the halfway point between the village and the castle.

Eadric notified his laird of their business, "Lass is looking for Charlotte Nicholson."

Marcus's gaze sat unfathomably upon Autumn as he hitched his thumb over his shoulder. "She is nae longer in the village. Reid came for her. Where they've gone I dinna ken."

Autumn sighed, more than only a little frustrated, and then more rueful to have taken Lewin from Lorain's side.

It hadn't been obvious yet, not in Charlotte's company, but it was now, how she didn't fit in at all.

"Well then, I don't know what to do with myself," she stated, lifting and dropping her arms.

Her present vexation was not only about depriving Lorain of Lewin's company, and it wasn't about the bath she clearly wasn't going to have. But even as she realized it was deeper, she couldn't quite put her finger on what stung her.

Marcus sensed her frustration. "Mayhap we will only stroll about," he offered, "without agenda."

"But aren't you busy?" She'd rarely seen him at all during the daytime since she'd come to Balla Àrd; he was always about some castle or laird or war business. Autumn lifted her hand to include his soldiers. "All of you?"

Gibbon laughed and walked around Marcus and past Autumn. "'Tis nae my hand he wants to hold skipping through the lea."

Lewin smirked and Eadric winked at Autumn as they made to follow Gibbon back to the castle. Osgar, his bald head reflecting today's hazy sunshine, was the last to leave, whistling a jaunty tune that was caught by the wind and taken away with him.

Autumn watched them go for a moment before turning back to Marcus, whose brown eyes were fixed on her.

"I don't want to say that you all seem purposeless today," Autumn said, when he seemed only to be waiting for her to say something, "but it's a little out of the ordinary for you and Gibbon and Osgar—all of them—to be without something to do. Am I right?"

"Aye, normally we would be training now. But we had planned to assist the cottars with the ploughing, getting the fields ready to receive the winter planting, but Cahal's oxen is lame, and the plough's beam snapped in half this morn after meeting with a sturdy rock. We wrestled the rock from the earth—'twas as large as Wilfrid's fat head—and are only waiting on the plough's beam to be repaired. But that will involve crafting an entirely new piece and will take some time." He shrugged. "It does the lads nae harm to ken some free time."

Before the battle with the MacPhails that would come, which loomed so large, Autumn thought. She said nothing though, reluctant to have her already tortured mind plagued by grief with thoughts of war and of those who might not return. But then it was there, with only that fleeting thought, and her brain expanded upon it, fearing for Marcus above all others.

And it sucked. Everything in this time period sucked and suddenly Autumn was desperate to get away from it.

She stepped forward and put her hand on Marcus's forearm, wringing a frown from his gaze.

"I want to go home," she said, anguish weakening her voice. "Charlotte won't help me. I need you to help me."

"And what would ye have me do?" He asked through clenched teeth.

"I don't know. Can we visit the place—that hill—where you found me? Wouldn't I have a better chance of being zapped through time from there?" Maybe there *were* portals, and she needed to be near one.

"Aye," he said, but not happily. "As soon as the MacPhails are in hand, I will—"

"No," Autumn cried. "Before that. Now. I can't do this anymore. I'm going nuts. I can't be here. I can't watch and wait for you to come back from a fight with the MacPhails and then—what? What happens if you don't come back? How am I supposed to survive that?"

"Calm yourself, lass." He laid his hand over hers.

"I will not calm myself, Marcus. Do you have any idea how awful this is for me? You don't seem to care whether you die or not, but I do—and not only because you're the only good thing I've found here."

Though his visage was twisted with whatever tormented him now, his voice was low and quiet when he spoke.

"Ye dinna care," he charged. "Ye vowed ye would nae."

Autumn gritted her teeth and snapped at him. "Honestly, that's starting to get on my nerves."

"What is?"

"You are." She yanked her hand from under his. "Marcus, I never would have guessed that you would have—three times now—thrown that back in my face. That's rude. And something else—manipulative, maybe. Or just mean, that you keep bringing it up. Fine, I have feelings for you. Are you happy? I didn't want to, but I do."

"And now you dinna, because I'm getting on your nerves?" He questioned severely.

Autumn rolled her eyes. "My God, sometimes you can be so medieval-ly obtuse. Being frustrated with you doesn't simply cancel out all emotions. Unless, you harping on those rules I installed is because you like to torment people, or you like to brandish your own superiority. Maybe you like rubbing my face in it, how ridiculous it was to even suggest it. I'll have you know, first it was desperate, yes I admit that. But mostly, it was just to safeguard my heart because I want—I need—to go home. But maybe I didn't need to protect myself. You're being a jerk about it, and it makes me wonder if I'm not in any danger of falling in love with you."

"Ye canna have it both ways—"

"I know that, Marcus," she cried. "That's why I'm upset!"

"For Chrissakes, lass, but what do ye want?" He shouted at her.

"I don't know what I want!" She hollered back at him, her hands fisting between them. And then she lost all her ferocity, her body deflating. She knew this fight was pointless, and that neither of them was in the wrong or to blame for their circumstance. She pushed out a ragged breath and stared at him, her gaze beseeching. "Maybe....maybe I just want a hug and one of those really sweet forehead kisses that you see in the movies, that make the woman feel like everything's going to be all right." When Marcus didn't move but continued to seethe at her, she lifted her hands helplessly. "I don't know, maybe I just need a grilled cheese cut diagonally on a pretty plate and several hours of stupid daytime TV."

Marcus opened his mouth, releasing a heavy sigh. He reached out and took Autumn's hand, gently pulling her closer at the same time he took one step forward.

Autumn's heart was heavy as she met his gaze, seeing the profound anguish etched in his eyes.

He took her face in his hands and closed his eyes, slowly lowering his head until his lips met her forehead.

Tears filled her eyes as she closed them. He let the kiss sit there a moment before he gathered her in his strong arms. Autumn fitted herself against his solid and warm chest.

He kissed her hair and said raggedly against her head, "But I canna give ye the other. I dinna ken grilled cheese, or daytime tee-vee."

Autumn smiled against his chest and let out one of those little sobs that was also a laugh. "This is perfect, actually."

They stayed like that for a long moment. Autumn wrapped her arms around him, her fingers twisted into the fabric of his tunic. Marcus's arms held her snugly, his left hand at the back of her head, holding her against him.

It was heaven, to be in his arms, but it simply wasn't possible to remain there and pretend that nothing else mattered to her. "I want to stay with you, Marcus," she said, having to raise her voice a bit to compete with the wind. "But I need to go home."

Though she felt him nod, he said nothing.

And then, as if those agonized words had the power to manifest, Autumn was aware of a change in the air. Though it didn't smell the same, it was similar to the odor of rain in the air, the scent non-distinct but instantly equated with the fact that rain would come. This one, whatever was its fragrance, had only been first known to her at the broch, but she recognized it now, the heaviness, the sense of vapor in the air, its elusive fragrance.

She stiffened and pushed away from Marcus, holding his forearms.

The wind stopped blowing. Her hair no longer whipped about but fell over her shoulders.

Marcus sensed it, too. Though he kept one hand on her waist, he turned a bewildered frown all around. Out came his sword, and with a ferocious scowl.

"Oh, no," Autumn whimpered, surging forward against his chest. She clung to him, trying to join her hands at his back. "No. I'm not ready."

Marcus shook her off, but only to meet her gaze. "What the bluidy hell is this?"

Shaking her head, she cried, "I don't know, but this feels like it did...before."

"Dinna go," he said simply, as if the choice were hers.

"Don't let me go, Marcus." Faced now with the absolute choice, she knew where she wanted to be. "I don't want to leave you."

With his sword held in one hand, and her arm in his other, he shook her furiously. "Fight it, Autumn," he demanded of her. "Dinna go."

Tears rolled down her cheeks. She knew the choice was not hers to make.

"Find me, Marcus," She begged him frantically. "Find me."

"When? Where?"

Whatever was the power that would move her, it was stronger than before. She felt its presence surrounding her.

She was nearly incoherent with fright, clawing at him as the wind returned with a ferocity that nearly toppled them.

"Don't let me go, Marcus," she pleaded. She locked her gaze on him. "Hold tight."

And then, most ridiculous, as if such a thing might be possible, she thought she might simply impress herself onto him forcibly, finding his hand and squeezing it tight with both of hers, closing her eyes, imbuing every ounce of energy to make him feel her, so that he wouldn't forget her. "Don't ever let me go," she whispered fervently.

"Where, Autumn? Tell me when and where! I will find ye!"

While her eyes were closed, an image flashed across her mind, a bird's eye view of her and Marcus standing upon the rocky slope, the grass bent sideways by the wind.

Marcus bellowed her name.

Autumn clung to him.

Closer to the keep, Gibbon and Lewin hollered unintelligible words. Osgar and Eadric sprinted toward their laird, brandishing their swords.

But when Autumn opened her eyes, nothing was as it was.

***

As quickly as the wind had kicked up, it blew away to naught until nary a blade of grass was disturbed.

Marcus stared at his hand, which Autumn had just been holding, and at the ground in front of him, where Autumn had stood a second ago.

She was gone. She simply...disappeared.

Jesu.

She'd begged him not to let go. She'd looked at him, directly into his eyes, putting all her faith in his strength.

Please don't let me go.

He consulted his hand again, his chest heaving and his jaw gaping. He hadn't. He hadn't let go.

His throat constricted and his nose burned. He hadn't hung on, either.

She'd looked to him to save her. It was powerful, her faith in him.. But then it was fleeting, his occasion of that. He'd failed her.

His palms were imprinted with her fingernails, little half-moons reddened and indented.

Don't ever let me go.

A ragged, anguished breath burst from him. He fell to his knees, his sword clanging to the ground.

She hadn't only been talking about her hand.

She'd just begged him to keep her in his heart.

He sat back on his heels, the wind knocked out of him. He didn't only want her in his bluidy heart. He wanted her here. With him!

He roared her name. "Autumn!"

Eadric crashed to the jagged earth in front of him, ducking his head to get a glimpse of Marcus's face.

"What—?" He croaked. "What was that?"

Lewin came next, bumping into Eadric as he, too, fell to his knees. "Where is she? Laird, where is she?"

Marcus signaled his own bewilderment with a shake of his head.. "I dinna ken." He gulped for breath. "Find her. Search everywhere. Turn o'er every rock. Leave nae any space unexplored. Find her."

Chapter Nineteen

She was much less surprised than she was apprehensive.

She knew she wasn't with Marcus anymore; she'd felt that coming. She wept inside for the heartbreaking tragedy of that. *Oh, Marcus!*

And then her heart dropped even more when she looked around, realizing that she stood within a small medieval hamlet but that this was not Balla Àrd's village. The village was similar in aesthetics to Balla Àrd's but not the same, the configuration of the lanes and cottages different, the church's bell tower spied above the thatched roof in front of her, in the middle of the village, not on the fringe of town. Nothing was familiar, not at all, so that Autumn understood almost immediately that she was still in medieval Scotland but was no longer at Balla Àrd.

People around her stared. A woman dressed in a long brown kirtle yanked the hand of her a little girl, putting the child behind her skirts. Another woman, with a ruddy complexion and mousy hair, stared gape-jawed at Autumn, her chin so low that her neck was unseen. An old man holding a tool that looked like something the Grim Reaper would carry, straightened in a garden, and showed a hostile glare, muttering inaudible words. Someone screamed, the ear-piercing shriek spinning Autumn around to see what had generated such a howl.

Autumn had, apparently.

The screamer, a young woman probably not twenty years old, collapsed to the ground in a heap of billowing skirts, covering her mouth while she fixed her watery, frightened gaze on Autumn.

Oh, shit.

One or more of these gawking people might have witnessed this, Autumn's coming—possibly appearing out of thin air. Even as she wondered what that might look like to any of these witnesses, she also questioned what had happened—how it had looked—at Marcus's end, where they'd been clinging to each other one minute and in the next, she simply wasn't there.

Several slow and awestruck seconds went by before anything happened. Though Autumn felt none of that heavy quality that had forewarned her of what had come, the air was inundated now with frightful suspicion and transparent horror.

A door opened and then another, the girl's scream bringing forth nosy neighbors from their huts. The old man with the scythe stepped out of his garden. Another man appeared, coming from between two houses. He went to the young girl, who let loose a barrage of Gaelic, in all likelihood telling him what she'd just seen.

More people came, men, women, and children, and more people squawked, screaming at the newcomers what they had seen. One curious young girl knelt, staring with wonder at Autumn before she dropped her head to the ground, stretching her hands out above her head on the dusty lane. Mouths gaped or lips thinned, brows furrowed or went wide in shock; they cried and shouted or stared, mute and dumbstruck. Their reactions were all over the board in appearance, except for the overriding sense of alarm written on each and every face.

A few men in the gathering crowd grouped together, talking over each other in their haste to understand, or to decide upon a response, or to formulate what action that should be taken. After only half a minute, they turned toward Autumn and moved themselves, so they were the foremost of the hostile audience.

"I can explain—" Autumn said, holding up her hands defensively. But should she? She recalled Marcus telling her shortly after the MacPhail ambush that she should keep quiet about time travel. She had some vague suspicion—something gleaned from history lessons, or maybe movies or books, she didn't know—that people in the Middle Ages were highly superstitious, that they might be less confused than they were eager to accuse her of witchcraft or sorcery—and to do something about it.

The seven men, several brandishing farm tools as weapons, stepped forward yet more.

Autumn's stomach roiled with queasiness. She felt suddenly as if she were spinning—or the village and its people were—and she struggled to breathe, able only to draw rapid, shallow breaths. Though the air was cool, her face flushed, and she began to sweat. An abrupt sense of disorientation struck her as her field of vision narrowed sharply, until the scene before her grew narrower and narrower.

And then everything went black.

**

When Autumn's eyes fluttered open, she found herself no longer outside but inside a poorly lighted room and sitting upon a chair. Her surroundings were a blur of earthen colors and fuzzy faces. There was no moment of confusion; she woke almost instantly understanding that she'd fainted—again; though not once in her twenty-seven years had she ever fainted before traveling through time—and that she'd been ripped from Marcus's arms and was possibly in the fourteenth century but no longer at Balla Àrd. She was a little less clear on the specifics, what had happened in that tiny village and with those people who had looked as if they'd been ready to tie her to a stake and light a bonfire beneath her. She tried to lift her trembling hand but found she could not move it. She glanced down at her hand, which sat upon the arm of the chair. She blinked foggily until her vision cleared and she saw that a cloth had been wrapped around her wrist, securing it to the chair. With a silent gasp, she turned her gaze to her other hand, finding it to be in the same condition. She wrenched both hands against the binds, to little effect. She tried to surge up and out of the chair, only to get nowhere, discovering that her ankles had also been bound, secured to the chair's legs.

She raised her head and found a dozen pair of eyes watching her, all of them male and none of their gazes compassionate. Gulping down her fright, she took in her surroundings, understanding that the chair sat in the middle of a cavernous hall, cleared or devoid of any benches or trestle tables, except for the lone table at the end of the room, straight in front of her, fully a dozen yards away, it seemed.

All but one man stood intimidatingly in front of the table, hands on the hilts of their swords, their stances wide, their posture and expressions threatening. From this distance, they were only stalwart figures with a malevolent gleam in their eyes. One man sat behind the long wooden table, his hand set before him, his fingers tapping impatiently.

Autumn squinted, leaning forward. Her mouth fell open. "Reid?"

Oh, but thank God for the familiar face, even if it did seethe with fury! She sagged with relief until she understood that he might not be the savior, not if she were tied to a chair in front of him.

At the sound of her voice, saying his name, his expression turned to icy coolness while his lips pressed into a thin line of expanding ferocity. More than one of his soldiers, some of whom Autumn now recognized by sight though she didn't know their names, turned to their laird to gauge his reaction.

No one seemed to know her.

Panic returned. In a shaky voice, she said his name again, hoping to see some spark of recognition.

"Ye dinna appear as I expected a witch might," he said, accusation in his gruff tone.

"I-I'm not a witch, I swear to you. Why are you pretending you don't know me? Where is Charlotte? Can I talk to Charlotte?"

"Cease!" He commanded, his voice filling the hall. "I dinna ken ye any more than ye do me."

"I do," she said weakly. "We met at Balla Àrd. You are married to—"

"Silence!" He roared.

Autumn jumped and bit her tongue, startled by the rage resonated in his voice. She was advised then that her body was sore and achy. But why was Reid pretending that he didn't know who she was? Oh, shit. Ideas and possibilities tangled in her brain, any one of them too impossible to grasp. She needed to think, to figure out how to approach this. She stalled presently, asking what had happened in the village.

"Why dinna ye tell me what happened, witch?" He asked, so much loathing in his voice.

Afraid to heighten his fury, Autumn sat mutely, her brain still whirring, trying to piece together what was going on.

"Ye materialized in the village, as well ye ken," he charged. "Simply come to life before many gawkers and what is your purpose?"

Aware at the moment of a pounding in her right temple that might have little to do with her utter uncertainty, she snapped at him, "Did they attack me?"

"They deduced a threat," he answered, his voice returned to a measure of calm, "and meant only to subdue it."

"Subdue is rather an understatement though, right?" She reproached tartly. She felt as if she'd been kicked and punched and thrown down a very rocky hill.

"Apologies to ye, lass," Reid Nicholson said without a hint of remorse, "for the vehemence of their reaction to ye, dropping from the sky."

Curiosity compelled her ask, "But did I drop from the sky?" She honestly had no idea.

"According to those who witnessed it, ye simply...came to life before them, being...*frothy*—said Tomas—and unformed and then...filling in, having the density of a true form."

Which certainly must have terrified them, of course. Autumn glanced at Reid, her gaze beseeching. "Please believe me. I'm not a witch. I'm not the one doing this, moving me around through time—"

"Ye are nae helping yerself," Reid hurled at her, this preceded by a scoffing snort.

Assuming she had nothing to lose—they obviously thought her a witch already—she dared to ask, "What year is it?" She knew she hadn't been sent home, to 2023, and now had a sinking suspicion that she'd actually been moved further back in time, to some point before Reid would have met her, possibly before he'd met Charlotte even.

He let out an angry chuckle. "A witch should ken the—"

"What year is it?" She persisted. "It's a simple question."

Reid clenched his teeth and stared hard at her.

But it was one of his silent minions who answered. "'Tis the year of our Lord, thirteen hundred and one."

Autumn had come to the middle ages in 1304. She'd been hurtled back another three years. But why? How? Autumn scoffed at herself now. Likely, as before, she would never know how or why or be able to make sense of any of it.

By Charlotte's recounting, Reid had met his wife in 1302—meaning not yet. He was thus, at this moment, very unlikely to believe any word Autumn uttered about journeying through time. Possibly, it would only add kindling to the fire of their fears that she was a witch.

Autumn swallowed down the dryness in her throat. She raised her chin and demanded, "I want to speak to Marcus McInnes." True, if this present circumstance were real, if what she feared might be reality, Marcus wouldn't have met her yet either. But he would know her, wouldn't he? He would, at least, know that same sense she'd had—that Marcus had admitted to feeling as well—that there was some incomprehensible but mighty bond between them. Marcus would know her.

Her startling request brought a new and different frown to Reid Nicholson's ferocious face.

He was slow to reply, though, and Autumn repeated her want. "Send for Marcus McInnes. He will be able to verify my...the truth, that I am not a witch."

While it appeared he'd been briefly startled by her mentioning his best friend's name, he covered his shock quickly and ably, his features returning to a brooding, angry man.

"The trial will commence forthwith," he said, ice dripping from his words, "and the punishment will be—"

"You can't simply hold some mock trial," Autumn yelled at him, "and not allow me any witnesses and then burn me at the stake without any real proof. That's..."—she sought a word that might have greater effect than *wrong*—"that's ungodly. It's sinful." Extreme anxiety obliged her to add, "Only a weak and...and terrified person would do that."

She wasn't surprised when he slanted a dark and dangerous look at her, clearly seeing through her transparent ploy.

"The trial will proceed," Reid declared again, "and ye will be charged with *maleficium*—harmful magic. If found guilty, ye will be executed, the method of death determined by the ecclesiastical court and our own Father Finlay MacCauley." He clamped his lips and studied her, his gaze narrowing, before he revealed, "Though a burning at the stake may nae be the chosen method for execution, yer body must be burned after the punishment is carried out, to prevent yer soul from creeping out to cause distress."

Astounded, and horrifically amused, Autumn repeated, "Prevent my soul from creeping out to cause distress? Yes, by all means, let us protect against that. Let us ignore the brutal monsters that would burn an innocent person to begin with."

Though his frown darkened again, she wasn't sure that he picked up on her sarcasm.

"I have the power to send for as many as three witnesses. Whom do ye name?"

"Only one," she said, lifting her chin. "I've said his name already. Marcus McInnes is my witness."

Reid shook his head. "Name another," he said calmly, but with an air of authority that suggested he was unaccustomed to being disobeyed. "I ken the McInnes, and I ken he will nae support your claim. I would ken if ye'd met him, or if he kent ye."

"You know nothing, Reid Nicholson," she said, probably putting herself in greater jeopardy but wanting—*needing*—to sound sure and superior and unintimidated. "Marcus McInnes is my witness," Autumn repeated with confidence. "Send to Balla Àrd for him."

***

Autumn languished for three days behind iron bars, beneath the ground in what appeared to be a dank and dismal medieval dungeon, subsisting on foul water, a thin, tasteless gruel, and one fat chunk of bread, about the size of her fist, that was delivered but once a day. The conditions were beyond inhumane. She was forced to relieve herself in a slop bucket in the darkest corner of the cell, the experience beyond degrading. She experienced a growing rage each time she squatted over that bucket and swore to herself that if she lived and if she remained in the fourteenth century she would make it her life's mission to improve the conditions of jailed persons in this time. How she might do that, she had no idea, but damn, this was cruel.

She had plenty of time to dwell upon her situation and fought almost hourly to keep hope alive. She wasn't certain if any message had been sent to Marcus. The only person she saw was the man who delivered her once-daily meal, but he had yet to answer any of her frantic questions, hadn't said even one word to her and so, she wasn't exactly sure if her circumstance was closer or further from dire.

With so much time on her hands, she gave plenty of thought to a myriad of ideas. For a while, she wrestled with what, if anything, to say about Charlotte when she saw Reid again. Autumn was a bit fearful of doing or saying anything that might upset the balance of the universe. She was afraid to jeopardize Reid and Charlotte's future by alerting him of what was to come, namely Charlotte. Autumn was well aware how deep was the love between Reid and Charlotte; she didn't want to do anything that might change what was supposed to happen next year.

Over the course of two and a half days, she supposed a hundred different scenarios for what a reunion with Marcus might look like, maintaining a fervent hope that he would somehow know her, or *feel* her. *If* he'd actually been summoned, as she'd commanded of Reid. *If* he came to Kingswood before they killed her.

Autumn scolded herself for not having seen the truth, or more honestly, for having resisted it, wanting only to get home. She'd fallen in love with him. She had to wonder if anything might be different if only she'd told him. But then, she allowed herself forgiveness as well; she gave herself a pass. Nothing had made sense over the last week and a half. How was she expected to act rationally, to make good and sensible decisions when nothing around her made sense? What was realistic about time travel?

What was logical about falling in love with a person who lived seven hundred years in the past? And doing so in a matter of days? Nothing. Nothing made sense.

Still, she couldn't imagine that this was to be her end. Why had she been moved through time, if she'd not been meant to do something significant, something meaningful? Was she truly about to die when she hadn't really begun to live? In either century?

And then she worried that Fate was going to do what Fate was going to do and that in all probability, Fate didn't care what she thought, what she'd done, who she missed and mourned, or who she loved. If she were meant to die, she would die. She only wasted a few minutes wondering what that did to her future self. Would she exist in the future, be born in 1996 if she died now? Autumn pondered this but fleetingly; she speculated that being dead now would rather make the point moot. At least to her. A dead person couldn't know what they wouldn't have, or had been cheated out of, would they?

More than once, when thinking about being brought abovestairs to face her trial she reminded herself that she was no shrinking violet. She would face whatever happened to her with her chin held high, would try so very hard not to crumble like a quivering mass of jelly, which was how she often felt.

I am not a shrinking violet, she repeated over and over. *I am stronger than my fear. Courage flows within me. I embrace strength. I embrace my own power.*

These oft-repeated mantras sadly deserted her when the time came.

On the third morning of her unjust captivity, the rattling of keys and clomping of feet on the stairs did not signify the coming of her bland breakfast down to the dungeon, but the arrival of four Nicholson soldiers. Only one spoke and because he did so in rapidly uttered Gaelic, she had no idea what he was saying. But the gate was opened and hands waved her forward. Autumn stood on wobbly legs, having to put her hands on the cold and damp dungeon wall to keep from toppling over.

She was, in reality, very grateful for how these men manhandled her, all but dragging her from her cell, carrying her up the stairs with beefy hands under her arms. She wasn't sure she could have made the climb or the subsequent walk to the hall on her own two feet.

This was it.

Inside the hall, her eyes darted all around, looking for him.

Marcus was not here.

Today, the trestle tables were placed precisely about Kingswood's hall, as if the dinner hour approached. And yet they were empty. Having been kept in utter darkness for more than two days, Autumn squinted against what seemed a very bright light from the small glowing candles hanging overhead. She glanced toward the door, the one that led to the courtyard. The door was fully open and bright white light filled the rectangular doorway so harshly that she jerked her hand upward to cover her eyes. For a split second, she thought it might be heaven beckoning her. That hope was swiftly squashed, the very medieval sound of hoofbeats on cobbles and the rhythmic pounding of the blacksmith's hammer on an anvil dashing it all to hell.

She was made to stand before the head table, which was now crowded with ten people, her jury she might presume.

None of them were Marcus.

What hope she'd known flickered like a candle's flame in a restless wind.

Reid was there, of course, as formidable as ever, primed to preside over this farce, to pronounce her guilty of witchcraft and sentence her to some gruesome death. After subjecting her to an expression of smug disdain, as if he expected her to be found out now, Reid slowly turned his gaze to the right.

Autumn's gaze followed.

A figure stepped from the shadows.

At first he was simply a dark and enigmatic form. But with each step forward he took, coming into the light provided by the open door, his presence grew more commanding, and more real. Sunlight played upon the contours of his rugged face, highlighting beloved lines and creases and the intensity of his chocolate brown eyes. The height and breadth of him, his broad shoulder and muscular frame, were so profoundly beautiful to her.

Autumn's heart leapt and screamed with joy and hope. A strangled cry burst from deep in her chest.

But his gaze reflected none of the same. In the depths of his beloved brown eyes, Autumn saw not one hint of recognition.

But she didn't care. So overcome with joy and relief was she that she ran toward him, lifting her arms.

He reacted by unsheathing his sword. But he didn't aim it directly at her, and she knew—she truly believed in her heart of hearts—that he wouldn't stab her.

She would never know for sure, though. While Marcus braced himself for impact, two of the Nicholson soldiers surged forward, blades reaching the space between Marcus and Autumn before she closed it. Their blades crossed and held, with Autumn trapped on one side.

She wasn't deterred though. But the fullness of her reaction to Marcus's presence dropped her to her knees. She tipped her face up to him, over those silver blades. Her eyes brimmed with grateful tears.

"Oh, thank God you're here," she said. "I love you. I'm sorry I didn't tell you sooner." She knew it would make no sense to him. She knew it might instead only pound another nail into her witch's coffin, but she had to tell him. He had to know. "I love you, Marcus."

She'd believed, she truly did, that Marcus would know her. Even if it were now three years earlier and they couldn't have met yet by his reckoning, he would know her. Their bond was strong enough. Wasn't it?

"Marcus," she pleaded when he said nothing, pleaded for consideration, simply to have him at least *feel* her. "You know me," she said brokenly.

He strode forward, waving his hand slowly in front of him to move the swords between them. When he stood directly in front of her, the muscles around his eyes tightened, causing a piercing, unyielding focus that seemed to bore straight into her, through her. Lips that had many times kissed her with utmost tenderness, had kissed many parts of her body, formed a stern line, hinting at suppressed rage.

The last of Autumn's optimism faltered. With each passing moment, the weight of his glare grew heavier, pressing down upon her.

Finally, he turned toward Reid, dismissing Autumn cruelly as he said, "I dinna ken who this is. Do what ye will."

Autumn fell forward, her hands reaching out to the cold stone floor, diminished by the icy and harsh removal of all hope.

"I'll thank ye nae to waste my time on such drivel ever again," Marcus said, presumably to Reid, his voice choked with fury.

He pivoted and strode angrily toward the door.

Driven by profound despair, Autumn cried out to the floor, "Your grandfather used to tell you tales of dragons. He said he fought with them. You might have believed him as a child but then you kind of questioned why you never challenged him on those implausible tales."

She picked up her head, turning her face toward him.

He stopped at the door, the shadow of his imposing figure silhouetted against the bright light outside. His face was turned ever so slightly to the right.

Knowing she had his attention, Autumn scrambled for more to shout at him, to force him to acknowledge her.

"You were engaged—betrothed," she corrected, "to Ysabella and then Agnes and then Miriam. You might have been in love with Miriam but when she betrayed you, you convinced yourself that you were not."

He turned and snarled at her, likely as perplexed as he was furious with what he might think was only witch's magic.

Autumn pushed herself to her feet, just as angry at him—ridiculously—for not recognizing her.

"Aelred has only one hand and Osgar is sometimes called a goblin by Gibbon. Eadric has a limp, one he was born with. He lost his inheritance due to his perceived weakness."

He stomped toward her, his snarl evolving into a growl. "By my oath, woman, I will nae hear of—"

"You have a scar on the top of your right shoulder," she rushed out. "It's shaped like a comma," she said, holding up her hand, curling her forefinger a bit. "It's one of dozens on your body." She wept. "I stroked it with my fingers. You said it brought you peace."

He stopped within a foot of her, his scowl a storm of rage, his eyes flashing with lightning.

Autumn was not cowed, but stiffened her spine and met his gaze.

They both went very still, silently seething at each other.

"Who the bluidy hell are ye?"

"I am Autumn and you are in love with me," she whispered to him. "I saw it on your face, before I was ripped from your arms."

He was not conceding anything, but he was questioning everything.

"I dinna ken ye, nae at all," he said gruffly, his wretched tone asking her to explain how she knew so much about him.

She didn't want to spook him, but she needed to touch him, or be touched by him.

She needed him to feel her.

"We loved in another time that is not yet...lived. I begged you not to let me go," she said, her voice very small now, not wanting to be heard by the audience that was slowly creeping forward around them. "I begged you to find me. You were as afraid as I was, and you said, *When? Where?* You promised you would find me."

He was, she was sure of it, beginning to waver.

"I...I dinna—I ken nothing of that. I'm sorry, lass." And he looked it, too, like he really was sorry that he couldn't trust her.

"Marcus," she said, and saw his scowl return at how easily his name came to her lips. "I won't touch you. I'm not a witch. I can't hurt you." She lifted her hand between them. "But just take my hand. You'll see."

He smirked meanly, as if he suspected her of some game.
Autumn remained determined. Confidence soared.
She only needed him to touch her.
"Please, Marcus," she implored him. "Take my hand."

Chapter Twenty

Kingswood Castle
1301

Her entreaty was hard to resist.

Bluidy hell, there was no part of her that was easy to dismiss. Though her hair was disheveled, and her face and garb were dusted with dirt, her eyes shone brightly, and the shape and color of her lips beckoned him.

Beneath the grime of what was surely the result of a few days underground in Reid's dungeon, he saw what she was, a striking beauty with gray eyes. But that was just it—how could he ever have forgotten her?

He knew he had never met her and yet...there was some awareness of her, a familiarity that shook him.

Marcus lifted his eyes from the hand she raised between them and fixed his gaze on her. In the depths of her striking gray eyes, he imagined an infinite well of understanding—she clearly looked as if *she* knew him, and beyond what clues she'd given about his grandfather, the scar on his shoulder from the battle at Falkirk, and about his men.

A moment ago, she had accused him of being in love with her, had said she saw it in his face when she was ripped from his arms. He knew not of what she spoke but upon hearing those words, there had been a hitch in his breath and briefly, a tight fist around his heart, it seemed, as if he were experiencing then what she claimed he'd lived.

He held her profoundly intimate gaze, was mesmerized by it. He sensed no wicked intent, but strangely found peace in her gaze. He comprehended nothing but was seized by a powerful notion that he should want to understand.

Marcus looked down at her hand and slowly lifted his own. Even before he clasped his hand to her, he was filled with some sense that he *had* done so before.

An undeniably stirring sensation engulfed him as soon as he took her hand, wrapping his much larger fingers around hers.

He lifted his eyes to hers, arching a brow. That was it?

The woman named Autumn smiled at him. She laid her free hand over the top of their joined ones and her gray eyes shimmered with hope.

"I love you, Marcus."

A searing light flashed before his eyes. And then an image of him holding Autumn's hand in another setting, in a moonlit wooded vale, assailed him. He knew he wasn't dreaming. It was broad daylight, and he was not abed, was inside Kingswood's hall. It came to him harshly, crashed into him really, as if someone had just smacked his chest hard with the blunt side of an axe, just enough to stun him.

Other pictures presented themselves, not slowly, but in a quick flash of images, depictions in his own brain of him and Autumn, at Balla Àrd and upon a meadow in the aftermath of a battle. And then another, of Autumn shrouding bodies in Balla Àrd's bailey with another woman; one of Autumn and that woman dancing inside Balla Àrd's hall, Autumn entrancing him with the way she swayed to the music. He saw them walking about the loch at Balla Àrd and most amazingly, at some time naked and entwined in each other's arms near the bathing spot and then again, in the chamber that had once been his sister's.

Most astonishingly, the images came to him not only as a visual recollection, but they were filled with emotion. He *felt* everything he experienced inside those moments: being curious and captivated; feeling protective; the wild desire for her; the rapture of his climax, the contentment found in her arms—all of this, even an odd skepticism he tried to ignore about her.

The images kept coming, and he was startled by one that showed Autumn tracing her finger along the very scar she named; she'd said it had brought him peace and he experienced that now, the peace he'd known then, as a sense of inner calm and as being in harmony with her, in a timeless manner.

He was shown the moment she'd been ripped from his arms, as she'd claimed. He and Autumn standing on the path beyond the keep, amid the jagged rocks and tall grass, clinging to each other as the wind howled around them. Gibbon and a few of the lads were there as well, close anyhow, but Marcus only saw him and her, and he suffered now what she insisted he'd known once already, watching her being yanked away from him. She'd simply faded to dust. He was smacked in the heart with what that felt like, the gut-wrenching pain, the shock, the grief, the anger, and the fear. And the ensuing hollowness.

He trembled where he stood, baring his teeth as he fought against the aching sorrow.

Somewhere, Reid called his name. He felt himself falling.

He blinked, or thought he did, and he was presented with additional images of himself and Autumn, surrounded by people he did not recognize, wearing garb that was unfamiliar, inside a chamber with impossibly smooth and plumb walls and ceiling and dancing shimmery lights entwined in crystals. He'd never seen these people, neither the adults nor the young weans, but knew somehow that they were Autumn's family, and that he and Autumn were pleased to be among them.

Another white light flashed inside his mind's eye, and it was done.

Though he'd not realized he'd closed his eyes, he opened them now, and saw the vaulted timber ceiling of Kingswood's hall. Muted noise and sound came to him. A shuffling of many feet; the metallic slither of a blade being removed from its scabbard; a cry of his name; Reid snapping out orders.

His heart hammered like a drum, inside his chest and in his ears.

He was laying on his back, on the cold stone of Kingswood's hall.

Intuitively, he understood that he had been shown all that for a reason. He was empowered with an idea to see it for what it was, something that was not meant to raise questions, to bring confusion, to make him ponder why or how, but was meant to give him—to allow him—to understand and see what had been, and thus, what could be. He pondered the beautiful weight of the joy in his chest, that came with the revelation.

He and Autumn were destined to be together—had been or would be, he'd just been shown.

He'd been torn to pieces by her leaving.

He was in love with her.

Reid appeared before him, on his haunches at Marcus's side.

"Bluidy hell," cursed Reid, helping Marcus to sit up. "Did she cast a spell on ye?"

Marcus ignored him, his gaze searching for and finding Autumn, held at bay by four of Reid's guards. None would dare to touch her but pointed the tips of their swords directly at her, one of them only inches from her throat.

She wasn't afraid. She stood with her chin raised and a proud defiance in her gaze. And somehow he realized he knew that about her. Autumn was, in her own way, fearless.

And everything he did in the next few seconds was rooted in desire, in want, in love. He couldn't lose her again.

"*Jesu,*" he rasped, intensely moved by what he'd been shown. The entirety of it was still unknown, parts incomprehensible, but the core of it was crystal clear and remained: he was in love with her. "Let her go," he panted, struggling to get the words out, feeling as if he'd run swiftly and for many miles.

"Marcus...?" Reid questioned.

"She is nae a threat," he said, still short of breath. With certainty, he added, "She is nae a witch."

Reid rose to his full height and made a motion with his head, which brought down the wall of the swords around Autumn.

She rushed forward, dropping to her knees beside him. She jerked forward as if she would have hurled herself in his arms, but caught herself before she did. Her eyes were glassy and skimmed over every inch of his face. Possibly she saw no more resistance and did then lean forward, taking her face in her hands. Softly, bravely, she laid her lips against his.

Her touch and her kiss were familiar.

He knew her.

Marcus shook with joy and took hold of her wrists, pushing her away, just enough to meet her gaze.

"How did ye do it?"

"Travel through time?" she asked softly, in deference to listening ears. "I didn't. Someone—or something—keeps moving me around. And I wanted very badly to go home to my family, but when I was taken from you three years from now, I realized that I wanted more to be with you."

Three years from now?

"I meant how did ye make me see all those images?"

The woman named Autumn, for whom he suddenly, inexplicably felt a vast and powerful emotion that he had to assume must be love, wrinkled her face in confusion. "I didn't do it, Marcus. But I held your hand tight before we were parted and I swear, I willed the memory of me into you. I tried, anyway. I thought I'd never see you again. I was simply hoping that you would keep me in your heart...as I would you."

"Was I in love with you?" He asked, less filled with doubt than he was wanting clarity, or confirmation.

"You didn't say you were," she answered. "But then I didn't say I loved you until today." Her exquisitely shaped mouth curved in a bittersweet smile. "I'm sorry it took being taken away from you for me to realize it." She bit her lip and then asked, "What did you see?"

"Us," he answered, the first thing that came to mind. "I saw us. At Balla Àrd. I saw ye...stripped from me."

"I was brought here. I don't know how or why, unless it was to show me that...that I did love you."

Marcus's brow knitted. "And I ye?"

Autumn's lips trembled with a burgeoning joy that was beautiful to behold.

"I canna breathe," he said, shaken by his inability to catch his breath.

Reid, obviously close yet, was there, extending his hand down to Marcus.

"Let us step outside," he offered, helping Marcus to his feet.

As Autumn scrambled out of the way and to her feet, Reid gripped Marcus's hand firmly, pulling him close until they were nearly nose to nose.

"What the bluidy hell is happening?"

Breathlessly, Marcus replied, "I dinna ken. But Reid, I *do* ken her...somehow." A memory was rekindled, an echo of the past—or the future—that bade Marcus say to Reid, "If anything should happen to me, today or at any time—when it does," he said, having some certainty that *something* would happen, "I need ye to assure that Balla Àrd survives. Petition the king," he instructed, even as he was a bit flustered about the certainty he felt. "Take Balla Àrd for the Nicholsons."

Reid's reaction to that was to stare at him as if he'd grown another head.

"She *has* cast a spell on ye," Reid accused hotly.

"She has nae," Marcus said, stepping to the side, but still needing Reid's hand to guide him, as he felt particularly weak, as if his legs might collapse under him. "Nae a spell of the black magic ilk. But I canna leave her, and nae can I have her taken away."

Reid walked him outside the door. And because the laird of Kingswood did not give any command to detain Autumn, she followed, hovering about at Marcus's right side.

Marcus was not surprised to find the bailey nearly empty. When Marcus had arrived today, at the behest of Reid's odd summons, and before Autumn had been retrieved from the dungeon, Reid had advised that her necessary trial would not take place until tomorrow. He'd not wanted to make a spectacle out of Marcus's arrival or his meeting with Autumn but had wanted that done in private, for which Marcus had been thankful earlier and was even more so now, after the fact.

Thus, no crowd gathered or waited in Kingswood's courtyard. It was supremely quiet, almost eerily so.

Ten feet outside the door, Marcus bent over, putting his hands on his knees, wondering why he was struggling to breathe still, why the air felt so heavy, as if it were laden with a dense, oddly unscented smoke.

He felt Autumn's hand on his back, rubbing a small soft circle. He was surprised Reid allowed it but was grateful for that as well, since her touch was soothing.

Just as Marcus straightened himself and drew a full breath, Autumn dropped her hand and turned away from him.

"Autumn?" He gave no thought to how effortlessly her name had just rolled off his tongue. But he sensed immediately her returned distress.

He was peripherally aware of storm clouds gathering overhead just as Autumn spun around to him, her face alive with panic.

"It's happening again, Marcus," she moaned. The briefly bright orbs of her gray eyes now darkened into a haunting, ashen hue. It seemed the weight of the world had settled there, in her eyes, and her darting frantic glances betrayed a rising turmoil within.

Marcus's heart twisted. "*What* is happening?" He ground out, turning his hand upward to hold her wrist. But he felt it, too, the changing atmosphere, as if more than only a storm brewed. The feeling was akin to standing in a windswept pasture, staring at the wall of a forest, knowing an army of thousands thundered toward you, even as they remained unseen and unheard because of the shrill ringing in your ears, inspired by rage and purpose.

"They're going to take me away again," Autumn cried. She threw her arms around his neck and wept against his ear. "I can't lose you again. Marcus, I love you."

"I will nae let them," he said with a compulsion born of love. He wrapped one arm around her waist while he drew his sword with the other. "I will nae let ye go."

Next to him, Reid drew his sword as well, though Marcus couldn't be sure if he felt the coming danger as well or if his reaction was simply a mirror of Marcus's.

Pivoting with Autumn in his arms, Marcus spun in circles to find and meet the threat. Autumn was turned with him, her feet nearly off the ground for his tight grip, her cheek against his, watching, their chests heaving.

He turned and the gate suddenly was gone. He pivoted further and Reid wasn't there and then Kingswood was gone.

An unknown, unrecognized force overwhelmed him and tossed him on his back. Autumn was pulled from his arms. His sword was yanked from his tight grip.

He bellowed Autumn's name, same as he had before.

He didn't believe he'd been knocked out, but suspected that might have been the case, when he opened his eyes and found only a cloudless sky above. The wind didn't blow, and no clouds churned angrily across the sky. The air was light and fine.

He was on his back. His first attempt to rise produced a stabbing pain in some muscle in his side. He flopped back down.

"Autumn," he said weakly. He cleared his throat and made a better effort at a shout. "Autumn!"

Something tickled the palm of his hand, which was flung out at his side. He turned his head against the earth and found Autumn laying next to him, staring at him. He didn't know if she was crying or laughing.

He knew an instant relief because she was at his side. Whatever had happened, they were together now.

He needed to get his bearings, felt as if he couldn't move just yet. He stared straight above, trying to make sense of what had just happened.

High above him, smack in the middle of the clear blue sky, a shiny bird flew straight as an arrow. It left a trail of white smoke in its wake, the plume thin where it was close to the bird and widening as the bird flew away from it.

He recalled a conversation with Autumn that had taken place...when? In her past? In his future?

"'Tis an airplane, is it nae?"

Autumn turned her face to the sky. In profile, Marcus watched as her mouth opened, slowly and with so much wonder. A tear slid from her eyes and rolled down into the tousled blonde hair near her ear.

"It is," Autumn said. "It's an airplane, Marcus." She covered her mouth and nose with two hands, her emotions overwhelming her as she stared at the sky. Her shoulders shook with her sobs.

Nearly undone by this, Marcus drew on every ounce of strength he had and rolled over toward her. Her face fell into shadow as he loomed over her. He searched her gaze, enthralled by the brilliant joy found within.

Though he had more questions than answers, he knew one thing with a certainty that defied logic but was accepted with so much tranquility. That he was where he was supposed to be—with her.

Softly, he bent and kissed her forehead.

"We're home, Marcus," she said when their eyes met again.

He knew it innately — it was simply alive inside him, the notion—that home was wherever she was.

"Aye, love."

Epilogue

*Near Chicago
Ten years later....*

Above the brick-fronted, wood encased fireplace hung a medieval sword. A few years ago, it had been sealed with a synthetic conservation wax, and it gleamed still as if it hadn't been made seven-hundred years ago. On the right side of the fireplace in the den at the back of the house was a set of French doors that led to the leaf-strewn, sandstone patio. To the left of the fireplace, bookshelves stretched from floor to ceiling. Little dust gathered there for the books were frequently perused. The shelves were organized by subject matter, the highest one holding costly, ancient tomes that had been collected over the years. Below were several shelves of academic books, covering everything from psychology to computer science, sociology to criminal justice, and business to ancient world history. Beneath those were novels: fantasy, romance, true crime, and plenty of thrillers, with a few cozy mysteries, and the occasional time travel story.

The bottom shelf was rather scattered, some books standing while a whole pile sat on their sides, stacked unevenly, the pile being rifled through on a nightly basis just before bedtime. That shelf housed the Harry Potter collection, a dozen different Dr. Seuss books, and an assortment of fairy tales, adventures, and even a few children's Westerns.

The den was dim save for those spots where standing lamps hung over the desk and the skirted chaise, each employed with enough frequency that the desk chair had been replaced twice now and the chaise reupholstered just last fall. A floppy, stuffed pink bunny was sprawled across the foot of the chaise. Two baseball mitts sat on the floor near the French doors. The baseball had rolled under the mahogany executive desk.

The family room, at the other side of the house, was similarly infested with evidence that children lived happily here. The green velvet sectional was decorated with more than one strategically placed throw or pillow, each meant to hide stains from dirty little shoes that should have been left at the door and fingers greased by popcorn butter on movie night. On any given day, between any two cushions, one might find barrettes or crayons, coins or candy wrappers, and until it was vacuumed out next week, an unpopped kernel, still slimy with butter. A plaid throw, in the McInnes colors, was draped and tucked in on the end of the long side of the sofa. Charlie, their German shepherd, spent more than half his day there. Charlie spent his nights in the bedroom at the top of the stairs, snuggled up against his favorite person in a twin bed with a sheer pink canopy.

The door inside the mudroom opened, and Marcus entered, carrying four year-old Eveyln in his arms. He toed off his gym shoes and held out his arm to prevent his two sons from running past him. "Shoes, lads."

William, nine, and Noah, eight, hastened to comply, kicking off their shoes and then hurriedly straightening them on the open shelf at the bottom of the huge hall tree before they dashed into the house, running straight for the family room. It was a race every day to claim the remote and thus be the one to find Channel 4 and announce if they made it in time to catch their mother on the news.

Marcus removed Evelyn's tiny sneakers and set her down. Charlie had come running as soon as he heard the door open and was waiting for her. She hugged the dog tightly and whispered something to him. Marcus never knew what they talked about, those two.

But he did always know in advance if his wife expected to have a segment live on the evening news, and usually did not ruin the anticipation for their boys. Tonight, she would be reporting on that Donnelly case she'd been working on for a week, since a fire, now known to be arson, had tragically killed a family of four. Marcus knew he didn't want the boys to bear witness to any reporting on that gruesome tale.

"No TV tonight, lads," he called out as he walked through the back hall into the kitchen, setting down the fancy boxed cake on the counter. "Your màthair said she would nae be on the air tonight and we've got a birthday dinner to get ready."

"I thought we were having Mom's birthday party at Nana's house," Noah said, shoulders slumping as he returned to the kitchen.

"That will be Sunday at Papa and Nana's house, when the whole family can make it," Marcus told him, pulling open cupboard doors, looking for a certain dish. "But today is her actual birthday, and I want just us to celebrate." He found what he was looking for. "Now let's get this cake out of the box and onto your màthair's favorite cake platter so she thinks we made it ourselves."

William scrunched up his face, his expression incredulous. "Mom's never gonna believe we made this."

"What?" Marcus questioned, moving his gaze to include Noah's dubious frown. "I've made a cake before. Just last year, I made that cake for you to bring to school on your own birthday," he reminded his son.

"Um yeah, and it looked like it rode under the bus and not on it."

"Another reason I prefer to drive yc to school." He winked at the lads. "C'mon now. I marinated steaks ere I left for work this morning. We need to scrub and bake potatoes—peasant food, your màthair calls them; I beg to differ. We are nae peasants but kings," he pronounced loudly, pumping his fist into the air.

Noah and William copied their father, throwing up their hands, reciting automatically, "Clarior hinc honos!"

"There ye have it, lads. Brighter hence the honor." He pulled open the fridge and began throwing items over his shoulder. "Look lively, lads," he warned, and the boys scrambled to catch all the falling produce. "Noah, ye will set the table. William, ye will put together the salad with your sister. Evelyn?" He called, closing the fridge. "Evelyn?"

Evelyn and Charlie came strolling out from the mudroom finally. Charlie was wearing Evelyn's jacket, walking stiffly as if he couldn't move his legs properly in the confines of the sleeves. Eveyln dragged her small pre-school back pack on the floor behind her, wiping her tired eyes—she had just recently gotten over a nasty bout with the flu—utterly unperturbed by all the attention fixed her way. She saw all the salad makings in Will's arms. "I don't like onion."

Marcus lifted her up onto the stool at the breakfast counter. "I dinna blame ye. Mayhap ye will simply sit here and look bonny." He kissed the top of her perfect blonde head.

Evelyn put her chin in her hands and slid her elbows along the counter, her face dropping lower as she smiled gratefully at her father.

Will rolled his eyes.

"Noah," Marcus called. "Give Charlie a hand, will ye?"

"Yep. One day, he's just gonna go off on her and eat her face off."

"He would nae ever," Marcus addressed idly, bringing out the glass dish from the fridge that contained all the steaks—and one small marinating chicken breast for Evelyn.

While the boys set the table and made the salad and Evelyn became drowsier and drowsier at the counter, Marcus quickly made Autumn's favorite dill dressing for the salad and ducked out the sliding glass door near the breakfast nook, onto the patio to start the grill.

When he came back inside, trying to organize everything in his head so that it would all be ready at the same time, he saw his wife leaning against the wall between the mudroom and the kitchen, slowly untying the belt of her coat.

She wore a dreamy expression on her face, silently watching her children at work, or about to fall asleep in Evelyn's case. Though Charlie was standing in front of her, furiously wagging his tail, waiting to be acknowledged, her children had yet to notice her. She bent and scratched Charlie behind his ears, bringing his snout close to her face, mouthing words to him. When she straightened, she saw Marcus walking toward her.

He backed her into the mudroom, out of view of the kids.

"Happy Birthday," he said, taking her beloved face in his hands. "You're nae supposed to be home this early."

She hadn't aged a bit in ten years, he often told her. Truth was, she had, as had he. She was even bonnier, though; her beauty had not been confined to youth, but had evolved into something more profound, more womanly, due in part to her happiness, her constant confidence, and the love she felt and radiated. Her gray eyes were surrounded by a few more creases; her blonde hair no longer fell to the middle of her back, but only touched her shoulders when loose. She lamented no longer being a size 4 but Marcus found her womanly curves all the more enticing. But even he was amazed that he never tired of looking at her. Nearly a decade of marriage had given him a treasure trove of joy-filled memories and not one of them didn't have Autumn at the center.

Autumn smiled and closed her eyes, tilting her face up to him.

Grinning, Marcus gave her the kiss she was after, but only a little one.

"We pre-recorded the segment," she told him, shrugging out of her coat. "God, I hope you can do better than that as a welcome home-slash-happy birthday kiss."

He could. He did. He slanted his mouth over hers at the same time he drew her up against his hard body, catching her falling coat at her back. He didn't fully plunder, but then he wanted to make her melt against him, which she obligingly did, her arms around his waist. It was some time before they came up for air.

"Now be a guid lass, will ye, and come in all surprised?" He asked, reaching out to hang her coat on the hooks to his right. "And make a fuss, will ye nae, over the lads helping with dinner?"

Autumn smiled brilliantly. "Did they?" She whispered.

"Aye, they did, they are. And ye can fix whatever I'm doing wrong, but ye're nae to fret at all about the table set or the salad."

Autumn winked at him. "Gotcha. All right. I'll wait a few minutes."

Marcus gave her one more kiss and returned to the kitchen. Will had his back to the kitchen, near the sink and the cutting board, slicing tomatoes. Noah was circling the table, laying out five plates. Evelyn had climbed down from the tall stool and made her way to the sectional in the family room. Charlie and she were presently snuggling on the plaid blanket.

Marcus washed his hands at the kitchen island, so that he faced the mudroom.

A moment later, she walked in, giving a feigned cry of shock, "What's going on here?"

Three little faces turned her way.

Noah reached her first, throwing his arms around her waist, crying, "Happy Birthday!"

William came next, forced to hug both is brother and his mother to be close. He tipped his face up to Autumn. "Happy Birthday, Mom."

Evelyn scurried off the sofa, squealing, "Happy Birf-day, Mama!" as she ran to her mother.

William, who could sometimes be a wonderful big brother, picked up his sister so she could kiss their mother.

Autumn put her arms around all of them. "Oh, my gosh! What a welcome! And dinner, too? I'm spoiled."

While her three children showered her with affection, Autumn lifted her eyes to Marcus. Her gaze was watery with her happiness.

He remained near the sink, fisting his hands and the towels he'd dried them with against the counter, pleased to take in the scene, which filled him with so much love. Possibly, his gaze mirrored his wife's as his heart swelled with indescribable joy.

He'd left behind an entire life, a purpose, kin and loved ones and friends, and not a day went by that he knew any regret. He missed them, missed Balla Àrd, but he never regretted what Autumn considered his sacrifice, to be here and stay here with her.

There was no sacrifice. Though he bemoaned the loss of those relationships he'd known for the first thirty years of his life, nothing could compare to what he had now.

Marcus adored his children, adored Autumn more, still. 'Twas a powerful connection between them, one that he cherished. Their love had grown and evolved over time, weathering life's peculiar storms, always emerging stronger.

He smiled with a deep contentment. The sight of her filled his heart with a love that transcended time, that had been tested and found unwavering.

They were simply meant to be.

The End

*Stay tuned for Reid & Charlotte's story in
the upcoming
Beloved Enemy
Book Six of the Far From Home: Scottish Time Travel Romance*

Far From Home: A Scottish Time-Travel Romance

*And Be My Love
Eternal Summer
Crazy In Love
Beyond Dreams
Only The Brave
When & Where
Coming 2024
Beloved Enemy
Winter Longing
Hearts on Fire
Here in Your Arms*

Other Books by Rebecca Ruger

Highlander: The Legends

*The Beast of Lismore Abbey
The Lion of Blacklaw Tower
The Scoundrel of Beauly Glen
The Wolf of Carnoch Cross
The Blackguard of Windless Woods
The Devil of Helburn by the Sea
The Knave of Elmwood Keep*

The Dragon of Lochlan Hall
The Maverick of Leslie House
The Brute of Mearley Hold
The Rebel of Lochaber Forest
The Avenger of Castle Wick

Heart of a Highlander Series
Heart of Shadows
Heart of Stone
Heart of Fire
Heart of Iron
Heart of Winter
Heart of Ice

The Highlander Heroes Series
The Touch of Her Hand
The Memory of Her Kiss
The Shadow of Her Smile
The Depths of Her Soul
The Truth of Her Heart
The Love of Her Life

www.rebeccaruger.com

Printed in Great Britain
by Amazon